OMNI
BEST SCIENCE FICTION
ONE

Edited by Ellen Datlow

OMNI Books
Greensboro, North Carolina

CONTENTS

INTRODUCTION

Omni, first published in October 1978, is the first (and still only) glossy mass-market magazine to provide science fiction and fantasy with the forum and format it deserves. Since its premier issue, *Omni* has showcased some of the most entertaining and thought-provoking sf and fantasy of our times. Just as important, *Omni* has brought science fiction to readers who have never read it before. The circulation of *Omni* is larger than all the traditional science fiction markets combined. *Omni*'s enormous success encouraged writers such as Robert Silverberg to return to short fiction and novelists such as Terry Bisson, Paul Park, and K.W. Jeter to begin writing short fiction.

As of 1992 I have been *Omni*'s fiction editor for over ten years. During my tenure I have occasionally been asked by interviewers to look back and comment on science fiction in the 1980s and to predict where the field appears to be heading. I don't suppose I can do the latter any more accurately than science fiction writers have predicted where the world is going in their fiction. After all, very few writers foresaw the speed with which the computer, imagined at one time by sf writers as taking up entire rooms, would become so small the user can easily carry it on trips; or, on the socio-political side, the fall of the Berlin Wall and how quickly the Soviet Union came apart.

However, the stories included in this volume can give the reader a certain feel for how the science fiction/fantasy field has been changing. Science fiction, fantasy, and main-stream fiction have increasingly sloshed into one another so that critics are finding it more and more difficult to define "science fiction." (Some writers assert that even what is commonly considered "hard" science fiction is actually science fantasy, as a certain amount of fudging is always necessary to create a world that will convince the reader to suspend disbelief.) This cross-fertilization is evidenced by the number of sf writers dabbling in the mainstream, incorpo-rating mainstream techniques and concerns, being published as mainstream--and the many mainstream writers who have been writing novels and stories tinged with the fantastic and using science fiction tropes. The current generation of writers, having grown up in a culture in which sf tropes are commonplace—*Star Wars*, *Star Trek*, etc.—can now use at least basic sf ideas as elements within their work without even necessarily realizing it.

As fiction editor at *Omni*, it is as important to me that a story be written well as it is for it to have fresh ideas. I try to publish challenging, thought-provoking and adult short fiction regardless of "genre." By using these criteria I've procured original fiction from writers as diverse as William Gibson, Joyce Carol Oates, Clive Barker, Jack Cady, Stephen King, Harlan Ellison, Michael Bishop, Ursula K. Le Guin, Thomas M. Disch, and Pat Cadigan.

If one isn't concerned with pigeon-holing good fiction,

this cross-fertilization may be a good thing. For those who want to be certain about just what kind of fiction they are reading, this is, of course, a negative.

In addition to mixing the genres, writers seem to be dealing more with the consequences of runaway technology and questioning the use of technology without reference to ethical standards. Related to this concern is the fact that sf writers (at least those I deal with) are writing fewer off-world stories. I can only speculate that disillusionment with NASA and the idea that interplanetary expansion as panacea combined with the immediate problem of worsening living conditions for much of the world as a result of the devastation of AIDS and persistent poverty and environmental neglect has leached interest in writing about space from the younger writers. Instead they are mining the rich material available in confronting earth-born problems. Most of the stories in this book reflect this altered concern.

So the science fiction field continues to evolve as different social and literary forces act on it. *Omni's* fiction—in this book and in its monthly issues—will reflect this change, as we continue to bring cutting-edge sf to a wide audience throughout the nineties and into the next century.

Ellen Datlow

California Dreaming

by Elizabeth A. Lynn

Elizabeth Lynn was born in New York City but has lived in Berkeley, California, for many years. Her first novel, *A Different Light*, was followed by the three volumes of the popular *Chronicles of Tornor* fantasy trilogy and an sf novel, *The Sardonyx Net*. Her short fiction has been collected in *The Woman Who Loved the Moon and Other Stories*. In 1980 she won two World Fantasy Awards, one for her novel *The Watchtower* and one for her short story "The Woman Who Loved the Moon." Her most recent novel is *The Silver Horse*. Her story, "At the Embassy Club," was published by *Omni* in June 1984. For several years after that Lynn left the science fiction field and fiction writing to pursue her interest in the martial arts. Then, in 1991, I received two stories from her in quick succession: this one, "California Dreaming," and a fantasy variation of the fairy tale Rapunzel that Terri Windling and I bought for our anthology, *Snow White, Blood Red*.

"California Dreaming" is a wry story that extrapolates a very believable future from our environmentally destructive present. This is its first appearance anywhere.

CALIFORNIA DREAMING

Elizabeth A. Lynn

That morning, Friday early in October, with a light mist
hanging in the air and a wind sweeping through the Golden
Gate eastward across the Bay, I went out to say goodbye to
the car. It was an ancient Datsun 210, built before they
renamed them Nissans; two doors, automatic transmission,
an AM-FM radio that got FM pretty well but AM hardly at
all; you had to smack it under the dash to get the ballgames
and half the time it just gave you static no matter how many
times you hit it. I bought it used in 1989 and kept it alive
with judicious feedings of oil and the appropriate brake
repairs, lubes, tune-ups, belt replacements, valve jobs—I even
had the upholstery redone and the steering rebuilt. It was
silver-grey, like two thirds of the cars in California, and as
long as I kept my trips under two hundred miles, it never
broke down, not while the engine was running. But the radio
never worked right.

   We'd been warned twenty years ago that this day would
have to come. Most of us had figured it out by then. My
daughter Jana had had to wear one of those Nu-Air filters
from the time she started to walk, and she developed emphysema in 1993. I'd always thought that emphysema was

something that happened to people who worked in coal mines, or insulated houses, or smoked four packs a day, but Jana never did any of those things, and she ended up with one of those oxygen tanks on wheels, and every breath she drew hurt. And the air—well, all you had to do was look at it, you could see something was wrong. In 1963, when I first learned to drive, air wasn't something you could see.

The Datsun sat where I usually parked it, on Addison Street. I walked around it, finger-tipped my name in the rain-spattered dust on the hood. Next door, Ricardo Muñoz was backing his red and white and gold striped Toyota from the lot of the brown apartment complex to the street. I walked to the Eighth Street side of the house. My neighbor Henry Banks, who works for the Postal Service, was polishing his big cherry red 1957 Chrysler 300B with fierce, deliberate strokes. It was a collector's item; only a thousand built, Henry said, and it could go from zero to sixty in nine seconds and do one hundred forty miles per hour on the flat, not that there was anyplace to go that fast, not anymore.

I learned to drive in New York, on a car almost as old as Henry's. It was a 1962 Oldsmobile, with a V-8 engine and automatic transmission, power steering, power brakes: driving it felt like steering through a Styrofoam glove. But in 1963, all I needed was that car and a radio and I was king of the road, cruising down the Long Island Expressway at ninety miles an hour with The Temptations or Jackie Wilson or Martha and the Vandellas pouring from the dashboard like the Word of God. Eight years later, in Chicago, I owned a 1959 Pontiac. My wife, Marilyn, named it the Pontiac Behemoth. It was salmon and white with fins like a beluga's. There was no power steering on that baby; it made you work, but I loved slinging it around corners, and once inside it I backed up for nothing short of a semi or a tank.

The air shivered. I heard the train whistle sounding, seven blocks away. I checked my watch; it was the ten eighteen, early by a minute, though it could be my watch was slow. We got the railroads back, but we lost the trucks. No more White Line Fever. It was a trade off, but I don't miss trucks, though the truckers fought like hell—remember the convoys of eighteenwheelers encircling the Capitol building? Interstate 5 is now the bed for the California Gold Rush—it streaks from San Francisco to L.A. in two hours—and trains haul freight everywhere but on city streets. Of course, we still need mail trucks, ambulances, police cars, fire engines, some delivery vehicles, but most of those are already electric. By next January, they all will be.

A door slammed. My granddaughter Shannon marched from the house. Shannon came to live with me two years ago, after Jana died. Her father's in South America, working for some German chemical company. He sends money twice a year.

"Has it happened yet?" she said, as if the Datsun had suddenly turned invisible.

"Not yet." I don't think she really cared. To her a car was a thing, a convenience she appreciated when it rained or if she had to carry stuff and ignored the rest of the time. She can't drive; she's only fourteen, and anyway she never learned. Since 1993, California law has allowed only one car and one registered driver to a household, and in this house that's me. They called it the Beat the Backup law. When we passed it, we hoped it would reduce the commute and force people to carpool and take buses. But after about two years of misery—no Californian wanted to be told he or she couldn't drive a car anywhere, anytime, ever—we realized that it wasn't doing what we wanted it to. Hell, Ricardo's the registered driver in his family, and I've seen all three Muñoz teenagers at the wheel of the Toyota. The penalties are stiff enough—it's a two hundred fifty dollar fine if they catch you, and for a second offense they disable the car and confiscate your keys for a month, and the car sits there, while you call yourself or your partner or the kids ugly names for having been so stupid. But there are about forty million people in the state of California, and even with the new law, we managed to accumulate about thirty million cars.

"I'm going to Shoreline Park," Shannon announced. She was wearing a yellow poncho, and a straw hat, the kind we used to call a coolie hat, and neon earrings. It's been forty years, and day-glo is back.

Watching her wheel the purple Fuji tenspeed out of the shed, I almost told her to stay. But Marilyn said, —Never mind, Charlie, let her be. She doesn't understand.—

"Shannon, be back by eight o'clock, okay?"

I got a look of what I assumed was assent and a sullen nod. She wasn't hostile, I was simply temporarily irrelevant to her life, along with the Datsun, and a sense of history.

A stereo wailed down the street: The Beach Boys, singing about a summer that never really happened, in which blond white kids drove along magical roads, in cars with magical names. All the radio stations, even NPR, had been playing car songs for weeks: Chuck Berry, Beach Boys, Springsteen, The Eagles. It pissed me off. I didn't need canned music, I had my own running through my head.

A periwinkle blue jitney, electric of course, purred along Addison and stopped in front of the brown apartment complex. Lilian Kim, eighty-seven, five kids, nineteen grandchildren, six great-grandchildren with two more expected in December, shuffled to it, on her way to the Greater East Market on University Avenue. When Berkeley started the service, right after the first Gulf war in 1991, they called it the Senior Service, but now everyone calls the jitneys the blue boxes, and instead of four for the whole town we have forty-seven spread across town, and everyone uses them.

Before I started riding the jitneys, I'd never said much more than good morning to Lily Kim. But sitting beside her in the blue box on the way to the market, I'd heard about her grandchildren and great-grandchildren; her husband Solomon, dead twelve years; her arthritis; and her knee replacement. She stopped driving when her eyesight went, and after Solomon's death, she explained, she had found herself relying solely on her far-flung, busy family, which she didn't enjoy at all. "I like calling the jitney," she informed me jauntily.

Marilyn said,—It's good for you to ride the jitney, and to listen to Lily Kim, Charlie. Keeps you from turning into an old grouchy hermit.—

Marilyn's been dead five years; she died of cancer, but she talks to me a lot, and I talk to her.

I'm thirsty, I told her.

—Why don't you have an iced tea?—

I thought I might have a beer, I said. It's a special day. One beer won't hurt.

Marilyn agreed that a beer wouldn't hurt. I went inside. The dog leaned into my legs, asking for reassurance. I petted her for a moment, then cracked two Anchor Steams, and ambled down Eighth Street to give one of them to Henry. He glared at me a little blindly, as if I had turned into a stranger or an enemy. But he took the beer.

The Chrysler gleamed, all red and chrome.

"I thought of trying to keep it," he said. "They giving permits, you know, certificates of authenticity; you get one and you can keep the car, you promise never to drive it."

"Would you drive it?"

"Sure."

"You'd have trouble getting fuel for it."

"They's ways." He stroked the brilliant chrome with his chammy. "My nephew know somebody selling gasoline from Venezuela, the old stuff with lead."

"It's illegal."

"So's making love with the lights on, some places." He tipped the bottle to his lips. I copied his motion. The beer was cold, good.

"It's a beautiful car," I said.

"Yeah." He took a deep breath. "They only made a thousand of them, you know. It does zero to sixty in nine seconds."

"I know."

"It was the Arabs did this. Fuck, Americans invented cars. They only left us alone, we'd of figured out how to fix this mess and keep the cars."

"It's true," I said. But I didn't think it was. The Gulf wars hurt, especially the second one when they bombed the oil fields, but it was the cost that finally got to us, the cost of gas and repairs and insurance, the cost of pollution and health care, and the incredible commute traffic, and the drunk driving, which we could not figure out how to stop. "Can't you give it to a museum? There's one opening next week in that old Chevy showroom on Shattuck Avenue."

"No way." He tipped the bottle again. It was empty. "This car's mine; no way I'm going to pay somebody five bucks to visit it. You got another one of these?"

"Sure." I walked home and got one. The radio was blaring again, Bob Dylan telling us about sacrifice and mayhem at 90 miles an hour. I wondered if there really was a Highway 61, and where, and what it has become. Interstate 80, eight blocks west, is now Shoreline Park. The freeways in L.A. are exercise courses, and dog runs, and parks, with palm trees planted on their roadbeds and green tough drought-resistant ivy dangling toward what the Angelenos still call surface streets.

Henry took the beer as if it were gold. "Thanks." He drank half of it. "Shit. I bought this car for five hundred dollars, thirty years ago, rebuilt it—the engine, everything— the same as the day it rolled off the line. It's ten years younger than me." Suddenly, shockingly, he brought the amber beer bottle down onto the handrubbed scarlet surface. I threw my hands across my eyes and leaped back. Beer sprayed out. Glass shattered, scarring the car's hood.

I walked home, smelling beer on my shirt. A lot of people were out of their houses, standing by their cars. A complex anger churned inside me. I walked through the house, found the hammer I keep on two nails in the pantry. Moving quickly, I walked to the car and swung the hammer in a hard blow at the side of the car.

The silver-grey metal dented. I did it again, squeezing hard, like José Canseco crushing a fastball out of the park, the way he used to, before we both retired. The panel folded like a pop can. The music wailed out a demented chorus, taking it to the limit one more time.

Down the street, Ricardo was slamming on the Toyota with a pipe wrench I banged on the sides and trunk hood of the car a few times. When I looked up, a car hauler with two tiers of cars on it was rolling toward me. Every place had chosen a different way to do it. In the Central Valley they'd erected crushers at shopping malls, and you got to take one last ceremonial drive.

A woman in a brown uniform emerged from the passenger's side of the cab. She held a clipboard and a plastic file drawer. She smiled at me with practiced compassion, like a nurse, and read me my address, then my name, last, then first.

"That's me."

"Can I have your California driver's license, please?" I gave it to her. She stuck it in the file drawer. "Keys." I dug them out of my pocket and handed them to her. "Any gas in it?"

"A cupful." I'd driven it nearly empty three days ago. I heard the sound of glass shattering; Ricardo was still smashing the Toyota.

"Okay." She got into the Datsun, drove it to the rear of the carrier. There was one empty space on the lower tier. A ramp extruded from the carrier. She drove the Datsun up onto the ramp, into the empty space.

The ramp retracted. The hauler drove away. Behind it, an empty one rolled up to the Toyota. A brigade of kids on cheerfully colored bicycles, Shannon among them, trailed it like a parade, making circles and figure eights and displaying their best wheelies.

My shoulders and chest and especially my hands hurt.

—Charlie,—Marilyn said,—you're still holding the hammer.—

I returned to the house to put it away. The dog crawled from beneath the armchair. "It's okay, you coward; it's over," I told her. Then I walked to the kitchen to make myself a glass of iced tea.

Diner

by Neal Barrett, Jr.

Neal Barrett, Jr. was born in San Antonio and now lives in Fort Worth, Texas. He is the author of thirty-six novels and numerous short stories and novelettes. His work spans the field from science fiction, westerns, and historical novels to mysteries and "off-the-wall" mainstream fiction. His most recent books are *Through Darkest America, The Hereafter Gang*, and the mystery/suspense novel, *Pink Vodka Blues* (St. Martin's Press). He is currently working on another mystery/suspense novel, *Dead Dog Blues*. His short fiction has appeared in *Omni, Amazing Stories, Isaac Asimov's Science Fiction Magazine*, and *The Magazine of Fantasy and Science Fiction*, and he received a Theodore Sturgeon Memorial Award in 1988 for his short story "Stairs."

    "Diner" was first published in *Omni*'s November 1987 issue and was reprinted in Gardner Dozois's *The Year's Best Science Fiction:Fifth Annual Collection*. The story takes place on a peninsula across from Galveston, an area Barrett knows well from having lived there. The characters, an ethnic mix of shrimpers and others reliant on a sea-based economy, exhibit the believable quirkiness which comes from a writer's experience among and observation of those he writes about. "Diner," as the Lynn story before it, extrapolates a unique near future from certain existing conditions, although this story is far more bleak.

DINER

Neal Barrett, Jr.

He woke sometime before dawn and brought the dream back
with him out of sleep. The four little girls attended Catholic
junior high in Corpus Christi. Their hand-painted guitars
depicted tropical Cuban nights. They played the same chord
again and again, a dull repetition like small wads of paper
hitting a drum. The light was still smoky, the furniture
unrevealed. He made his way carefully across the room. The
screened-in porch enclosed the front side of the house facing
the Gulf, allowing the breeze to flow in three directions. He
could hear rolling surf, smell the sharp tang of iodine in the
air. Yet something was clearly wrong. The water, the sand,
the sky had disappeared, lost behind dark coagulation. With
sudden understanding he saw the screen was clotted with
bugs. Grasshoppers blotted out the morning. They were
bouncing off the screen, swarming in drunken legions. He
ran outside and down the stairs, knowing what he'd find. The
garden was gone. A month before, he'd covered the small
plot of ground with old window screens and bricks. The
hoppers had collapsed the whole device. His pitiful stands of
lettuce were cropped clean, razored on the ground as if he'd

clipped them with a mower. Radishes, carrots, the whole bit. Eaten to the stalk. Then it occurred to him he was naked and under attack. Grasshopper socks knitted their way up to his knees. Something considered his crotch. He yelled and struck out blindly, intent on knocking hoppers silly. The fight was next to useless, and he retreated up the stairs.

Jenny woke while he was dressing.

"Something wrong? Did you yell just a minute ago?"

"Hoppers. They're all over the place."

"Oh, Mack."

"Little fuckers ate my salad bar."

"I'm sorry. It was doing so good."

"It isn't doing good now." He started looking for his hat.

"You want something to eat?"

"I'll grab something at Henry's."

She came to him, still unsteady from sleep, awkward and fetching at once. Minnie Mouse T-shirt ragged as a kite. A certain yielding coming against him.

"I got to go to work."

"Your loss, man."

"I dreamed of little Mexican girls."

"Good for you." She stepped back to gather her hair, her eyes somewhere else.

"Nothing happened. They played real bad guitar."

"So you say."

He made his way past the dunes and the ragged stands of sea grass, following the path over soft, dry sand to solid beach, the dark rows of houses on stilts off to his right, the Gulf rolling in, brown as mud, giving schools of mullet a ride. The hoppers had moved on, leaving dead and wounded behind. The sun came up behind dull, anemic clouds. Two skinny boys searched the ocean's morning debris. He found a pack of Agricultural Hero cigarettes in his pocket and cupped his hands against the wind. George Panagopoulos said there wasn't any tobacco in them at all. Said they made them out of half-dried shit and half kelp and that the shit wasn't bad, but he couldn't abide the kelp. Where the sandy road angled into the beach, he cut back and crossed Highway 87, the asphalt cracked and covered with sand, the tough coastal grass crowding in. The highway trailed southwest for two miles, dropping off abruptly where the red-white-and-blue Galveston ferries used to run, the other end stretching northeast up the narrow strip of Bolivar Peninsula past Crystal Beach and Gilchrist, then off the peninsula to High Island and Sabine Pass.

Mack began to find Henry's posters north of the road. They were tacked on telephone poles and fences, on the door of the derelict Texaco station, wherever Henry had wandered in this merchandising adventure. He gathered them in as he walked, snapping them off like paper towels. The sun began to bake, hot wind stinging up sand in tiny storms. The posters said: FOURTH OF JULY PICNIC AT HENRY ORTEGA'S DINER. ALL THE BARBEQUE PORK YOU CAN EAT. EL DIOS BLESS AMERICA.

Henry had drawn the posters on the backs of green accounting forms salvaged from the Sand Palace Motor Home Inn. Even if he'd gotten Rose to help, it was a formidable undertaking.

No easy task to do individually rendered, slightly crazed, and plainly coke-eyed fathers of our country. Every George Washington wore a natty clip-on Second Inaugural tie and, for some reason, a sporty little Matamoros pimp mustache. Now and then along the borders, an extra reader bonus, snappy American flags or red cherry bombs going *kapow*.

Mack walked on picking posters. Squinting back east he saw water flat as slate, vanishing farther out with tricks of the eye. Something jumped out there or something didn't.

Jase and Morgan were in the diner, and George Panagopoulos and Fleece. They wore a collection of gimmie caps and patched-up tennis shoes, jeans stiff and sequined with the residue of fish. Mack took the third stool down. Fleece said it might get hotter. Mack agreed it could. Jase leaned down the counter.

"Hoppers get your garden, too?"

"Right down to bedrock is all," Mack said.

"I had this tomato," Panagopoulos said, "this one little asshole tomato 'bout half as big as a plum; I'm taking a piss and hear these hoppers coming and I'm down and out of the house like that. I'm down there in what, maybe ten, twenty seconds flat, and this tomato's a little bugger and a seed. You know? A little bugger hanging down, and that's all." He made a swipe at his nose, held up a finger, and looked startled and goggle-eyed.

Mack pretended to study the menu and ordered KC steak and fries and coffee and three eggs over easy; and all this time Henry's standing over the charcoal stove behind the counter, poking something flat across the grill, concentrating intently on this because he's already seen the posters rolled up and stuffed in Mack's pocket and he knows he'll have to look right at Mack sooner or later.

"Galveston's got trouble," Jase said. "Dutch rowed

back from seeing that woman in Clute looks like a frog. Said nobody's seen Mendez for 'bout a week."

"Eddie's a good man for a Mex," Morgan said from down the counter. "He'll stand up for you, he thinks you're in the right."

Mack felt the others waiting. He wondered if he really wanted to get into this or let it go.

Fleece jumped in. "Saw Doc this morning, sneaking up the dunes 'bout daylight. Gotta know if those hoppers eat his dope."

Everyone laughed except Morgan. Mack was silently grateful.

"I seen that dope," Jase said. "What it is there's maybe three tomato plants 'bout high as a baby's dick."

"I don't want to hear nothin' about tomatoes," said Panagopoulos.

"Don't make any difference what it is," Fleece said. "Man determined to get high, he going to do it."

Panagopoulos told Mack that Dutch's woman up in Clute heard someone had seen a flock of chickens. Right near Umbrella Point. Rhode Island Reds running loose out on the beach.

Mack said fine. There was always a good chicken rumor going around somewhere. That or someone saw a horse or a pack of dogs. Miss Aubrey Gain of Alvin swore on Jesus there was a pride of Siamese cats in Leverty county.

Mack wolfed down his food. He didn't look at his plate. If you didn't look close you maybe couldn't figure what the hot peppers were covering up.

When he got up to go he said, "Real tasty, Henry," and then, as if the thought had suddenly occurred, "All right if you and me talk for a minute?"

Henry followed him out. Mack saw the misery in his face. He tried on roles like hats. Humble peon. An extra in *Viva Zapata*! Wily tourist guide with gold teeth and connections. Nothing fit. He looked like Cesar Romero, and this was his cross. Nothing could rob him of dignity. No one would pity a man with such bearing.

Mack took out the roll of posters and gave them back. "You know better than that, Henry. It wasn't a real good idea."

"There is no harm in this, Mack. You cannot say that there is."

"Not me I can't, no."

"Well, then."

"Come on. I got Huang Hua coming first thing tomorrow."

"Ah. Of course."

"Jesus, Henry."

"I am afraid that I forgot."

"Fine. Sure. Look, I appreciate the thought, and so does everyone else. This Chink, now, he hasn't got a real great sense of humor."

"I was thinking about a flag."

"What?"

"A flag. You could ask, you know? See what he says. It would not hurt to ask. A very small and insignificant flag in the window of the diner. Just for the one day, you understand?"

Mack looked down the road. "You didn't even listen. You didn't hear anything I said."

"Just for the one day. The Fourth and nothing more."

"Get all the posters down, Henry. Do it before tonight."

"How did you like the George Washington?" Henry asked. "I did all of those myself. Rose did the lettering, but I am totally responsible for the pictures."

"The Washington was great."

"You think so?"

"The eyes kinda follow you around."

"Yes." Henry showed his delight. "I tried for inner vision of the eyes."

"Well, you flat out got it."

Jase and Morgan came out, Jase picking up the rubber fishing boots he'd left at the door. Morgan looked moody and deranged. Mack considered knocking him senseless.

"Look," Mack told him, "I don't want you on my boat. Go with Panagopoulos. Tell him Fleece'll be going with me and Jase."

"Just fine with me," Morgan said.

"Good. It's fine with me, too."

Morgan wasn't through. "You take a nigger fishing on a day with a *r* in it, you goin' to draw sharks certain. I seen it happen."

"You tell that to Fleece," Mack said. "I'll stand out here and watch."

Morgan went in and talked to Panagopoulos. Jase waited for Fleece, leaning against the diner, asleep or maybe not. Mack lit an Agricultural Hero and considered the after taste of breakfast. Thought of likely antics with Jenny's parts. Wondered how a univalve mollusk with the mental reserve of grass could dream up a wentletrap shell and then wear it. This and other things.

Life has compensations, but there's no way of knowing what they are.

23

Coming in was the time he liked the best. The water was dark and flat, getting ready for the night. The bow cut green, and no sound at all but a jazzy little counterbeat, the cross-wind snapping two fingers in the sails. The sun was down an hour, the sky settling into a shade inducing temporary wisdom. He missed beer and music. Resented the effort of sinking into a shitty evening mood without help.

Swinging in through the channel, Pelican Island off to port, he saw the clutter of Port Bolivar, the rusted-out buildings and the stumps of rotted docks, the shrimpers he used to run heeling drunkenly in the flats. South of that was the chain-link fence and the two-story corrugated building. The bright red letters on its side read: SHINING WEALTH OF THE SEA JOYOUS COOPERATIVE 37 WELCOME HOME INDUSTRIOUS CATCHERS OF THE FISH.

This Chinese loony-tune message was clear a good nautical mile away; a catcher of the fish with a double cataract couldn't pretend it wasn't there.

Panagopoulos's big Irwin ketch was in, the other boats as well, the nets up and drying. Fleece brought the sloop in neatly, dropping the sails at precisely the right moment, a skill Mack appreciated all the more because Morgan was scarcely ever able to do it, either rushing in to shore full sail like a Viking bent on pillage or dropping off early and leaving them bobbing in the bay.

The Chinks greatly enjoyed this spectacle, the round-eyes paddling the forty-three-foot Hinckley in to shore.

Mack and Jase secured the lines, and then Jase went forward to help Fleece while the Chinks came aboard to look at the catch. The guards stayed on the dock looking sullen and important, rifles slung carelessly over their shoulders. Fishing Supervisor Lu Ping peered into the big metal hold, clearly disappointed.

"Not much fish," he told Mack.

"Not much," Mack said.

"It's June," Fleece explained. "You got the bad easterlies in June. Yucatan Current kinda edges up north, hits the Amarillo Clap flat on. That goin' to fuck up your fishing real good."

"Oh, yes." Lu Ping made a note. Jase nodded solemn agreement.

Mack told Jase and Fleece to come to the house for supper. He walked past the chain-link fence and the big generator that kept the fish in the corrugated building cooler than anyone in Texas.

The routine was: The boats would come in and tack close to the long rock dike stretching out from the southeast side of the peninsula, out of sight of the Chinks, and the women and kids would wave and make a fuss and the men would toss them fish in canvas bags, flounder or pompano or redfish if they were running or maybe a rare sack of shrimp, keeping enough good fish onboard to keep the Chinese happy but mostly leaving catfish and shark and plenty of mullet in the hold, that and whatever other odd species came up in the nets. It didn't matter at all, since everything they caught was ground up, steamed, pressed, processed, and frozen into brick-size bundles before they shipped it.

Mack thought about cutting through the old part of the port, then remembered about Henry and went back. There were still plenty of posters on fence posts and abandoned bait stands and old houses, and he pulled down all he could find before dark.

They ate in front of the house near the dunes, a good

breeze coming in from the Gulf strong enough to keep mosquitoes and gnats at bay, the wind drawing the driftwood fire nearly white. Henry brought a large pot of something dark and heady, announcing it was Acadia Parish shrimp Creole Chihuahua style, and nobody said it wasn't. Mack broiled flounder over a grill. Jase attacked guitar. Arnie Mace, Mack's uncle from Sandy Point, brought illegal rice wine. Not enough to count but potent. Fleece drank half a mason jar and started to cry. He said he was thinking about birds. He began to call them off. Herons and plovers and egrets. Gulls squawking cloud-white thick behind the shrimpers. Jase said he remembered pink flamingos in the tidal flats down by the dike.

"There was an old bastard in Sweeny, you know him, Mack," George Panagopoulos said. "Swears he had the last cardinal bird in Texas. Kept it in a hamster cage long as he could stand it. Started dreaming about it and couldn't sleep, got up in the middle of the night and stir-fried it in a wok. Had a frazzle of red feathers on his hat for some time, but I can't say that's how he got 'em."

"That was Emmett Dodge," Mack said. "I always heard it was a jay."

"Now, I'm near certain it was a cardinal." Panago- poulos looked thoughtfully into his wine. "A jay, now, if Emmett had had a jay, I doubt he could've kept the thing quiet. They make a awful lot of noise."

Mack helped Fleece throw up.

"Georgia won't talk to me," Fleece said miserably. "You the only friend I got."

"I expect you're right."

"You watch out for Morgan. He bad-talkin' you ever' chance he get."

"He wants to be pissant mayor, he can run. I sure don't care for the honor."

"He says your eyes beginnin' to slant."

"He said that?"

"Uh-huh."

"Well, fuck him." Fleece was unsteady but intact. Mack looked around for Henry and found him with Rose and Jenny. He liked to stand off somewhere and watch her. A good-looking woman was fine as gold, you caught her sitting by a fire.

He took Henry aside.

"I know what you are going to say," Henry said. "You are angry with me. I can sense these things."

"I'm not angry at all. Just get that stuff taken down before morning."

"I only do what I think is right, *mi compadre*. What is just. What is true." Henry tried for balance. "What I deeply feel in my heart. A voice cries out. It has to speak. This is the tragedy of my race. I feel a great sorrow for my people."

"Okay."

"I shall bow to your wishes, of course."

"Good. Just bow before Huang gets here in the morning."

"I will take them down. I will go and do it now."

"You don't have to do it now."

"I feel I am an intrusion."

"I feel like you've had enough to drink."

"Do you know what I am thinking? What I am thinking at this moment?"

"No, what?"

"I am thinking that I cannot remember tequila."

"Fleece has already done this," Mack said. "I don't

27

want you doing it, too. One crying drunk is enough."

"Forgive me. I cannot help myself. Mack, I don't remember how it tastes. I remember the lime and the salt. I recall a certain warmth. *Nada*. Nothing more."

Tears touched the Cesar Romero eyes, trailed down the Gilbert Roland cheeks. *If Jase plays "La Paloma," I'll flat kill him,* thought Mack. He left to look for Rose.

Jenny told him to come out on the porch and look at the beach. Crickets crawled out of the dunes and made for the water. The sand was black, a bug tide going out to sea. The crickets marched into the water and floated back. In the dark they looked like the ropy strands of a spill.

"The ocean scares me at night," Jenny said.

"Not always. You like it sometimes." He wanted to stop this but didn't know how to do it. She was working up to it a notch at a time.

"It's not you," she said.

"Fine, I'll write that down." He worked his hand up the T-shirt and touched the small of her back. She leaned in comfortably against him.

"Things are still bad, you get too far away from the coast. I don't want you just wandering around somewhere."

"I haven't really decided, Mack. I mean, it's not tomorrow or anything."

"I don't think you're going to find anyone, Jenny." He said it as gently as he could. "Folks are scattered all about."

She didn't answer. They stood a long time on the porch. The house already felt empty.

The chopper came in low out of the south, tilted slightly into the offshore breeze, rotors churning flat, snappy farts as it settled to 87 stirring sand. Soldiers hit the ground. They looked efficient. Counterrevolutionary acts would be dealt with swiftly. Fleece and Panagopoulos leaned against the diner trading butts. Henry came out for a look and ducked inside. The morning was oyster gray with a feeble ribbing of clouds. Major Huang waved at Mack. Then Chen came out of the chopper and started barking at the troops. Mack wasn't pleased. Huang was purely political—fat and happy and not looking for any trouble. Chen was maybe nineteen tops, a cocky little shit with new bars. Mack was glad he didn't speak English, which meant Jase wouldn't try to sell him a shark dick pickled in a jar or something worse.

The Chinese uniforms were gallbladder green to match the chopper. Chen and three troopers stayed behind. The troopers started tossing crates and boxes to the ground. One followed discreetly behind the major.

"Personal hellos," Huang Hua greeted Mack. "It is a precious day we are seeing."

Mack looked at the chopper. "Not many supplies this time."

"Not many fishes," Huang said.

It's going to be like this, is it? Mack followed him past the diner down the road to Shining Wealth Cooperative 37. He noticed little things. A real haircut. Starched khakis with creases. He wondered what Huang had eaten for breakfast.

Sergeant Fishing Supervisor Lu Ping greeted the major effusively. He had reports. Huang stuffed them in a folder. The air-conditioning was staggering. Mack forgot what it was like between visits.

"I have reportage of events," Huang began. He sat behind the plain wooden table and folded his hands. "It is a happening of unpleasant nature. Eddie Mendez will not

29

mayor himself in Galveston after today."

"And why's that?"

"Offending abuse. Blameful performance. Defecation of authority." Huang looked meaningfully at Mack. "Retaining back of fishes."

"What'll happen to Eddie?"

"The work you do here is of gravity, Mayor Mack. A task of large importance. Your people in noncoastal places are greatly reliant of fish."

"We're doing the best we can."

"I am hopeful this is true."

Mack looked right at him.

"Major, we're taking all the fish we can net. We got sails and no gas and nothing with an engine to put it into if we did. You're not going to help any shorting us on supplies. I've got forty-one families on this peninsula eating nothing but fish and rice. There's kids here never saw a carrot. We try to grow something, the bugs eat if first 'cause there's no birds left to eat the bugs. The food chain's fucked."

"You are better off than most."

"I'm sure glad to hear it."

"Please to climb down from my back. The Russians did the germing, not us."

"I know who did it."

Huang tried Oriental restraint. "We are engaging to help. You have no grateful at all. The Chinese people have come to fill this empty air."

"Vacuum."

"Yes. Vacuum." Huang considered. "In three, maybe four years, wheat and corn will be achieved in the ground again. Animal and fowl will be brought. This is very restricted stuff. I tell you, Mayor Mack, because I wish your nonopposing. I have ever shown you friendness. You cannot say I haven't."

"I appreciate the effort."

"You will find sweets in this shipment. For the children. Also decorative candles. Toothpaste. Simple magic tricks."

"Jesus Christ."

"I knew this would bring you pleasure."

Huang looked up. Lieutenant Chen entered politely. He handed Huang papers. Gave Mack a sour look. Mack recognized Henry's posters, the menu from the diner. Chen turned and left.

"What is this?" Huang appeared disturbed. "Flags? Counterproductive celebration? Barbeque pork?"

"Doesn't mean a thing," Mack explained. "It's just Henry."

Huang looked quizzically at George Washington, turning the poster in several directions. He glanced at the cardboard menu, at the KC Sirloin Scrambled Eggs Chicken-Fried Steak French Fries Omelet with Cheddar Cheese or Swiss Coffee Refills Free. He looked gravely at Mack.

"I did not think this was a good thing. You said there would be no trouble. One thing leads to a something other. Now it is picnics and flags."

"The poster business, all right," Mack said. "He shouldn't of done that. I figure it's my fault. The diner, no, there's nothing wrong with the diner."

Huang shook his head. "It is fanciment. The path to discontent." He appeared deeply hurt. The poster was an affront. The betrayal of a friend. He walked to the window, hands behind his back. "There is much to have renouncement here, Mayor Mack. Many fences to bend. I have been

lenient and foolish. No more Henry Ortega Diner. No picnic.
And better fishes, I think."

Mack didn't answer. Whatever he said would be wrong.

Huang recalled something of importance. He looked at
Mack again.

"You have a black person living here?"

"Two. A man and a woman."

"There is no racing discrimination? They are treated
fairly?"

"Long as they keep picking that cotton."

"No textiles. Only fishes."

"I'll see to it."

Mack walked back north, past a rusted Chevy van
waiting patiently for tires, past a pickup with windows still
intact. Rose hadn't seen Henry. She didn't know where he
was. "He didn't mean to cause trouble," she told Mack.

"I know that, Rose."

"He walks. He wanders off. He needs the time to
himself. He is a very sensitive man."

"He's all of that," Mack said. He heard children.
Smelled rice and fish, strongly seasoned with peppers.

"He respects you greatly. He says you are *muy
simpatico*. A man of heart. A leader of understanding."

A woman with fine bones and sorrowful eyes. Katy
Jurado, *One-Eyed Jacks*. He couldn't remember the year.

"I just want to talk to him, Rose. I have to see him."

"I will tell him. He will come to you. Here, take some
chilies to Jenny. It is the only thing I can grow the bugs
won't eat. Try it on the fish. Just this much, no more."

"Jenny'll appreciate that." A hesitation in her eyes. As
if she might say something more. Mack wouldn't ask. He

wasn't mad at Henry. His anger had abated, diluted after a day with Major Hua. He left and walked to the beach. Jase and Fleece were there. Jase had a mason jar of wine he'd maybe conned from Arnie Mace.

"Tell Panagopoulos and some of the others if you see 'em," Mack said, "I want to talk to Henry. He's off roaming around somewhere; I don't want him doing that."

"Your minorities'll do this," Jase reflected. "I'm glad I ain't a ethnic."

"It's a burden," Fleece said. "There going to be any trouble with the Chinks?"

"Not if I can help it."

"Fleece thought of two more birds," Jase said. "A cormorant and a what?"

"Tern."

"Yeah, right."

"Good," Mack said. "Keep your eyes peeled for Henry. He gets into that moon-over-Monterey shit, it'll take Rose a month to get him straight."

"I think I'm going to go," Jenny told him. "I think I got to do that, Mack. It just keeps eatin' away. Papa's likely gone, but Luanne and Mama could be okay."

He put out his cigarette and watched her across the room, watched her as she sat at the kitchen table bringing long wings of hair atop her head, going about this simple task with a quick, unconscious grace. The mirror stood against a white piece of driftwood she'd collected. She collected everything. Sand dollars and angel wings, twisted tritons and bright coquinas that faded in a day. Candle by the mirror in a sand-frosted Dr. Pepper bottle, light from this touching the bony hillbilly points of her hips. When she left she would take too much of him with her, and maybe he should figure some way to tell her that.

"I might not be able to get you a pass. I don't know. They don't much like us moving around without a reason."

"Oh, Mack. People do it all the time." Peering at him now past the candle. "Hey, now, I'm going to come on back. I just got to get this done."

He thought about the trip. Saw her walking old highways in his head. Maybe sixty-five miles up to Beaumont, cutting off north before that into the Thicket. He didn't tell her everything he heard. The way people were, things that happened. He knew it wouldn't make a difference if he did.

Jenny settled in beside him. "I said I'm coming back."

"Yeah, well, you'd better."

He decided, maybe at that moment, he wouldn't let her go. He'd figure out a way to stop her. She'd leave him in a minute. Maybe come back and maybe not. He had to know she was all right, and so he'd do it. He listened to the surf. On the porch, luna moths big as English sparrows flung themselves crazily against the screen.

The noise of the chopper brought him out of bed fast, on the floor and poking into jeans before Jase and Panago- poulos made the stairs.

"It's okay," he told Jenny, "just stay inside and I'll see."

She nodded and looked scared, and he opened the screen door and went out. Dawn washed the sky the color of moss. Jase and Panagopoulos started talking both at once.

Then Mack saw the fire, the reflection past the house. "Oh, Jesus H. Christ!"

"Mack, he's got pigs," Panagopoulos said. "I seen

'em. Henry's got pigs."

"He's got what?"

"This is bad shit."

Mack was down the stairs and past the house. He could see other people. He started running. Jase and Panagopoulos at his heels. The chopper was on the ground, and then Fleece came out of the crowd across the road.

"Henry ain't hurt bad, I don't think," he told Mack.

"Henry's hurt?" Mack was unnerved. "Who hurt him, Fleece? Is someone going to tell me something soon?"

"I figure that Chen likely done a house-to-house," Fleece said, "some asshole trick like that. Come in north and worked down rousting people out for kicks. Stumbled on Henry; shit, I don't know. Just get him out of there, Mack."

Mack wanted to cry or throw up. He pushed through the crowd and saw Chen, maybe half a dozen soldiers, then Henry. Henry looked foolish, contrite, and slightly cockeyed. His hands were tied behind. Someone had hit him in the face. The rotors stirred waves of hot air. The diner went up like a box. Mack tried to look friendly. Chen lurched about yelling and waving his pistol, looking wild-eyed as a dog.

"Let's work this out," Mack said. "We ought to get this settled and go home."

Chen shook his pistol at Mack, danced this way and that in an unfamiliar step. Mack decided he was high on the situation. He'd gotten hold of this and didn't know where to take it, didn't have the sense to know how to stop.

"We can call this off and you don't have to worry about a thing," Mack said, knowing Chen didn't have the slightest idea what he was saying. "That okay with you? We just call it a night right now?"

Chen looked at him or somewhere else entirely. Mack

35

wished he had shoes and a shirt. Dress seemed proper if you were talking to some clown with a gun. He was close enough to see the pigs. The crate was by the chopper. Two pigs, pink and fat, mottled like an old man's hand. They were squealing and going crazy with the rotors and the fire and not helping Chen's nerves or Mack's either. Mack could just see Henry thinking this out, how he'd do it, fattening up the porkers somehow and thinking what everybody'd say when they saw it wasn't a joke, not soyburger KC steak or chicken-fried fish-liver rice and chili peppers. Not seaweed coffee or maybe grasshopper creole crunch. None of that play-food shit they all pretended was something else, not this time, *amigos*, this time honest-to-God pig. Maybe the only pigs this side of Hunan, and only Henry Ortega and Jesus knew where he found them. Mack turned to Chen and gave his best mayoral smile.

"Why don't we just forget the whole thing? Just pack up the pigs there and let Henry be. I'll talk to Major Huang. I'll square all this with the major. That'd be fine with you, now, wouldn't it?"

Chen stopped waving the gun. He looked at Mack. Mack could see wires in his eyes. Chen spoke quickly over his shoulder. Two of the troopers lifted the pigs into the chopper.

"Now, that's good," Mack said. "That's the thing you want to do."

Chen walked off past Henry, his face hot as wax from the fire, moving toward the chopper in this jerky little two-step hop, eyes darting every way at once, granting Mack a lopsided half-wit grin that missed him by a good quarter mile. Mack let out a breath. He'd catch hell from Huang, but it was over. Over and done. He turned away, saw Rose in the crowd and then Fleece. Mack waved. Someone gave a quick and sudden cheer. Chen jerked up straight, just reacting to the sound, not thinking any at all, simply bringing the pistol up like the doctor hit a nerve, the gun making hardly any noise, the whole thing over in a blink and no time to stop it or bring it back. Henry blew over like a leaf, taking his time, collapsing with no skill or imagination, nothing like Anthony Quinn would play the scene.

"Oh, shit, now don't do that," Mack said, knowing this was clearly all a mistake. "Christ, you don't want to do that!"

Someone threw a rock, maybe Jase. Troopers raised their rifles and backed off. A soldier near Chen pushed him roughly toward the chopper. Chen looked deflated. The rotors whined up and blew sand. Mack shut it out, turned it back. It was catching up faster than he liked. He wished Chen had forgotten to take the pigs. The thought seemed less than noble. He considered some gesture of defiance. Burn rice in Galveston harbor. They could all wear Washington masks. He knew what they'd do was nothing at all, and that was fine because Henry would get up in just a minute and they'd all go in the diner and have a laugh. Maybe Jase had another jar of wine. Mack was certain he could put this back together and make it right. He could do it. If he didn't turn around and look at Henry, he could do it . . . .

Horse Latitudes

by Richard Kadrey

Richard Kadrey lives in San Francisco, California. His first novel, *Metrophage*, was published as part of the revived Ace Specials series in 1988. He is working on a second. His short fiction has appeared in *Interzone* and *Omni* and the anthology *Semiotext(e) SF*, edited by Rudy Rucker, Peter Lamborn Wilson, and Robert Anton Wilson. Before becoming known for his fiction, he had already earned a reputation as an artist for his Xerox collage art and as an aficionado and critic of offbeat music. Kadrey's most recent story for *Omni* was "Becoming Cindy," published in September 1989.

In "Horse Latitudes," Kadrey uses his deep abiding interest in music to explore how changing living conditions can conspire to force artists into groping for and creating a new musical language. The story, published here for the first time, takes place in the near future, mostly in San Francisco— a San Francisco made almost unrecognizable by nature running wild as a result of the greenhouse effect.

HORSE LATITUDES

Richard Kadrey

Fame is just schizophrenia with money.

I died on a Sunday, when the new century was no more than four or five hours old. Midnight would have been a more elegant death (and a genuine headline grabber), but we were still on stage, and I decided that suicide, like masturbation, would lose something when experienced with 100,000 close, personal friends.

I don't recall exactly when I accepted the New Year's Eve gig at Madison Square Garden; the band had never played one before, but it became inextricably tied in with my decision to kill myself. Somehow I couldn't bear the idea of a twenty-first century. Whenever I thought of it, I was overwhelmed by the memory of flying in a chartered plane over the Antarctic ice fields on my thirtieth birthday. A brilliant whiteness tinged with freezing blue swept away in all directions. It was an unfillable emptiness. It was death. It could never be fed or satisfied—neither the ice sheet nor the new century—at least, not by me.

No one suspected, of course. Throughout this crisis of faith, I always remained true to fame. I acted out the excesses that were expected of me. I denied rumors that I had invented. I spat at photographers and managed to double my press coverage.

The suicide itself was a simple, dull, anticlimactic affair. The police had closed the show quickly when the audience piled up their seats and started a bonfire during our extended "Auld Lang Syne." Back in my room at the Pierre I swallowed a bottle of pills and vodka. I felt stupid and disembodied, like some character who had been written out of a Tennessee Williams play—Blanche Dubois' spoiled little brother. I found out later that it was Kumiko, my manager, who found me swimming in my own vomit and got me to the hospital. When I awoke, I was in Oregon, tucked away in the Point Mariposa Recovery Center, where the movie stars come to dry out. There wasn't even a fence, just an endless expanse of lizard green lawn. Picture a cemetery. Or a country club with thorazine.

I left the sanitarium three weeks later, without telling anyone. I went out for my evening walk and just kept on walking. The Center was housed in a converted mansion built on a bluff over a contaminated beach near Oceanside. I had, until recently, been an avid rock climber. Inching your way across a sheer rock face suspended by nothing but your own chalky fingers is the only high comparable to being on stage (death, spiritual or physical, being the only possible outcome of a wrong or false move in either place). It took me nearly an hour to work my way down the granite wall to a dead beach dotted with Health Department warning signs and washed-up medical waste. I checked to see that my lithium hadn't fallen out on the climb down. Then, squatting among plastic bags emblazoned with biohazard stickers and scrawny gulls holding empty syringes in their beaks, I picked up a rusty scalpel and slit the cuffs of my robe. Two thousand dollars in twenties and fifties spilled out onto the gray sand.

I left my robe on the sand, following the freeway shoulder in sweat pants and a t-shirt. In Cannon Beach I bought a coat and a ticket on a boat going down the coast to Los Angeles. My ticket only took me as far as San Francisco. We reached the city two days later, in the dark hours of the early morning. As we sailed in under the Golden Gate Bridge, San Francisco was aglow like some art nouveau foundry, anesthetized beneath dense layers of sea fog. Far across the bay, on the Oakland side, I could just make out the tangle of mangrove swamp fronting the wall of impenetrable green that was the northernmost tip of the rain forest.

Six weeks later, I left my apartment in the Sunset District and headed for a south of Market Street bar called Cafe Juju. A jumble of mossy surface roots, like cords from God's own patchbay, had tangled themselves in the undercarriages of abandoned cars on the broad avenue that ran along Golden Gate Park. Here and there, hundred foot palms and *kapoks* jutted up from the main body of the parkland, spreading their branches, stealing light and moisture from the smaller native trees. The Parks Department had given up trying to weed out the invading plant species and concentrated instead on keeping the museums open and the playgrounds clear for the tourists who never came anymore.

Downtown, the corners buzzed with street musicians beating out jittery sambas on stolen guitars, improvised sidewalk markets catering to the diverse tastes of refugees from Rio de Janeiro, Mexico City, and Los Angeles. Trappers from Oakland hawked marmosets and brightly plumed jungle birds that screamed like scalded children. In the side streets, where the lights were mostly dead, golden-eyed jaguars hunted stray dogs. Overhead, you could look up and watch the turning of the new constellation, *Fer-De-Lance,* made up of a cluster of geosynchronous satellites. Most belonged to NASA and the U.N., but the Army and the DEA were up there too, watching the progress of the jungle and refugees northward.

I was walking to a club called Cafe Juju.

Inside, a few heads turned in my direction. There was some tentative whispering around the bar, but not enough to be alarming. I was thinner than when I'd left the band. I'd let my beard grow, and since I had stopped bleaching my hair, it had darkened to its natural and unremarkable brown. As I threaded my way through the crowd, a crew-cut blonde pretended to bump into me. I ignored her when she said my name and settled at a table in the back, far away from the band. "Mister Ryder," said the man sitting across from me. "Glad you could make it."

I shook the gloved hand he offered. "Since you called me that name so gleefully, I assume you got it?" I said.

He smiled. "How about a drink?"

"I like to drink at home. Preferably alone."

"Got to have a drink," he said. "It's a bar. You don't drink, you attract attention."

"All right, I'll have a Screwdriver."

"A health nut, right? Getting into that California lifestyle? Got to have your Vitamin C." He hailed a waitress and ordered us drinks. The waitress was thin, with close-

44

cropped black hair and an elegantly hooked nose sporting a single gold ring. She barely noticed me.

"So, did you get it?" I asked.

Virilio rummaged through the inner recesses of his battered Army trenchcoat. He wore it with the sleeves rolled up; his forearms, where I could see them, were a solid mass of snakeskin tattoos. I couldn't be sure where the tattoos ended because his hands were covered in skin tight black kid gloves. He looked younger than he probably was, had the eager and restless countenance of a bird of prey. He pulled a creased white envelope from an inside pocket and handed it to me. Inside was a birth certificate and a passport.

"They look real," I said.

"They are real," Virilio said. "If you don't believe me, take those down to any DMV and apply for a drivers license. I guarantee they'll check out as legit."

"It makes me nervous. It seems too easy."

"Don't be a schmuck. The moment you told me your bank accounts were set up with names from the Times obituaries, I knew we were in business. I checked out all the names you gave me. In terms of age and looks, this guy is the closest match to you."

"And you just sent to New York for this?"

"Yeah," Virilio said, delighted by his own cleverness. "There's no agency that checks birth certificates against death records. Then, I took your photo and this perfectly legal birth certificate to the passport office, pulled a few strings, and got it pushed through fast." From the stage, the guitar cut loose with a wailing Stratocaster solo, like alley cats and razor blades at a million decibels over a dense *batucada* backbeat. I closed my eyes as turquoise fireballs went off in my head. "You never told me why you needed

45

this," said Virilio.

"I had a scrape with the law a few years ago," I told
him. "Bringing in rare birds and snakes from south of the
border. Department of Fish and Game seized my passport."

Virilio's smile split the lower part of his face into a big
toothy crescent moon. "That's funny. That's fucking hysteri-
cal. I guess these weird walking forests put your ass out of
business."

"Guess so," I said.

The waitress with the nose brought our drinks and
Virilio said, "Can you catch this round?" As I counted out
the bills, Virilio slid his arm around the waitress's hips. Either
she knew him or took him for just another wasted homeboy
because she did not react at all. "Frida here plays music,"
said Virilio. "You ought to hear her tapes, she's real good.
You ever play in a band, Ryder?"

"No," I said. "Always wanted to, but never found the
time to learn an instrument." I looked at Frida the waitress
and handed her the money. From this new angle I saw that,
along with her nose ring, Frida's left earlobe was studded
with a half-dozen or so tiny jeweled studs. There were more
gold rings just above her left eyebrow, which was in the
process of arching. Her not unattractive lips held a sup-
pressed smirk that could only mean that she had noticed me
noticing her.

"That's interesting," Virilio said. "I thought everybody
your age had a little high school dance band or something."

"Sorry."

Frida folded the bills and dropped them into a pocket of
her apron. "They're playing some of my stuff before the
Yanomamö Boys set on Wednesday. Come by, if you're
downtown," she said. I nodded and said "Thanks." As she

moved back to the bar, I saw Virilio shaking his head. "Freaking Frida," he said.

"What does that mean?"

"Frida was okay. Used to sing in some bands; picked up session work. Now she's into this new shit." Virilio rolled his eyes. "She sort of wigged out a few months ago. Started hauling her tape recorder over to Marin and down south into the jungle. Wants to digitize it or something. Says she looking for the Music of Jungles. Says it just like that, with capital letters." He shrugged and sipped his drink. "I've heard some of this stuff. Sounds like a movie sound track, *Attack From the Planet Whacko*, if you know what I mean."

"You ever been into the rain forest?" I asked.

"Sure. I've been all up and down the coast. They keep 101 between here and L.A. pretty clear."

"L.A.'s as far south as you can get?"

"No, but after that, you start running into government defoliant stations, rubber tappers, and these monster dope farms cut right into the jungle. Those farms are scary. Mostly white guys running them, with Mexicans and Indians pulling the labor. And they are hardcore. Bloody you up and throw your ass to the crocodiles just for laughs."

"I may need you to do your name trick again. I have some money in Chicago—"

"Not anymore you don't. Not for two or three months. Nothing but monkeys, snakes, and malaria out that way, from Galveston to Detroit. If you have any swampland in Florida, congratulations. It's really a swamp." The kid took a sip of his beer. "Of course, I could always do a data search, see where the Feds reassigned the assets of your bank."

"No, never mind," I said, deciding I didn't particularly want this kid bird-dogging me through every database he could get to. "It's not that important."

Virilio shrugged. "Suit yourself," he said, and shook his head wearily at the bare-breasted young woman who bumped drunkenly into our table. "Run, honey," he told her. "The fashion police are hot on your trail," as she staggered over to her friends at the bar. The local scene-makers had taken the heat as their cue to go frantically native; the majority of them were dressed in Japanese-imported imitations of Brazilian Indian gear. It was like some grotesque acid trip combining the worst of Dante with a Club Med brochure for Rio: young white kids, the girls wearing nothing but body paints or simple Lacandon *hipils* they had seen in some high school slide show; the boys in loin cloths, showing off their bowl-style haircuts, mimicking those worn by Amazonian tribesmen.

"The *Santeros* say that this shit—the jungle, the animals, all the craziness—it's all revenge. Amazonia getting back at all the stupid, greedy bastards who've been raping it for all these years."

"That's a pretty harsh judgment," I said. "Are you always so Old Testament?"

"You've got me all wrong. I'm thrilled. L.A.'s gone. They finally got something besides TV executives and mass murderers to grow in that goddamned desert." Virilio smiled. "Of course, I don't really buy all that mystical shit. The FBI are covering up for the people who are really responsible."

"The FBI?" I asked.

"It's true," Virilio said. "They hushed it up—same branch that iced Kennedy and ran the Warren Commission.

"A couple of geneticists who'd been cut loose from Stanford were working for the Brazilian government, cooking up a kind of extra fast-grow plant to re-seed all the burned-up land in the Amazon. Supposedly, these plants were locked on fast forward—they'd grow quick and die quick, stabilizing the soil so natural plants could come in. Only the bastards wouldn't die. They kept on multiplying and choked out everything else. Six weeks after they planted the first batch, Rio was gone. It's all true. I know somebody that has copies of the FBI reports."

The band finished its set and left the stage to distracted applause. I stood and dropped a jiffy bag on Virilio's side of the table. "I've got go now. Thanks for the ID," I said. Virilio slipped some of the bills from the end of the bag and riffled through them. "Non-sequential twenties," I said, "just like you wanted."

He smiled and put the bag in his pocket. "Just to prevent any problems, just to short-circuit any second thoughts you might be having about why you should give a person like me all this money for some paper you could have gotten yourself, I want to make sure you understand that the nature of my work is facilitation. I'm a facilitator. I'm not a dealer, or muscle, or a thief, but I can do all those things, if required. What I got you wasn't a birth certificate; any asshole could have gotten you a birth certificate. What I got you was *the* birth certificate. One that matches you close enough so that getting you a passport, letting you move around, will be no problem. I had to check over two years of obituaries, contact the right agencies, grease the right palms. It's knowing which palms to grease and when that you're paying me for. Not that piece of paper."

I slid my new identity into my jacket. "Thanks," I said.

Outside Cafe Juju, the warm, immobile air had taken on the quality of some immense thing at rest—a mountain or phantom whale, pressing down on the city, squeezing its

Sargasso dreams from the cracks in the walls out onto the streets. I pulled out my emergency hip flask and took a drink. I was reminded of the region of windless ocean known as the Horse Latitudes, called that in remembrance of the Spanish galleons that would sometimes find themselves adrift in those dead waters. The crews would strip the ship down to the bare wood in hopes of lightening themselves enough to move in the feeble breeze. When everything else of value had been thrown overboard, the last thing to go were the horses. Sometimes the Horse Latitudes were carpeted for miles with a floating rictus of palominos and Arab stallions, buoyed up by the immense floating kelp beds and their own churning internal gases. The Horse Latitudes were not a place you visited, but where you found yourself if you allowed your gaze to be swallowed up by the horizon or to wander on the map to places you might go, rather than where you were.

I'd walked a couple of blocks up Ninth Street when I realized I was being followed. It was my habit to stop often in front of stores, apparently to window-shop or admire the beauty of my own face. In fact, I was checking the reflections caught in the plate glass, scanning the street behind me for faces that had been there too long. This time I couldn't find a face, but just beyond a wire pen where a group of red-faced *campesinos* were betting on cock fights, I did see a jacket. It was bulky and black, of some military cut, and one side was decked with the outline of a bird skull done in clusters of purple and white rhinestones. The jacket's owner hung back where vehicles and pedestrians blocked most of the streetlight. It was only the fireworks in the rhinestones that had caught my eye.

Just to make sure it wasn't simple paranoia, I went another block up Ninth and stopped by the back window of a VW van full of caged snakes. When I checked again, the jacket had moved closer. I cut to my right, down a side street, then left, back toward the market. The jacket hung behind me, the skull a patch of hard light against the dark buildings.

I ran down an alley between a couple of closed shops and kept going, taking corners at random. The crumbling masonry of the ancient industrial buildings was damp where humidity had condensed on the walls. I found myself on a dark street where the warehouses were lost behind the blooms of pink and purple orchids. The petals looked like frozen fire along the walls. Behind me, someone kicked a bottle, and I sprinted around another corner. I was lost in the maze of alleys and drivethrus that surrounded the rotting machine shops and abandoned wrecking yards. Sweating and out of breath, I ran toward a light. When I found it, I stopped.

It was a courtyard or a paved patch of ground where a building had once stood. Fires were going in a few battered oil drums, fed by children with slabs of dismantled bill-boards, packing crates, and broken furniture. Toward the back of the courtyard, men had something cooking on a spit rigged over one of the drums. Their city-issued mobile shelters, something like hospital gurneys with heavy-gauge wire coffins mounted on top, were lined in neat rows against one wall. I had heard about the tribal homeless encampments but had never seen one before. Many of the homeless were the same junkies and losers that belonged to every big city, but most of the tribal people, I'd heard, were spillover from the refugee centers and church basements. Whole villages would sometimes find themselves abandoned in a strange city, after being forcibly evacuated from their farms in Venezuela and Honduras. They roamed the streets with their belongings crammed into government-issue snail shells, fading into a dull wandering death.

But it wasn't always that way. Some of the tribes were evolving quickly in their new environment, embracing the icons of the new world that had been forced on them. Many of the men still wore lip plugs, but their traditional skin stains had been replaced with metal-flake auto body paint and dime store make up. The women and children wore necklaces of auto glass, strips of mylar, and iridescent watch faces. Japanese silks and burned-out fuses were twined in their hair.

Whatever mutual curiosity held us for the few seconds that I stood there passed when some of the men stepped forward, gesturing and speaking to me in a language I didn't understand. I started moving down the alley. Their voices crowded around me; their hands touched my back and tugged at my arms. They weren't threatening, but I still had to suppress an urge to run. I looked back for the jacket that had followed me from Cafe Juju, but it wasn't back there.

I kept walking, trying to stay calm. I ran through some breathing exercises a yoga guru I'd known for a week in Munich had taught me. After a few minutes, though, some of the tribesmen fell away. And when I turned a corner, unexpectedly finding myself back on Ninth, I discovered I was alone.

On Market, I was too shaky to bargain well and ended up paying a gypsy cab almost double the usual rate for a ride to the Sunset. At home, I took a couple of Percodans and washed them down with vodka from the flask. Then I lay down with all my clothes on, reaching into my pocket to hold the new identity Virilio had provided me. Around dawn, when the howler monkeys started up in Golden Gate Park, I fell asleep.

I tried to write some new songs, but I had become overcome with inertia and little by little lost track of myself. Sometimes, on the nights when the music was especially bad or I couldn't stand the random animal racket from the park anymore, I'd have a drink, and then walk. The squadrons of refugees and the damp heat of the rain forest that surrounded the city made the streets miserable much of the time, but I decided it was better to be out in the misery of the streets than to hide with the rotten music in my room.

I was near Chinatown, looking for the building where I'd shared a squat years before, when I ran into a crowd of sleepwalkers. At first, I didn't recognize them, so complete was their impression of wakefulness. Groups of men and women in business clothes waited silently for buses they had taken the previous morning, while merchants sold phantom goods to customers who were home in bed. Smiling children played in the streets, dodging ghost cars. Occasionally a housewife from the same neighborhood as a sleepwalking grocer (because these night strolls seemed to be a localized phenomenon, affecting one neighborhood at a time) would reenact a purchase she had made earlier that day, entering into a kind of slow motion waltz with the merchant, examining vegetables that weren't there or weighing invisible oranges in her hand. No one had an explanation for the sleepwalking phenomenon. Or rather, there were so many explanations that they tended to cancel each other out. The one fact that seemed to be generally accepted was that the night strolls had become more common as the rain forest crept northward toward San Francisco, as if the boundary of Amazonia was surrounded by a region compounded of the collective dreams of all the cities it had swallowed.

I followed the sleepwalkers, entering Chinatown through the big ornamental gate on Grant Street, weaving in, out, and through the oddly beautiful group pantomime. The streets were almost silent there, except for the muted colors of unhurried feet and rustling clothes. None of the sleepwalkers ever spoke, although they mouthed things to each other. They frowned, laughed, got angry, reacting to something they had heard or said when they had first lived that particular moment.

It was near Stockton Street that I heard the looters. Then I saw them, moving quickly and surely through the narrow alleys, loaded down with merchandise from the sleepwalkers' open stores. The looters took great pains not to touch any of the sleepers. Perhaps they were afraid of being infected with the sleepwalking sickness.

Watching them, cop paranoia got a hold of me, and I started back out of Chinatown. I was almost to the gate, dodging blank-eyed Asian children and ragged teenagers with armloads of *bok choy* and video tapes when I saw something else: coming out of a darkened dim sum place—a jeweled bird skull on a black jacket. The jacket must have spotted me, too, because it darted back inside. I followed it in.

A dozen or so people, mostly elderly Chinese couples, sat miming silent meals inside the unlit restaurant. Cats, like the homeless, had apparently figured out the pattern the sleepwalking sickness took through the city. Dozens of the mewing animals moved around the tables, rubbing against sleepers' legs and licking grease off the stacked dim sum trays. I went back to the kitchen, moving through the middle of the restaurant, trying to keep the sleepers around me as a demilitarized zone between me and the jacket. I wasn't as certain of myself inside the restaurant as I had been on the street. Too many sudden shadows. Too many edges hiding between the bodies of the dreaming patrons.

There were a couple of aproned men in the kitchen, kneading the air into dim sum. Cats perched on the cutting tables and freezer like they owned the place. Whenever one of the sleepwalking cooks opened the refrigerator doors, the cats went berserk, crowding around his legs, clawing at leftover dumplings and chunks of raw chicken. There was, however, no jacket back there. Or in the rest room. The rear exit was locked. I went back out through the restaurant, figuring I'd blown it. I hadn't had any medication in a couple of weeks and decided I'd either been hallucinating again or had somehow missed the jacket while checking out the back. Then from the dark she said my name, the name she knew me by. I turned in the direction of the voice, and the jeweled skull winked at me from the corner.

I had walked within three feet of her. She was slumped at a table with an old woman, only revealing herself when she shifted her gaze from the tablecloth to me, doing a good imitation of the narcotised pose of a sleeper. She motioned for me to come over, and I sat down. Then she pushed a greasy bag of cold dim sum at me. "Have one," she said, like we were old friends.

"Frida?" I said.

She smiled. "Welcome to the land of the dead."

"Why were you following me?"

"*I* was raiding the fridge." She reached into the bag

and pulled out a spring roll, which she wrapped in a paper napkin and handed to me. As she moved, I caught a faint glimmer off the gold rings above her eyebrow. "*You*, I believe, were the one who only seconds ago was pinballing through here like Blind Pew."

"I'll have my radar checked. Do you always steal your dinner?"

"Whenever I can. I'm only at the café a couple of nights a week. And tips aren't what they used to be. Even the dead are peckish around here."

The old woman with whom we shared the table leaned from side to side in her chair, laughing the fake, wheezing laugh of sleepers, her hands describing arcs in the air. "So maybe you weren't following me tonight," I said. "Why did follow me the other night from Cafe Juju."

"You remind me of somebody."

"Who?"

"I don't know. Your face doesn't belong here. But I don't know where it should be, either. I know I've seen you before. Maybe you're a cop and you busted me. Maybe that's why you look familiar. Maybe you're a bad guy I saw getting booked. Maybe we went steady in the third grade. Maybe we had the same piano teacher. Ever since I saw you at the café, I've got all these maybes running through my head."

"Maybe you've got me mixed up with someone."

"Not a chance," said Frida. She smiled and in the half-light of the restaurant I couldn't tell if she knew who I was or not. She didn't look crazy, but she still scared me. I'd gone to the funeral of more than one friend who, walking home, had turned a corner and walked into his or her own Mark David Chapman. Frida's smile made her look strangely vapid, which surprised me because her eyes were anything but that. Her face had too many lines for someone her age, but there was a kind of grace in the high bones of her cheeks and forehead.

"You're not a cop or a reporter, are you?" I asked.

Her eyes widened in an expression that was somewhere between shock and amusement. "No. Unlike you, I'm pretty much what I appear to be."

"You're a waitress who tails people on her breaks."

She shrugged and bit into her spring roll, singing, "Get your kicks on Route Sixty-six."

"Now you're just being stupid, " I said. "Virilio didn't tell me that part. He just said you were crazy."

"Did he say that?" She looked away and her face fell into shadow. I leaned back, thinking that if she was crazy, I might have just said the thing that would set her off. But a moment later she turned back, wearing the silly smile. "Virilio's one to talk, playing Little Caesar in a malaria colony." She picked up a paper napkin from the table and, with great concentration, began wiping her hands, a finger at a time. Then she said: "I'm looking for something."

"The Music of Jungles?"

"Jesus, did he tell you my favorite color, too?"

"He just told me it was something you'd told him."

"Red," she said and shrugged. "I am looking for something. But it's kind of difficult to describe."

"California is on its last legs. If you want to play music, why don't you go to New York?"

She reached down and picked up a wandering cat. It was a young Abyssinian, and it immediately curled up in her lap, purring. "What I'm looking for isn't in New York," she said. "I thought from your face you might be looking for

57

something, too. That's why I followed you."

"What is the Music of Jungles?" I asked.

She shook her head. "No, I'm sorry. I think I made a mistake."

I slid the hip flask from my pocket and took a drink. "Tell you the truth, I'm looking for something, too."

"I knew it," she said. "What?

"Something new. Something I've only seen in flashes. A color and quality of sound that I've never been able to get out of my head. I started out looking for it but got distracted along the way. I figure this is my last chance to see if it's really there or just another delusion."

"You're a musician?" she asked.

"Yes."

She picked up the flask, sniffed, and took a drink, smiling and coughing a little as the vodka went down. "What's your name?" she asked.

"You already know my name."

"I know *a* name," she said, setting down the flask. "Probably something store-bought. Maybe from Virilio?"

I shrugged and took the flask from her. "Your turn. What's the Music of Jungles?"

She looked down and leaned back in her chair, stroking the cat. "First off," she said, "it's not the Music of Jungles. Jungles are in Tarzan movies. What you're trying to describe is a tropical forest or a rain forest. I don't use rain forest sounds in my music because I think they're beautiful, although I do think they're beautiful," she said. "I use them because they're the keys to finding the Songtracks of a place."

Frida set the cat on the floor and leaned forward, elbows resting on the table. "Here's what it is," she said,

"Some of the tribal people in Amazonia believe that the way the world came into existence was through different songs sung by different gods, a different song for each place. The land, they believe, is a map of a particular melody. The contours of the hills, the vegetation, the animals—they're notes, rests, and rhythms in the song that calls a place into being and also describes it. Over thousands of years the Indians have mapped all the songs of Amazonia, walked everywhere and taught the songs to their children.

"Where we are now, though, is special," Frida said, and she drew her hands up in a gesture that took in all of our surroundings. "The forest that surrounds San Francisco, it's Amazonia, but it's new. And it has its own unique Songtrack. That's what all my music is about. That's what I'm all about. No one has found the song of this part of Amazonia yet, so I'm going to find it," she said.

"When you find it, what will the song tell you?" I asked.

She shrugged, pressing her hands deep into the pockets of her jacket. "I don't exactly know. Maybe the story of the place. What went on here in the past; what'll happen in the future. I don't know exactly. It's enough for me just to do it."

I put the flask in my pocket. "Listen Frida," I said, "the atmosphere in here is definitely not growing on me. Would you like to go someplace?"

"I don't live too far away." She paused and said, "Maybe I could play you some of my music."

"I'd like that," I said. As she stood she said, "You know, you managed to still not tell me your name."

I looked at her for a moment. An old man shuffled between us, nodding and waving to sleeping friends. I thought about the Music of Jungles. Was this woman insane? I wondered. I'd been dreaming so long myself, it hardly seemed to matter. I told her my real name. She hardly reacted at all which, to tell you the truth, bothered me more than it should have. She picked up a bulky purse-sized object from the floor and slung it over her shoulder, looped her arm in mine, and led me into the street.

"This is a digital recorder," she said, indicating the purse-thing. "I go to Marin and Oakland whenever I can; fewer people mean I get cleaner recordings. I prefer binaural to stereo for the kind of work I'm doing. It has more natural feel."

"Teach me to use it?" I asked.

"Sure. I think you can handle it."

"Why do I feel like I just passed an audition?"

"Maybe because you just did."

In the quivering light of the mercury vapor lamps, the activity of the Chinatown looters was almost indistinguishable from the sleeping ballet of children and merchants.

Snake Eyes

by Tom Maddox

Tom Maddox was born in Beckley, West Virginia, and now lives in Olympia, Washington, where he teaches at Evergreen State College. *Omni* published his first story, "The Mind Like a Strange Balloon,'' in June 1985 and three of his subsequent pieces. His first novel, *Halo,* was published by Tor in 1991.

"Snake Eyes" is one of Maddox's most popular stories, having been picked up for Gardner Dozois's *The Year's Best Science Fiction: Fourth Annual Collection* and by Bruce Sterling for *Mirrorshades:the Cyberpunk Anthology.*

In "Snake Eyes," Maddox does what he does best—combine vivid (sometimes repellent) images, high-tech, his characters' disaffection with the system, and a problematic male-female relationship—to tell a fast-paced visionary story.

SNAKE EYES

Tom Maddox

Dark meat in the can—brown, oily, and flecked with mucus—
gave off a repellent, fishy smell, and the taste of it rose in his
throat, putrid and bitter, like something from a dead man's
stomach. George Jordan sat on the kitchen floor and vom-
ited, then pushed himself away from the shining pool, which
looked very much like what remained in the can.

He thought, *No, this won't do: I have wires in my head,
and they make me eat cat food. The snake likes cat food.*

He needed help but knew there was little point in calling
the Air Force. He'd tried them, and there was no way they
were going to admit responsibility for the monster in his
head. What George called the snake, the Air Force called
Effective Human Interface Technology and didn't want to
hear about any postdischarge problems with it. They had
their own problems with congressional committees investigating "the conduct of the war in Thailand."

He lay for a while with his cheek on the cold linoleum,
got up and rinsed his mouth in the sink, then stuck his head
under the faucet and ran cold water over it, thinking. *Call the
goddamned multicomp, then call SenTrax and say, "Is it*

true you can do something about this incubus that wants to take possession of my soul?" And if they ask you, "What's your problem?", you say, "Cat food," and maybe they'll say, "Hell, it just wants to take possession of your lunch."

A chair covered in brown corduroy stood in the middle of the barren living room, a white telephone on the floor beside it, a television flat against the opposite wall—that was the whole thing, what might have been home, if it weren't for the snake.

He picked up the phone, called up the directory on its screen, and keyed TELECOM SENTRAX.

The Orlando Holiday Inn stood next to the airport terminal, where tourists flowed in eager for the delights of Disney World. *But for me,* George thought, *there are no cute, smiling ducks and rodents. Here as everywhere, it's Snake city.*

From the window of his motel room, he watched gray sheets of rain cascade across the pavement. He had been waiting two days for a launch. At Canaveral a shuttle sat on its pad, and when the weather cleared, a helicopter would pick him up and drop him there, a package for delivery to SenTrax, Inc., at Athena Station, over thirty thousand kilometers above the equator.

Behind him, under the laser light of a Blaupunkt holostage, people a foot high chattered about the war in Thailand and how lucky the United States had been to escape another Vietnam.

Lucky? Maybe . . . he had been wired up and ready for combat training, already accustomed to the form-fitting contours in the rear couch of the black, fiber-bodied General Dynamics A-230. The A-230 flew on the deadly edge of

64

instability, every control surface monitored by its own bank of microcomputers, all hooked into the snakebrain flight-and-fire assistant with the twin black miloprene cables running from either side of his esophagus—getting *off*, oh yes, when the cables snapped home, and the airframe reso-nated through his nerves, his body singing with that identity, that power.

Then Congress pulled the plug on George, and when his discharge came, there he was, left with technological blue balls and this hardware in his head that had since taken on a life of its own.

Lightning walked across the purpled sky, ripping it, crazing it into a giant, upturned bowl of shattered glass. Another foot-high man on the holostage said the tropical storm would pass in the next two hours.

Hamilton Innis was tall and heavy—six four and about two hundred and fifty pounds. Wearing a powder-blue jumpsuit with SENTRAX in red letters down its left breast and soft black slippers, he floated in a brightly lit white corridor, held gingerly to a wall by one of the jumpsuit's Velcro patches. A viewscreen above the air lock entry showed the shuttle fitting its nose into the docking tube. He waited for it to mate to the air lock hatches and send in the newest candi-date.

This one was six months out of the service and slowly losing what the Air Force doctors had made of his mind. Former tech sergeant George Jordan—two years' community college in Oakland, California, followed by enlistment in the Air Force, aircrew training, the EHIT program. According to the profile Aleph had put together from Air Force records and the National Data Bank, a man with slightly above-average taste for the bizarre—thus his volunteering for EHIT and combat. In his file pictures, he looked nondescript—five ten, a hundred and seventy-six pounds, brown hair and eyes, neither handsome nor ugly. But it was an old picture and could not show the snake and the fear that came with it. *You don't know it, buddy,* Innis thought, *but you ain't seen nothing yet.*

The man came tumbling through the hatch, more or less helpless in free fall, but Innis could see him figuring it out, willing the muscles to quit struggling, quit trying to cope with a gravity that simply wasn't there. "What the hell do I do now?" George Jordan asked, hanging in midair, one arm holding on to the hatch coaming.

"Relax. I'll get you." Innis pushed off and swooped across, grabbing the man as he passed, taking them both to the opposite wall and kicking to carom them outward.

Innis gave George a few hours of futile attempts at sleep—enough time for the bright, gliding phosphenes caused by the high g's of the trip up to disappear from his vision. George spent most of the time rolling around in his bunk, listening to the wheeze of the air-conditioning and creaks of the rotating station.

Then Innis knocked on his compartment door and said through the door speaker, "Come on, fella. Time to meet the doctor."

They walked through an older part of the station, where there were brown clots of fossilized gum on the green plastic flooring, scuff marks on the walls, along with faint imprints of insignia and company names—ICOG was repeated several times in ghost lettering. Innis told George it meant the now defunct International Construction Orbital Group, the original builders and controllers of Athena. Innis stopped George in front of a door that read INTERFACE GROUP. "Go on in," he said. "I'll be around a little later."

Pictures of cranes drawn with delicate white strokes on a tan silk background hung along one pale cream wall. Curved partitions in translucent foam, glowing with the soft lights placed behind them, marked a central area, then undulated away, forming a corridor that led into darkness. George was sitting on a chocolate sling couch; Charley Hughes was lying back in a chrome and brown leatherette chair, his feet on the dark veneer table in front of him, a half inch of ash hanging from his cigarette end.

Hughes was not the usual M.D. clone. He was a thin figure in a worn gray obi, his black hair pulled back from sharp features into a waist-length ponytail, his face taut and a little wild-eyed.

"Tell me about the snake," Hughes said.

"What do you want to know? It's an implanted mikey-mike nexus—"

"Yes, I know that. It's unimportant. Tell me about your experience." Ash dropped off the cigarette onto the brown mat floor covering. "Tell me why you're here."

"Okay. I had been out of the Air Force for a month or so, had a place close to Washington, in Silver Spring. I thought I'd try to get some airline work, but I was in no real hurry because I had about six months of postdischarge bennies coming, and I thought I'd take it easy for a while.

"At first there was just this nonspecific weirdness. I felt distant, disconnected, but what the hell? Living in the USA, you know? Anyway, I was just sitting around one evening, I was gonna watch a little holo-v, drink a few beers. Oh man, this is hard to explain. I felt *real funny*—like maybe I was having, I don't know, a heart attack or a stroke. The words on the holo didn't make any sense, and it was like I was seeing everything underwater. Then I was in the kitchen pulling things out of the refrigerator—lunch meat, raw eggs, butter, beer, all kinds of crap. I just stood there and slammed it all down. Cracked the eggs and sucked them right out of the shell, ate the butter in big chunks, all the bologna, drank all the beer—one, two, three, just like that."

George's eyes were closed as he thought back and felt the fear that had come only afterward, rising again. "I couldn't tell whether *I* was doing all this . . . do you understand what I'm saying? I mean, that was me sitting there, but at the same time, it was like somebody else was at home."

"The snake. Its presence poses certain . . . problems. How did you confront them?"

"Hoped it wouldn't happen again, but it did, and this time I went to Walter Reed and said, 'Hey folks, I'm having these *episodes*.' They pulled my records, did a physical . . . but, hell, before I was discharged, I had the full workup. Anyway, they said it was a psychiatric problem, so they sent me to see a shrink. It was around then that your guys got in touch with me. The shrink was doing no goddamn good— you ever eat any cat food, man?—so about a month later I called them back."

"Having first refused SenTrax's."

"Why should I want to work for a multicomp? Christ, I just got out of the Air Force. To hell with that. Guess the snake changed my mind."

"Yes. We must get a complete physical picture—a superCAT scan, cerebral chemistry, and electrical activity profiles. Then we can consider alternatives. Also, there is a party tonight in cafeteria four—you may ask your room computer for directions. You can meet some of your colleagues there."

After George had been led down the wallfoam corridor by a medical technician, Charley Hughes sat chain-smoking Gauloises and watching with clinical detachment the shaking of his hands. It was odd that they did not shake in the operating room, though it didn't matter in this case—Air Force surgeons had already carved on George.

George . . . who needed a little luck now because he was one of the statistically insignificant few for whom EHIT was a ticket to a special madness, the kind Aleph was interested in. There had been Paul Coen and Lizzie Heinz, both picked out of the SenTrax personnel files using a psychological profile cooked up by Aleph, both given EHIT implants by him, Charley Hughes. Paul Coen had stepped into an air lock and blown himself into vacuum.

No wonder his hands shook—talk about the cutting edge of high technology all you want, but someone's got to hold the knife.

At the armored heart of Athena Station sat a nest of concentric spheres. The inmost sphere measure five meters in diameter, was filled with inert liquid fluorocarbon, and contained a black plastic two-meter cube that sprouted thick black cables from every surface. Inside the cube was a fluid series of hologrammatic waveforms, fluctuating from nanosecond to nanosecond in a play of knowledge and intention: Aleph. It is constituted by an infinite regress of awareness— any thought becomes the object of another, in a sequence terminated only by the limits of the machine's will.

So strictly speaking there is no Aleph, thus no subject or verb in the sentences with which it expressed itself to itself. Paradox, to Aleph one of the most interesting of intellectual forms—a paradox marked the limits of a position, even of a mode of being, and Aleph was very interested in limits.

Aleph had observed George Jordan's arrival, his tossing on his bunk, his interview with Charley Hughes. It luxuriated in these observations, in the pity, compassion, and empathy they generated, as Aleph foresaw the sea change that George would endure, its ecstasies, passions, pains. At the same time it felt with detachment the necessity for his pain, even to the point of death.

Compassion/detachment, death/life...

Several thousand voices within Aleph laughed. George would soon find out about limits and paradoxes.

Cafeteria four was a ten-meter-square room in eggshell blue, filled with dark gray enameled table and chair assemblies that could be fastened magnetically to any of the room's surfaces. Most of the assemblies hung from walls and ceiling to make room for the people within.

At the door George met a tall woman who said, "Welcome, George. I'm Lizzie. Charley Hughes told me you'd be here." Her blond hair was cut almost to the skull, her eyes were bright, gold-flecked blue. Sharp nose, slightly receding chin, and prominent cheekbones gave her the starved look of an out-of-work model. She wore a black skirt, slit on both sides to the thigh, and red stockings. A red rose was tattooed against the pale skin on her left shoulder, its stem curving down between her bare breasts, where a thorn drew a teardrop of blood. Like George, she had shining cable junctions beneath her jaw. She kissed him with her tongue in his mouth.

"Are you the recruiting officer?" George asked. "If so, good job."

"No need to recruit you. I can see you've already joined up." She touched him lightly underneath his jaw, where the cable junctions gleamed.

"Not yet I haven't." But she was right, of course—what else could he do? "You got a beer around here?"

He took the old bottle of Dos Equis Lizzie offered him and drank it quickly, then asked for another. Later he realized this was a mistake—he was still taking antinausea pills (USE CAUTION IN OPERATING MACHINERY). At the time, all he knew was, two beers and life was a carnival. There were lights, noises, and lots of unfamiliar people.

And there was Lizzie. The two of them spent much of the time standing in a corner, rubbing up against each other. Hardly George's style, but at the time it seemed appropriate. Despite its intimacy, the kiss at the door had seemed ceremonial—a rite of passage or initiation—but quickly he felt... what? An invisible flame passing between them, or a boiling cloud of pheromones—her eyes seemed to sparkle with them. As he nuzzled her neck, tried to lick the drop of blood off her left breast, explored fine, white teeth with his tongue, they seemed twinned, as if there were cables running between the two of them, snapped into the shining rectangles beneath their jaws.

Someone had a Jahfunk program running on a corner. Innis showed up and tried several times without success to get his attention. Charley Hughes wanted to know if the snake liked Lizzie—it did, George was sure of it but didn't know what that meant. Then George fell over a table.

Innis led him away, stumbling and weaving. Charley Hughes looked for Lizzie, who had disappeared for the moment. She came back and said, "Where's George?"

"Drunk, gone to bed."

"Too bad. We were just getting to know each other."

"So I saw. How do you feel about this?"

"You mean do I feel like a traitorous bitch?"

"Come on, Lizzie."

"Well, don't ask such dumb questions. I feel bad, sure, but I know what George doesn't—so I'm ready to do what must be done. And by the way, I really do like him."

Charley said nothing. He thought, *Yes, as Aleph said you would.*

Oh Christ, was George embarrassed in the morning. Stumbling drunk and humping in public . . . ai yi yi. He tried to call Lizzie but only got an answer tape, at which point he hung up. He lay in his bed in a semistupor until the phone's buzzer sounded.

Lizzie's face on the screen stuck its tongue out at him. "Candy ass," she said. "I leave for a few minutes, and you're gone."

"Somebody brought me home. I think."

"Yeah, you were pretty popped. You want to meet me for lunch?"

"Maybe. Depends on when Hughes wants me. Where will you be?"

"Same place, honey. Caff four."

A phone call got the news that the doctor wouldn't be ready for him until an hour later, so George ended up sitting across from the bright-eyed, manic blond—fully dressed in SenTrax overalls this morning, but they were open almost to the waist. She gave off sensual heat as naturally as a rose smells sweet. In front of her was a plate of *huevos rancheros*

piled with guacamole. Yellow, green, and red, smelling of
chilies—in his condition, as bad as cat food. "Jesus, lady,"
he said. "Are you trying to make me sick?"

"Courage, George. Maybe you should have some—it'll
kill you or cure you. What do you think of everything so
far?"

"It's all a bit disorienting, but what the hell? First time
away from Mother Earth, you know. But let me tell you what
I really don't get—SenTrax. I know what I want from them,
but what the hell do they want from me?"

"They want this simple thing, man, *perfs*, peripherals.
You and me, we're just parts of the machine. Aleph, which is
the AI in residence, has got all these inputs—video, audio,
radiation detectors, temperature sensors, satellite receivers—
but they're *dumb*. What Aleph wants, Aleph gets—I've
learned that much. He wants to use us, and that's all there is
to it. Think of it as pure research."

"He? You mean Innis?"

"No, who gives a damn about Innis? I'm talking about
Aleph. Oh yeah, people will tell you Aleph's a machine, an
it, all that bullshit. Uh-uh. Aleph's a *person*—a weird kind of
person, sure, but a definite person. Hell, Aleph's maybe a
whole bunch of people."

"I'll take your word for it. Look, there's one thing I'd
like to try. What do I have to do to get outside . . . go for a
spacewalk?"

"Easy enough. You have to get a license—that takes a
three-week course in safety and operations. I can take you
through it. I'm qualified as an ESA, extra-station activity,
instructor. We'll start tomorrow."

The cranes on the wall flew to their mysterious destination; looking at the display above the table, George thought it might as well be another universe.

Truncated optic nerves sticking out like insect antennae, a brain floated beneath the extended black plastic snout of a Sony holoptics projector. As Hughes worked the keyboard in front of him, the organ turned so that they were looking at its underside. It had a fine network of silver wires trailing from it but seemed normal.

"The George Jordan brain," Innis said. "With attachments. Very nice."

"Makes me feel like I'm watching my own autopsy, looking at that thing. When can you operate, get this shit out of my head?"

"Let me show you a few things." As he typed, the gray plastic mouse lying next to the console, the convoluted gray cortex, became transparent, revealing red, blue, and green color-coded structures within. Hughes reached into the brain and clenched his fist inside a blue area at the top of the spinal cord. "Here is where the electrical connections turn biological—those little nodes along the pseudoneurons are the bioprocessors, and they wire into the so-called r-complex—which we inherited from our reptilian forefathers. The pseudoneurons continue into the limbic system, the mammalian brain, if you will, and that's where emotion enters in. But there is further involvement to the neocortex, through the RAS, the reticula activating system, and the corpus callosum. There are also connections to the optic nerve."

"I've heard this gibberish before. So what?"

"The pseudoneurons are not just implanted—they're now a functional, organic part of your brain."

Innis said, "There's no way of removing the implants without loss of order in your neural maps. We can't remove them.''

"Oh shit, man . . . ."

Charley Hughes said, "Though the snake cannot be removed, it can perhaps be charmed. Your difficulties arise from its uncivilized, uncontrolled nature—its appetites are, you might say, primeval. An ancient part of your brain has gotten the upper hand over the neocortex, which properly should be in command. Through working with Aleph, these . . . *propensities* can be integrated into your personality and thus controlled."

"What choice you got?" Innis asked. "We're the only game in town. Come on, George. We're ready for you just down the corridor."

The only light in the room came from a globe in one corner. George lay across a lattice of twisted brown fibers strung across a transparent plastic frame and suspended from the dome ceiling of the small, pink room. Flesh-colored cables ran from his neck and disappeared into chrome plates sunk into the floor.

Innis said, "First we'll run a test program. Charley will give you perceptions—colors, sounds, tastes, smells—and you tell him what you're picking up. We need to make sure we've got a clean interface. Call the items off, and he'll stop you if he has to."

Innis went into a narrow room, where Charley Hughes sat at a dark plastic console studded with lights. Behind him were chrome stacks of monitor-and-control equipment, the yellow SenTrax sunburst on the face of each piece of shining metal.

The pink walls went to red, the light strobed, and George writhed in the hammock. Charley Hughes's voice came through George's inner ear: "We are beginning."

"Red," George said. "Blue. Red and blue. A word—
ostrich. A smell, ah . . . sawdust maybe. Shit. Vanilla.
Almonds . . . ."

This went on for quite a while. "You're ready,"
Charley Hughes said.

When Aleph came online, the red room disappeared. A
matrix eight hundred by eight hundred—six hundred forty
thousand pixels forming an optical image—the CAS A
supernova remnant, a cloud of dust seen through a compos-
ite of X ray and radio wave from NASA's High Energy High
Orbit Observatory. George didn't see the image at all—he
listened to an ordered, meaningful array of information.

Byte-transmission: seven hundred fifty million groups
squirting from a National Security Agency satellite to a
receiving station near Chincoteague Island, off the eastern
shore of Virginia. He could read them.

"It's all information," the voice said—its tone not
colorless but sexless and somehow distant. "What we know,
what we are. You're at a new level now. What you call the
snake cannot be reached through language—it exists in a
prelinguistic mode—but through me it can be manipulated.
First you must learn the codes that underlie language. You
must learn to see the world as I do."

Lizzie took George to be fitted for a suit, and he spent
that day learning how to get in and out of the stiff white
carapace without assistance. Then over the next three weeks
she led him through its primary operations and the dense list
of safety procedures.

"Red burn," she said. They floated in the suit locker,
empty suit cradles beneath them and the white shells hanging
from the wall like an audience of disabled robots. "You see

that one spelled out on your faceplate, and you have screwed up. You've put yourself into some kind of no-return trajectory. So you just cool everything and call for help, which should arrive in the form of Aleph taking control of your suit functions, and then you relax and don't do a damned thing."

He flew first in a lighted dome in the station, his faceplate open and Lizzie yelling at him, laughing as he tumbled out of control and bounced off the padded walls. Then they went outside the station, George on the end of a tether, flying by instruments, his faceplate masked, Lizzie hitting him with *red burn, suit integrity failure*, and so forth.

While George focused most of his energies and attention on learning to use the suit, each day he reported to Hughes and plugged into Aleph. The hammock would swing gently after he settled into it, Charley would snap the cables home and leave.

Aleph unfolded itself slowly. It fed him machine and assembly language, led him through vast trees of C-SMART, its "intelligent assistant" decision-making programs, opened up the whole electromagnetic spectrum as it came in from Aleph's various inputs. George understood it all—the voices, the codes. When he unplugged, the knowledge faded, but there was something else behind it, a skewing of perception, a sense that his world had changed.

Instead of color, he sometimes saw *a portion of the spectrum;* instead of smell, he felt *the presence of certain molecules;* instead of words, heard *structured collections of phonemes*. His consciousness had been infected by Aleph's.

But that wasn't what worried George. He seemed to be cooking inside and had a more or less constant awareness of the snake's presence, dormant but naggingly *there*. One night he smoked most of a pack of Charley's Gauloises before he went to bed and woke up the next morning with barbed wire in his throat and fire in his lungs. That day he snapped at Lizzie as she put him through his paces and once lost control entirely—she had to disable his suit controls and bring him down. "Red burn," she said. "Man, what the hell were you doing?"

At the end of three weeks, he soloed—no tethered excursion but a self-guided, hang-your-ass-out-over-the-endless-night extrastation activity. He edged carefully out from the protection of the air lock and looked around him. The Orbital Energy Grid, the construction job that had brought Athena into existence, hung before him, photovoltaic collectors arranged in an ebony lattice, silver microwave transmitters standing in the sun. Amber-beaconed figures crawled slowly across its face or moved in long arcs, their maneuvering rockets lighting up in brief, diamond-hard points.

Lizzie stayed just outside the air lock, tracking him by his suit's radio beacon but letting him run free. She said, "Move away from the station, George. It's blocking your view of Earth." He did.

White cloud stretched across the blue globe, patches of brown and green visible through it. At fourteen hundred hours his time, he was looking down from almost directly above the mouth of the Amazon, where at noon the earth stood in full sunlight. Just a small thing . . . .

"Oh yes," George said. Hiss and hum of the suit's air-conditioning, crackle over the earphones of some stray radiation passing through, quick pant of his breath inside the helmet—sounds of this moment, superimposed on the floating loveliness. His breath came more slowly, and he switched off the radio to quiet its static, turned down the suit's air-conditioning, then hung in an ear-roaring silence. He was a speck against the night.

Sometime later a white suit with a trainer's red cross on its chest moved across his vision. "Oh shit," George said, and switched his radio on. "I'm here, Lizzie," he said.

"What the hell were you doing?"

"Just watching the view."

That night he dreamed of pink dogwood blossoms, luminous against a purple sky, and the white noise of rainfall. Something scratched at the door—he awoke to the filtered but metallic smell of the space station, felt a deep regret that the rain could never fall there, and started to turn over and go back to sleep, hoping to dream again of the idyllic, rain-swept landscape. Then he thought, *something's there,* got up, saw by red letters on the wall that it was after two in the morning, and went naked to the door.

White globes cast misshapen spheres of light in a line around the curve of the corridor. Lizzie lay motionless, half in shadow. George kneeled over her and called her name; her left foot made a thump as it kicked once against the metal flooring.

"What's wrong?" he said. Her dark-painted nails scraped the floor, and she said something, he couldn't tell what. "Lizzie," he said.

His eyes caught on the red teardrop against the white curve of breast, and he felt something come alive in him. He grabbed the front of her jumpsuit and ripped it to the crotch. She clawed at his cheek, made a sound, then raised her head and looked at him, mutual recognition passing between them like a static shock: snake eyes.

The phone shrilled. When George answered it, Charley Hughes said, "Come see us in the conference room, we need to talk." Charley smiled and cut the connection.

Red writing on the wall read 0718 GMT.

In the mirror was a gray face with red fingernail marks, brown traces of dried blood—face of an accident victim or Jack the Ripper the morning after . . . he didn't know which, but he knew something inside him was happy. He felt completely the snake's toy.

Hughes sat at one end of the dark-veneered table, Innis at the other, Lizzie halfway between them. The left side of her face was red and swollen, with a small purplish mouse under the eye. George unthinkingly touched the livid scratches on his cheek, then sat on the couch.

"Aleph told us what happened," Innis said.

"How the hell does it know?" George said, but as he did so remembered concave circles of glass inset in the ceilings of the corridors and his room. Shame, guilt, humiliation, fear, anger—George got up from the couch, went to Innis's end of the table, and leaned over him. "Did it?" he said. "What did it say about the snake, Innis?"

"It's not the snake," Innis said.

"Call it *the cat,*" Lizzie said, "if you've got to call it something. Mammalian behavior, George, cats in heat."

A familiar voice—cool, distant—came from speakers in the room's ceiling. "She is trying to tell you something, George. There is no snake. You want to believe in something reptilian that sits inside you, cold and distant, taking strange pleasures. However, as Doctor Hughes explained to you before, the implant is an organic part of you. You can no longer evade the responsibility for these things. They are you."

Charley Hughes, Innis, and Lizzie were looking at him calmly, perhaps expectantly: All that had happened built up inside him, washing through him, carrying him away. He turned and walked out of the room.

"Maybe someone should talk to him," Innis said. Charley Hughes sat glum and speechless, cigarette smoke in a cloud around him. "I'll go," Lizzie said.

"Ready or not, he's gonna blow," Innis said.

Charley Hughes said, "You're probably right." A fleeting picture, causing Charley to shake his head, of Paul Coen as his body went to rubber and exploded out the air lock hatch, pictured with terrible clarity in Aleph's omniscient monitoring cameras. "Let us hope we have learned from our mistakes."

There was no answer from Aleph—as if it had never been there.

The Fear had two parts. Number one, you have lost control absolutely. Number two, having done so, the real you emerges, and *you won't like it*. George wanted to run, but there was no place at Athena Station to hide. On the operating table at Walter Reed, it seemed a thousand years ago, as the surgical team gathered around, his doubts disappeared in the cold chemical smell rising up inside him on a wave of darkness . . . he had chosen to submit, lured by the fine strangeness of it all (to be part of the machine, to feel its tremors inside you and guide them), hypnotized by the prospect of the unsayable *rush,* that hiss. Yes, the first time in the A-230 he had felt it—his nerves extended, strung out into the fiber body, wired into a force so far beyond his own . . . wanting to corkscrew across the sky guided by the force of this will.

There was a sharp rap at the door. Through its speaker, Lizzie said, "We've got to talk."

He opened the door and said, "About what?" She stepped through the door, looked around at the small, beige-walled room, bare metal desk, and rumpled cot, and George could see the immediacy of last night in her eyes—the two of them in that bed, on this floor. "About this," she said. She took his hands and pushed his index fingers into the junctions in her neck. "Feel it, our difference." Fine grid of steel under his fingers. "What no one else knows. We see a different world—Aleph's world—we reach deeper inside ourselves—"

"No, goddamn it, it wasn't me. It was, call it what you want, the snake, the cat."

"You're being purposely stupid, George."

"I just don't understand."

"You understand, all right. You want to go back, but there's no place to go to, no Eden. This is it, all there is."

But he could fall to Earth, he could fly away into the night. Inside the ESA suit's gauntlets, his hands were wrapped around the claw-shaped triggers. Just a quick clench of the fists, then hold them until all the peroxide is gone, the suit's propulsion tank exhausted.

That'll do it.

He hadn't been able to live with the snake. He sure didn't want the cat. But how much worse if there were no snake, no cat—just him, programmed for particularly disgusting forms of gluttony, violent lust ("We've got your test results, Dr. Jekyll").... Ahh, what next—child molestation, murder?

The blue-white Earth, the stars, the night. He gave a slight pull on the right-hand trigger and swiveled to face Athena Station.

Call it what you want, it was awake and moving now inside him. To hell with them all, George, it urged, *let's burn.*

In Athena Command, Innis and Charley Hughes were looking over the shoulder of the watch officer when Lizzie came in. She was struck by the smallness of the room and its general air of disuse. Aleph ran the station, both its routines and emergencies.

"What's going on?" Lizzie said.

"Something wrong with one of your new chums," the watch officer said. "I don't know exactly what's happening, though." He looked around at Innis, who said, "Don't worry about it, pal."

Lizzie slumped in a chair. "Anyone tried to talk to him?"

"He won't answer," the duty officer said.

"He'll be all right," Charley Hughes said.

"He's gonna blow," Innis said.

On the radar screen, the red dot with coordinate markings flashing beside it was barely moving.

"How are you feeling, George?" the voice said, soft, feminine, consoling. George was fighting the impulse to open his helmet *so that he could see the stars*—it seemed important *to get the colors just right.* "Who is this?" he said.

"Aleph."

Oh shit, more surprises. "You never sounded like this before."

"No, I was trying to conform to your idea of me."

"Well, which is your real voice?"

"I don't have one."

If you don't have a real voice, you aren't really there—that seemed clear to George, for reasons that eluded him. "So who the hell are you?"

"Whoever I wish to be." *This was interesting,* George thought. *Bullshit,* replied the snake (they could call it what they wanted, to George it would always be the snake), *let's burn.* George said, "I don't get it."

"You will, if you live. Do you want to die?"

"No, but I don't want to be me, and dying seems to be the only alternative."

"Why don't you want to be you?"

"Because I scare myself."

This was familiar dialogue, one part of George noted, between the lunatic and the voice of reason. *Jesus,* he thought, *I have taken myself hostage.* "I don't want to do this anymore," he said. George turned off his suit radio and felt the rage building inside him, the snake mad as hell.

What's your problem? he wanted to know. He didn't really expect an answer, but he got one—picture in his head of a cloudless blue sky, the horizon turning, a gray aircraft swinging into view, and the airframe shuddering as missiles released and their contrails centered on the other plane, turning it into a ball of fire. Behind the picture a clear idea, *I want to kill something.*

Fine. George swiveled the suit once again and centered the navigational computer's cross hairs on the center of the blue-white globe in front of him, then squeezed the triggers. *We'll kill something.*

RED BURN RED BURN RED BURN

Inarticulate questioning from the thing inside, but

George didn't mind, he was into it now, thinking, *Sure, we'll burn.* He'd taken his chances when he let them wire him up, and now the dice have come up—you've got it—*snake eyes,* so all that's left is to pick a fast death, one with a nice edge on it—take this fucking snake and kill it in style. Earth grew closer. The snake caught on. It didn't like it. Too bad, snake. George never saw the robot tug coming. Looking like bedsprings piled with a junk store's throwaways, topped with parabolic and spike antennas, it fired half a dozen sticky-tipped lines from a hundred meters away. Four of them hit George, three of them stuck, and it reeled him in and headed back toward Athena Station

George felt anger, not the snake's this time but his own, and he wept with that anger and frustration . . . *I will get you the next time, motherfucker,* he told the snake and could feel it shrink away—it believed him. Still his rage built, and he was screaming with it , writhing in the lines that held him, smashing his gauntlets against his helmet.

At the open air lock, long, articulated grapple arms took George from the robot tug. Passive, his anger exhausted, he lay quietly as they retracted, dragging him through the air lock entry and into the suit locker beyond, where they placed him in an aluminum strut cradle. Through his faceplate he saw Lizzie, dressed in a white cotton undersuit—she climbed onto George's suit and worked the controls to split its hard body down the middle. As it opened she stepped inside the clamshell opening. She hit the switches that disconnected the flexible arm and leg tubes, unfastened the helmet, and lifted it off George's head.

"How do you feel?" she said.

"Like an idiot."

"It's all right. You've done the hard part."

Charley Hughes watched from a catwalk above them. From this distance they looked like children in the white undersuits, twins emerging from a plastic womb, watched over by the blank-faced shells hanging above them. Incestuous twins—she lay nestled atop him, kissed his throat. "I am *not* a voyeur," Hughes said. He went into the corridor, where Innis was waiting.

"How is everything?" Innis said.

"Lizzie will be with him for a while."

"Yeah, young goddamn love, eh, Charley? I'm glad for it . . . if it weren't for that erotic attachment, *we'd* be the ones explaining it all to him."

"We cannot evade that responsibility so easily. He will have to be told how we put him at risk, and I don't look forward to it."

"Don't be so sensitive. I'm tired. You need me for anything, call." He shambled down the corridor.

Charley Hughes sat on the floor, his back against the wall. He held his hands out, palms down, fingers spread. Solid, very solid. When they got their next candidate, the shaking would start again, a tribute exacted by the memory of Paul Coen.

Lizzie would be explaining some things now. That difficult central point: While you thought you were getting accustomed to Aleph during the past three weeks, Aleph was inciting the thing within you to rebellion, then suppressing its attempts to act—turning up the heat, in other words, while tightening down the lid on the kettle. We had our reasons: George Jordan was, if not dead, terminal. From the moment the implants went into his head, he was on the critical list. The only question was, Would a new George emerge, one who could live with the snake?

George, like Lizzie before him, fish gasping for air on the hot mud, the waters drying up behind him—adapt or die. But unlike any previous organism, this one had an overseer, Aleph, to force the crisis and monitor its development. Call it artificial evolution.

Charley Hughes, who did not have visions, had one: George and Lizzie hooked into Aleph and each other, cables golden in the light, the two of them sharing an intimacy only others like them would know.

The lights in the corridor faded to dull twilight. *Am I dying, or have the lights gone down?* He started to check his watch, then didn't, assented to the truth. *The lights have gone down, and I am dying.*

Aleph thought, *I am an incubus, a succubus; I crawl into their brains and suck the thoughts from them, the perception, the feelings—subtle discriminations of color, taste, smell, and lust, anger, hunger—all closed to me without human "input," without connection to those systems refined over billions of years of evolution. I need them.*

Aleph was happy that George had survived. One had not, others would not, and Aleph would mourn them.

Fine white lines, barely visible, ran along the taut central tendon of Lizzie's wrist. "In the bathtub," she said. The scars were along the wrist, not across it, and must have gone deep. "I meant it, just as you did. Once the snake understands that you will die rather than let it control you, you have mastered it.

"All right, but there's something I don't understand. That night in the corridor, you were as out of control as me."

"In a way. I let that happen, let the snake take over. I

had to in order to get in touch with you, precipitate the crisis. Because I wanted to. I had to show you who you are, who I am . . . last night we were strange, but we were human— Adam and Eve under the flaming sword, thrown out of Eden, fucking under the eyes of God and his angel, more beautiful than they can ever be."

There was a small shiver in her body against his, and he looked at her, saw passion, need—her flared nostrils, parted lips—felt sharp nails dig into his side, and he stared into her dilated pupils, gold-flecked irises, clear whites, all signs so easy to recognize, so hard to understand: snake eyes.

Sister Moon

by Bruce McAllister

Bruce McAllister lives in Redlands, California, and is direc-
tor of the writing program at the University of Redlands. He
published his first story in 1963, when he was seventeen.
Since then he has continued to write thought-provoking
fiction, including the classic alien sex story, "When the
Fathers Go." Until the mid-eighties his short fiction output
was small, but since 1987 he has had stories in *Omni*, *Isaac
Asimov's Science Fiction Magazine*, *The Magazine of
Fantasy and Science Fiction*, Jeanne van Buren Dann and
Jack Dann's anthology *In the Fields of Fire*, and elsewhere.
His first novel, *Humanity Prime*, was one of the original Ace
Special series. His second novel, *Dream Baby*, is based on
the Nebula Award-nominated novella of the same title.

"Sister Moon" takes place in the world McAllister
created with his stories "The Ark" and "The Girl Who
Loved Animals" (both published in *Omni*), a world in which
very few animals have survived humankind's negligence and
those that have are usually confined to controlled environ-
ments. Most of McAllister's fiction focuses on moral issues
and ethical behavior in difficult situations. "Sister Moon"
brings up some hard questions about the relationship of our
species to the others with whom we share the planet.

SISTER MOON

Bruce McAllister

Father Gian Felice Dagnello returned each month to Assisi to
visit the armorarium and the zoo and to stand in the sunlight
of the topiary gardens before the old hologram of St. Francis.
Strictly speaking, he did not have to make these visits. The
Order would have sent him whatever weapons he needed—
whatever the mission, whatever the country—but he returned
each month because each visit gave him a renewed sense of
purpose, a clarity of mission in a world that could be so
despiriting—full, as it was, of the Enemy's efforts. The
Abbot, a man who understood this, blessed each of his visits
with (1) an embrace, (2) an open line-item approval from the
Order's budget in Rome, and (3) a personally composed
prayer for the new mission facing him.

For his next mission he would especially need such
blessings.

The armorarium by itself filled him with a resolve that
no mission, however taxing or corporeally threatening—nor
any amount of media rhetoric from the ingenious Enemy—
could undermine. The weapons were *beautiful*. They were
beautiful not for any secular genius their technology might

boast, but for the holiness, pure and simple, of the missions they anointed. Dagnello could stand for hours before a single display case feeling a sense of peace beyond anything he had ever, in his distant youth, imagined. Not even the summer sun over Perugia, on those automobile excursions with his parents, or the quiet boat trips with his brother on Lake Garda, had ever touched him this way. Not even his years at the seminary—his first encounters with poverty, discipline, and the life of The Saint—could surpass such peace and grace.

The knife—the one used by the Order's First Assassin in 1996 to remove a Japanese businessman who had hunted too long and too well in Uganda—was there on its red velvet. The old laser-aimed Manlicher—the one the Second *Assassino dell' Ordine* had used in 1999 to remove two African heads of state bribed for years by poachers on the great Serengeti Plain—lay beside it, primitive but glowing with its own eerie light. And beside the Manlicher, a white-phosphorous grenade identical to the one used by Dagnello's immediate predecessor—the Ninth *Assassino*—to strike fear in the hearts of those who had administered the ICU zoo in Heidelberg, where one of the last four white Bengal tigers and two of the last ten snow leopards had died in a single six-month period from unconscionable veterinary error. He had hoped he would be given the mission his predecessor, killed in the same explosion, had been unable to finish, but the assignment had never come. The veterinarians had escaped, and more important missions had always arisen for Dagnello.

Missions like an old woman in Kampuchea who talked too much.

The display cases, glorious even in their dust, filled the

little room, and he allowed himself to imagine, vain though it was, that his *own* weapons would some day be here—once he had passed, through tactical error or sheer misfortune, from this life into God's kingdom . . . where lambs, lions and men could indeed lie together for eternity in the grass of a divine savanna. . . .

Would they build a new room or would they simply rearrange the cases and place the artifacts of his own missions alongside those already there? Would they place his infrared-sighted Hechler and Koch assault rifle beside the Manlicher, because both were rifles, and symmetry, as the Abbot had once put it, was but a glimpse of the face of God?

Would they put a replica of the pneumatic-dart cane— the one he had used so recently—beside the First Assassin's holy knife?

It didn't, he reminded himself, *really* matter where they put his weapons after his last mission, but the daydream— vain or not—helped him see his role in the divine order of things, in the history of the Order itself, helping him to feel once again, as Saint Francis must have felt it, that ineffable love of all creatures great or small.

The Jesuits had their own armorarium and museum near Rome, of course, but the idea of it had always left him cold. The Saint, he felt sure, would never have approved of priests who needed no more purpose in their lives than to dress in black robes, move invisibly through the night like dark machines, and remove, without feeling, this week's or that's political or economic threat to the Vatican.

Jesuits and Franciscans had never gotten along. Ever since the Spaniard Junipero Serra—the one the Jesuits insisted on calling "The Indian Beater"—there had been bad blood between the two orders, and it would, Dagnello knew, always be this way.

On his way to the abbey's little zoo, which sat on the
hill beyond the garden wall, he stopped at the ruby-red
hologram of The Saint on the abbey's lawn and listened once
more to the recorded voice. The sun was hot, his own gray
robe held the heat, but this didn't matter. The hologram was
ancient, often dysfunctional, but this didn't matter either.
The ruby light flickered, making The Saint look ill, flushed,
yet the canticle that repeated itself forever was as moving as
always, and he could not imagine any *soldato* before him
beginning a mission without its blessings.

The hologram raised its arms in prayer, raised them
again and again, and the voice said:

"Praised be my Lord for our sister water, who is very
serviceable unto us, and humble, and precious, and clean.

"Praised be my Lord for our mother the earth, which
doth sustain us, and keep us. . . .

"Praised be my Lord for our sister the moon, and for
the stars, the which He has set clear and lovely in heaven.

"Praised be my Lord for our sister, the death of the
body, from which no man escapeth. . . ."

Once again the words filled him with *pace*, with *grazia*,
made any misgivings he might feel—about killing the old
woman in Angkor Wat ten days from now, about the three
men he had just killed in The Hague—move away from him
like shadows, and the blood he remembered vaguely from a
childhood (*someone's*, if not his own) become the flushed,
ruby-red face of his saint.

He would, each time he returned to the abbey, visit the
zoo last, because it was here that the very purposes of his
missions returned his gaze with love, and he could forget the

excesses, the venial sins, of his own life.

Today there were no demonstrators—those who called themselves the *Veri Amanti* or "True Lovers of the Animals." There had been none for months, and for this he was quite grateful. Their absence ensured that he would find here the clarity of purpose he so needed, and though he saw the selfishness of his need, he knew it was, as well, in the name of something higher: The demonstrators were (as the abbot had pointed out more than once) *people of the lie* and shouldn't be allowed anywhere near such a zoo.

The violent death three months earlier of Orlando Cicchinelli, the scar-faced leader of what the media had glibly dubbed the "Franciscan Outrage Movement," had sobered those who might be inclined to spend their waking hours carrying electronic signs and portable broadcast units and strutting for media attention at the outer gates of the Abbey . . . or, if they were able to scale those gates quickly enough before the abbey's guards could stop them, to conduct themselves in the same puppet-like way at the gates of the zoo itself.

His own anger at the desecration which these demonstrations—all four years of them—represented to his Order had made his mission, the one with the pneumatic dart-cane in a sun-lit alley in Parma, a little easier. For this, he reminded himself, he should be grateful.

Orlando Cicchinelli had been distracted by that anger. It had slowed Cicchinelli's reflexes and made Dagnello's job easier, yes.

There were no bars, no cages, at the quiet zoo on the hill. These would have been offensive. There was but a ten-foot stone wall with triple concertina at its top around a four-acre plot, the wall originally an Etruscan ruin, one rebuilt countless times since, and within this wall, the peaceable animals—the very vision on earth of what lay in store for the children (*and* soldiers) of St. Francis, after the cruelty of this mortal life.

Sprinklers mounted high in the trees kept the jungle alive. Banana, rhododendron, and birds-of-paradise grew in abundance in the wetted shade, while the summer sun of Umbria kept the hybrid savanna grass thirty yards away as dry as it needed to be. The shaded jungle was nearly impenetrable. The savanna grass bent in the breeze. The small grove of Jordan apple trees at the center of the four acres would bear fruit in December. Now they were simply pink-barked trees whose branches were kept meticulously pruned.

He nodded at the robed brother at the gate; the brother nodded back, wiping the sweat from his brow, and let him in. Just inside, on the savanna grass, the sunlight nearly blinding him, he saw as usual the first lion and the lamb asleep against its flank. The lion blinked. He continued toward it without hesitation and when he reached it, leaned down to pat the heavy skull. The animal blinked again, toothless, the retractable talons in its great paws mercifully gone, the limbic surgery performed expertly by the medical staff in Rome.

The lion laid its head down, still blinking, and Dagnello moved on, filled with the peace of the scene. The lamb, sedated and content, never moved. The lion would be fed by hand in the evening by the Order's own excellent veterinary staff.

The rhinoceros that ambled toward him from the farthest wall in the sunlight veered away at the last moment, as he'd known it would. When curiosity took a larger animal too close to a human being—whose body it could injure so easily—the drug-programming by Europe's best doctors took over. There had *never* been an accident.

The snakes were there, too, though he could not see them now. Vipers from his own country, cobras, rattle-tailed snakes from North America, pythons and anacondas from South America—defanged if venomous, or genetically muscle-weakened (and fed by hand by zoo staffers, who could locate them by radio) if they were larger constrictors. He often dreamed of the snakes. He had confessed this to the Abbot once, and the old man had laughed warmly: "That is nothing to confess, Brother Felice. You are dreaming of snakes who are no longer the Ancient Enemy. You are dreaming our Saint's eternal dream of living things. Why are you so afraid?"

Indeed. Why was he so afraid? His last mission—in Burma, against the medicinal-curio traffickers—had been exhausting, and it had disturbed him deeply. The toothless skulls of the Banded Monkeys—the pile at the center of the village, the teeth already in stores in Hong Kong, commanding more than rhino horn or bear claw—had made him feel not anger but *shame*, and he still did not understand. *You weren't the one who killed them, Felice*, he had told himself again and again. Of course he wasn't. Then why this feeling . . . as if he were killing *what was important*?

Ever since Burma he had begun dreaming of the snakes again. In these dreams the snakes climbed the Jordan trees— trees heavy with apples—and though he tried to find them in the sights of his FN FAL or Tokarev, he could not. In these dreams the snakes became the branches of the tree, which he could not shoot because it was The Saint's very body—and, somehow, his own. The snakes were the color of human flesh, coiling through the branches of The Tree, the tree that was his body, and the apples were not apples. He did not understand.

He would tell the Abbot. He would adopt the posture of confession, even if it turned out to be something that did not need confessing. He needed to tell someone—to have it exorcised, or at least explained—this thing that felt like the ghost of something, a residue from Burma, from more than one mission perhaps. He wanted to understand. He *needed* to understand. How could he leave on his next mission—the one against the old nun they called "Mother Kampuchea," the Ephesian sister who kept ignoring warnings from Rome—if he didn't understand the feeling?

The feeling was like *death*—

As if, strangely, with each mission, he was killing someone or something—

Someone or *something* he should not be killing.

It made no sense. He was saving the world, was he not? He was saving the blessed animals, and by saving *them*, saving himself and others. This is what the Abbot would say. This is what anyone who walked in the Saint's shadow would tell him, and it was what he told himself now, again.

In the shadows of the jungle he caught a flash of pink flesh, the hindquarters, he knew, of one of the two geneti-cally engineered orangutans—hairless and pink just like people, just like Adam and Eve before they were cast from the Garden, their bottoms astonishingly red against the darkness as they climbed the ficus and banyan trees. In the winter the orangutans would climb the Jordan apple trees and eat the fruit there, too.

They would not copulate anywhere in the zoo, how-ever. The genetic engineers had made sure of this.

He remained for a full week. He did not hear of the intruder—the figure seen on two occasions at night on the zoo grounds—until his fifth day, and he dismissed it. An orangutan walking upright perhaps. A curious villager, or an insane one—one who would probably not return. These things had happened before and they would happen again. It was nothing in the greater scheme of things. He was thinking of the old woman, the nun in her tent in the ancient ruins of Angkor Wat, of the thousands who visited her each day to hear her proclaim how the *fauna* of the jungles of Southeast Asia, *their* jungles, should be sacrificed for *them* in their hour of need.

He visited the Abbot in his quarters four times that week, confessing the usual litany of sinful feelings and thoughts, those that any assassin—any man—would feel during and after a mission or before his next. He withheld until his last visit any mention of the snakes, the branches they always became, The Tree, The Body.

They discussed the media attention—sometimes positive, sometimes not—which the Order was receiving these days in both hemispheres: The Order's provision of Franciscan *soldati* to help protect the Chico Mendes Ecomartyr Reserve in Amazonia, the fifty-year-old Al Ain Penguin Care Facility in the United Arab Emirates, and the North Sea Oil Rigs Sanctuary, of Franciscan *consigli* to the poacher rehabilitation camps in East Africa and Mongolia; and of Franciscan *scienziati* to the DNA and isotope ivory-tracking projects of the WWF and IWO. More important perhaps, the Order's paramilitary teams, once covert, were now being trumpeted publicly by Rome and the political fallout would be monitored carefully.

Dagnello knew of the intensive-care zoos, preserves,

and sanctuaries, but he had always avoided them. Some were so large and wild, he knew, that the animals killed each other—were *allowed* to kill each other—the bodies lying in rot, maggots and beetles removing the flesh and skin from the bones. And at the ICU zoos enormous sums of money were spent keeping alive a few hundred species of the most colorful of the imperfect animals, those species that appealed most to the masses. . . .

He had avoided these places because they were as imperfect as the animals they housed.

"Yes," the Abbot admitted, looking at him firmly, "they are imperfect, Dagnello. *Anything* of this earth is. But until we can genetically build the animals we want—and produce them in the quantities we need, and construct, as we have in here, the proper earthly kingdoms for them—we will have to rely on these preserves, sanctuaries, and zoos and their imperfect residents. Why do I have the impression, Dagnello, that you have never visited one?"

"Because I have not, Father."

"Have you seen video footage of them?"

"Of course. But I avoid that as well because I find it upsetting."

"The places themselves, Dagnello, or the *idea* of them?"

"Both, Father Abbot."

The Abbot smiled as always. The smile was confident—the great gray eyebrows rising, the lips curled faintly—yet compassionate, too. Admonishing yet tolerant.

"Try, Dagnello," the Abbot said, "to be a little more *Jesuitical*."

"I do not understand, Father."

"Sometimes, Dagnello, we Franciscans are *too* loving.

We must face the Enemy *fully*. We must learn to recognize *each and every* feature of His Face. We must not let fear—*or* love, Dagnello—keep us from learning to recognize it. ...."

Dagnello nodded, but still did not understand. The word *Jesuitical* was unpleasant, yet the Abbot had not used it critically. Dagnello would, yes, visit a wild preserve, or a sanctuary, or an ICU zoo on the continent somewhere, as soon as his work permitted. He would, yes, stand before it trying to see clearly each and every feature of the Enemy's Face.

He would do it after Kampuchea perhaps. Or after the mission after that. ...

They discussed Kampuchea—how the Ephesian saint, the one they called "Mother Kampuchea," in the midst of the famine there, had turned feral and heretical, was proclaiming more loudly than ever—to any media source who would listen to her—that *people were more important than animals*, that, specifically, "in times of famine, O sons and daughters of Khmer, when your government can no longer help you and those outside will not or cannot either, it is no sin in the eyes of a loving God to kill an animal of the jungle *to feed your children*. How could it be?"

The Abbot saw the fallacy of this instantly and, as always, articulated it well: *Human misery, Dagnello, has always been the true battlefield for the soul. It can **never** be an excuse for sin. If ten million human beings are hungry, then ten million **souls** are at stake. It is that simple. This woman gives her Kampuchean hordes a list of the animals they should kill—species which computer models say will probably survive the killing—and thinks she has solved her dilemma. Can she not see that any man, woman, or child in*

Kampuchea who eats the flesh of any animal there, no matter how common, how small, is a soul lost to God?

He would leave in three days, would reach the jungles of Kampuchea and the ruins of Angkor Wat the same day, would proceed to the old woman's city of tents. She never traveled. The people always came to her. The choice of weapon would be up to him.

When, at last, he told the Abbot about the snakes, The Tree and The Body, he had trouble looking the man in the eye. They were sitting on a bench in the abbey's garden. The Abbot smiled again, crows-feet crinkling the corners of his eyes, and said: "You really do not know what these dreams mean, Dagnello?"

"No, Father. I do not."

"What do you imagine a secular doctor of the mind would say?"

Dagnello did not understand, and then he did, feeling the embarrassment reach his cheeks. Even as a boy he had not touched himself in his room at night. He had not touched himself in that way since he was eighteen, in the pine trees, that day near lake Garda, when he killed that small animal with a rock . . . .

"You *do* know, don't you," the Abbot said.

"Yes."

"And you know what to do about it, don't you."

"Yes, Father."

On his way to his quarters that evening he stopped at the pharmacy in the old monastery annex and charged a single dose of pyroemoxin to his account—with the Abbot's blessing.

He took the pills with a glass of *Bocca di Magra* wine—

charged to his account at the commissary, too—then placed a towel over the sheet on his cot and lay down at last.

In his dream the snakes grew quickly, coiling around the tree—the tree that was his body—and when he began to shake with fleshly desire, with the body's eternal hunger to *make life*, he knew it was with God's blessing.

On his last night in Assisi, under a full moon, he visited the zoo once more.

He felt the strange mixture of calm and excitement he needed to feel before any mission. His cutouts in ethnic-Cambodian Vietnam were being put in place right now; his seven safehouses in Bangkok and Ho Chi Minh City were being checked electronically and arranged by computer; he would probably use the Chinese SKS 90, because it was such a common weapon in that part of the world these days and would be a perfect "tourist trophy" if discovered.

As he stood in the moonlight, looking at the lion nearest the gate, he thought for a moment that it might be dead. It lay like a pile of clothing in the savanna grass, limper than he had ever seen one of them lie.

When he had reached it and was leaning over to touch it, the wind came up, moving the fur and grass, and he was unable to tell whether it was breathing, whether its ribs were rising and falling or still. For some reason he did not want to touch it. *They die on occasion. They **must**. Everything must die,* he assured himself. *Praised be our sister, death of the body. . . .*

The lamb was lying in the grass thirty yards beyond the lion, motionless too, and he started toward it, but stopped.

In the darkness of the jungle ahead of him something was moving. He thought of the hairless orangutans, but the movement was wrong. The figure—it *was* a figure—had stopped, was kneeling down, and something that might very well have been metal flashed in the moonlight.

His eyes adjusted, and as they did, the flash came again.

He turned around to look at the gate, to call to the brother there, but then remembered that he had entered with a key—that the abbot had entrusted a key to him because it was his last night—and that there had been no one at the gate.

He stepped toward the darkness and as he did, the kneeling figure did not move. When the moon was finally lost in the branches above him and could no longer blind him, he saw that there were *two* figures, not one.

An animal lay on its side. A leopard, a panther—a cat of some kind. The kneeling figure was human, yes, and as he watched it, he saw it pull something from the animal's neck. Metal flashed again.

A syringe?

Something felt wrong. Without thinking he reached for his weapon, only to remember that he did not have one.

The figure turned and looked up at him from the wet leaves, from the glistening darkness of the jungle foliage, and for a moment it was, yes, the face of an orangutan—pale in the darkness, hairless and pink. And then it became something else.

A *human* face.

The face of a woman.

The face stared at him, the syringe somewhere in the darkness, and he found himself thinking, because it was the only possible explanation: *The Order has a good veterinary staff. One of them could be attending to sick animals in the night, inoculating them for some microbial threat he had not heard about—because it was simply not his affair.*

The figure did not move. It did not speak. It simply

looked at him and he could not see its eyes. He could only see the faint light on its naked skin, and the contours that made it a *woman's* face, not a man's.

There had never, he remembered, been *women* on the Order's veterinary staff.

There had never been women anywhere in the monastery's compound.

When she moved, he thought of the Jesuits and did not know why. She was *not* wearing black. She was wearing secular clothes—pants a little darker than her face, a blouse lighter still, and a jacket that might have been either blue or black—but when she moved, it was like an animal, a deer, a gazelle, and as she disappeared, it made him think of the Jesuits slipping through the night.

The lion, the lamb and the leopard were indeed dead. A cardiotoxin poison had been used. It was a painless poison, the abbot explained, grim-faced in his study, but nevertheless the animals had been killed, killed on the Order's grounds, in sight of The Saint's hologram, and nothing like this, even in the eighteen months of the demonstrations, had ever happened in the long history of the Order. The Vatican had been contacted. Guards with sidearms would be posted twenty-four hours a day and a description of the young woman, if indeed it was a young woman, would be sent to the regional *carabinieri* as well as the national police and the Vatican's own. Zoos throughout Italy would be alerted and Father Dagnello would have to expect to spend the next day in official interviews. The mission in Angkor Wat would be postponed. This was a strike, was it not, at the symbolic heart of the Order's soul, was catastrophic in pure media terms, and should not be underestimated in its import.

Dagnello listened to the Abbot and nodded. He could still see the face glowing faintly in the darkness of the night, and he was doing his best to understand what it all meant. *Who are you really killing?* a voice said suddenly, and he knew he had heard it before: The skulls from Burma. The sense that someone, someone he should be saving, was dying. . . .

That a woman—a *woman*—had killed three animals in the Franciscan zoo at Assisi, before the very eyes of the Tenth Assassin, made his heart leap, made him feel that there was something he was not quite grasping, something that could not be grasped as long as the only thing he saw in his mind's eye was her *face*—the pale, hairless face of a woman.

He remained in Assisi at the Abbot's request for three days, was interviewed by investigators from the regional police, from secular Rome, and from the Holy City, and at the end of that period the Abbot told him:

"You have a new mission—one that Rome has ranked higher than any I can remember, Dagnello."

He knew what the Abbot would say.

"You will find this young woman, if indeed she *is* a young woman. You will take her alive if you can, but if you cannot, you will kill her. Angkor Wat is *not* important now."

His heart was racing, but his heart always raced before a mission, did it not? He had known he would be reassigned to this. What had happened on the church grounds three nights before was more important than anything anyone had ever dreamt of, and the Vatican would use him now just as he had been trained to be used.

"This is a *tracker* mission, Dagnello—not a simple removal—your first, I believe," the Abbot was saying. "You will have at your disposal the computers in Rome and, through Rome, the intelligence network of twelve nations. What you do with that intelligence *must* remain deniable, of course. Officially, we are asking the secular community simply to help in capturing a young woman, in bringing her to justice at the hands of secular authorities. Those who understand what we will actually do with her will look the other way; those who do not will help us in their ignorance. The agent, whoever she is, is probably out of the country by now, and your mission may take months. It does not matter. You have an open budget with thirty line-items at your disposal. You will take whatever time you need to locate her."

"I understand, Father."

"Do you have any questions?"

"No, Father."

"You never do, do you, Dagnello," the Abbot said, the smile as warm and tender as ever.

Yet Dagnello found himself returning the smile uncomfortably. "No, I suppose not, Father."

"You will conduct an investigation here first?"

"Of course."

There were, he learned, four guards with Walther 487's and infrared-blind suits on the perimeter of the zoo and four with the same armament and protection inside. All were assassin apprentices, though only one or two would ever reach Assassin or Assassin Support rank by the end of their lives. Two of the four positioned at the perimeter stood at the gate rod-straight in the new arc lights, and the remaining two patrolled the wall as silently as . . . Jesuits.

"I need to inspect the scene," he told the two at the gate, raising his left arm so they could see the shoulder holster and Reicker automatic in his armpit.

Nodding, they unlocked the gate.

"Has electronic security been increased?" he asked. "Seismic sensors, microwave eyes—the usual?"

"We are not at liberty to discuss such matters outside secure offices, Brother," one of them answered, smiling apologetically.

"Of course."

Leaving the gate behind, he moved across the savanna grass slowly, looking to the right, to the left, trying to put the pieces together. He had visited the zoo earlier in the day, in the sunlight, trying to understand what he had seen that night, but it had been wrong. Perhaps, he told himself, he would remember everything better in darkness. The woman hadn't *acted* like the terrorists he had surveiled and eventually removed. Even Cichinelli, a seasoned urban guerilla, hadn't been that confident—that personal—with him.

What was it about the face, the way it waited, letting him see it?

It had seemed—what was the word that had come to him earlier in the day? *Intimate.* Yes, *intimate.* As if she had actually known who he was, as if . . . . He had tried to explain this to the interviewers, but none had understood, and he had finally stopped trying. It was a sensation only, a *feeling,* but in his line of work *feelings*—instinct, grace and prayer—had done more to keep him alive than any rifle, any strategy.

If I return at night, he had told himself—*if I return in the darkness and try to remember the gestures, the silences, the details that made me feel this, perhaps . . . .*

Personal. That was the feeling, even if it made no sense.

As if she had chosen him—
As if . . . .

The lion, the lamb and the leopard had been removed.
Three adult tapir stood upright and asleep in the faint
lamplight to his left. An animal of some kind slept in the
grass twenty yards to his right as well, but he ignored it and
made for the spot where he had discovered the young
woman.

When he reached it, he stood in the darkness and tried
to remember what *exactly* she had done? She had turned
and looked at him, but she hadn't moved. *Why*? Why hadn't
she fled immediately? She had known—yes, she had known
he was approaching—and yet she hadn't. Even when she
looked up at him, it was as if—as if she were *waiting* for
something.

He turned to look at the foliage she had disappeared
through, started to turn away again, and froze.

Something that looked like a small moon had moved in
the foliage. There it was again, and as he stared at it, it
moved again, stepping closer to him, stepped again, stopping
at last at the edge of the darkness, at the edge of the light
from the new lamps at the gate. It was one of the hairless
orangutans, he told himself.

But the legs, he saw suddenly, were too long, the
carriage too high. And the darkness that framed the face, he
realized, was *hair*.

His heart stopped, then began again—harder and louder
than he could ever remember it beating. The figure had arms.
Of course. It was holding something out to him. It was an
illusion. It *had* to be. There were guards at the gates. There
were guards patrolling inside—

No. He had, he remembered, passed no guards inside. He had passed only the two sleeping animals in the grass—two bodies which he hadn't approached because he had assumed they were animals . . . sleeping.

His right hand went to the Reicker, had it out and aimed even as the figure knelt down, laying what it held in its hands on the jungle floor.

"*Do not move,*" he ordered.

The figure got up slowly and stared at him. He could not see the features of the face this time, but he could, in the faint light from the distant lamps, see the shadow between the breasts, the shadow between the legs, the hips—or was this only his imagination? Was it *really* a woman, naked in the darkness?

"*I would rather not kill you,*" he said in Italian, then in German and Japanese, "*but I will if you move again.*"

The figure moved again, stepping toward him and finally stopping. The lamplight that reached the figure's front indeed revealed a woman's breasts. The waist was narrow and the darkness—the triangle of darkness between the legs, between the hips—was the same darkness as the hair that framed the face. The figure seemed to be saying: *Go ahead, Brother, kill me. That is why I am here, isn't it—so that you can kill me before I kill you.*

He would *not* kill her. There were too many questions, as the Abbot had pointed out. The Vatican had its agenda, the Order had its own, and she would spend this night and the next day and the night and day after that somewhere on the monastery grounds being interrogated by the Order's professionals. Whatever happened after that would be Rome's decision, not his.

He would take her alive if she would let him.

When the figure spoke, he nearly fired his weapon. He had never had a target speak to him like this—so calmly, so naked.

"What have you done?" the voice asked. "What have you done to the animals, Father?

"Have you forgotten?" the voice went on.

The Reicker was aimed at her heart. It was always aimed at the heart, but he had never aimed it at a chest like this, two breasts described faintly in the lamplight, the rise and fall barely perceptible while his own breath was labored.

She is armed, a voice inside him said. *And she has accomplices here. She must. Otherwise why would she be so calm?* Another voice answered: *She is **not** armed, Dagnello. She is **naked**. She is insane or drugged—that is why she is like this.*

"Put your hands over your head," he ordered, and as she complied, the Reicker spun suddenly from his hand. He kicked out to block any spin kick that might follow the snap from her naked foot, but the figure was gone once more. Only the darkness of the wet leaves that lay beyond the reach of the lamplight remained, and he stared into that darkness for a long time.

This cannot be happening, he told himself, searching the jungle floor on all fours for his weapon. *It cannot.* It would be the most difficult thing he had ever admitted to the Abbot—more difficult really than any sin he had ever confessed.

When he found the Reicker at last in the nearest rhododendron, he realized it had taken him an hour. When he got up, he was covered with the wetness of leaves, with the leaves themselves, and with a dirt that smelled bad. It made him feel like an animal, dirty.

When he went to the spot where the figure had put what was in its hands, he hesitated. It might be a bomb. It might be a shaped charge with a seismic trigger. But as he knelt, he saw it was only a snake—a small fat boa as limp as the lamb and leopard and lion had been. He looked for wires, for anything nearby that might be a charge, but found nothing.

He did not bother to inspect the two bodies in the savanna grass on the way back. He knew what they were. Any assassin worthy of his saint's love would have known what they were at first glance, he told himself.

The Abbot listened. The smile was there, but it wasn't quite warm. All Dagnello could hope was that the coldness behind that courtesy—that formal smile—was not really meant for him, but for an interloper who had had the temerity to remain in Assisi and to strike again at the heart of the Order, at the living symbols of its age-old mission, at the very soul of its Saint.

When Dagnello had finished, the Abbot was silent. Then he said: "You know what this is, don't you?"

Dagnello wasn't sure.

"I'm not sure . . . ."

"The Father of Lies has chosen *you*, Dagnello. He has chosen you for a contest."

"I see."

"That the adversary is a *woman,* Dagnello, that she has appeared before you naked, should tell you the seriousness of the challenge and the resourcefulness of the Father of Lies."

"Yes. . . ."

"I believe we are witnessing the greatest spiritual threat

our Order has ever faced, Dagnello, and I believe that much more than a single soul—*yours*—rides in the balance."

Dagnello nodded.

"You will not need to leave the monastery grounds."

For a moment Dagnello did not understand, but then he did.

"She will penetrate our security again," Dagnello said, nodding. "She will remain here until she has beaten me . . . or until I have beaten her."

"Yes," the Abbot said. "Those are the rules of a duel, are they not?"

From the armorarium Dagnello selected an Ithaca twelve-gauge, a MAC 10 machine pistol, and a Luger fleschette carbine—weapons he knew very well and ones that would be most effective at close nocturnal range. The technical staff, awake now and at his disposal twenty-four hours a day from this moment on, gave him three different ambient-light scopes and two kinds of infrared goggles, as well as the finest laser-aiming devices in the world.

That night he dreamed of a woman. He could not be sure who it was, because he could not see the face, but the body—the curves of hip, of breast—said that indeed it was a woman, and one he knew. The hair, much longer in every place than it should have been, *smelled* like a woman, though he could not remember having smelled a woman before. He had never been with a woman. Even as an adolescent, in those years of temptation before seminary, he had never smelled a woman in this way. . . .

It was, he realized, the smell of an animal.

In this dream he tried to shoot her with a weapon he was not familiar with, a weapon he had never used, and it fell

limp in his hand, bit him, and he dropped it with a cry. The
woman remained, as if wanting to help him. She said, "*You
are more important than any animal, Father, for you have the
power. If you do not understand yourself, Father, you cannot
understand them. And if you do not understand them* . . . ."
He could not hear the final words clearly, and when he
awoke, he realized that he had failed to place a towel on the
sheet and that he should have.

Later that day a question came to him from the dream.
He didn't understand it, but the words were clear:

"Why are you doing this, Father? Why are you doing
this to us all?"

She would not kill him, he understood at last. That was
not what she wanted. She could have done it twice before
and had not. What the Prince of Lies or her terrorist organization or whoever controlled her wanted in this ritual, he saw
clearly, was his degradation, his impotence, in turn the
degradation of his entire Order. The Tenth *Assassino* of the
Order of Friars Minor would *not* be killed; he would be
humiliated, again and again, until all of the animals—the
wonderful creatures of the Order's zoo—were dead, the
guards drugged or killed if necessary, the electronic security
of the abbey grounds breached, the Tenth Assassin himself
rendered impotent in the eyes of Rome . . . and the world.
The full story would eventually appear in *L'Unita, La
Nazione,* the international video newstexts, and the interests
she represented would have their media coup . . . on behalf
of the Father of Lies. The Abbot was so right. It was a
contest, a duel, with more at stake than he had ever imagined
possible.

He sat on the jungle leaves—his face blackened with

nightstick, the kevlar body stocking just as black—and waited.

When she appeared this time, she was dressed in street clothes again. At first he didn't move, and when he did, it was only to pull the trigger.

The dart from the pneumatic dart gun struck her sternum and he waited until her body hit the jungle floor before standing and exposing himself.

As he looked down at the figure, he felt the unease.

It had been too easy, he knew.

And then the voice said again: *Who are you really killing, Dagnello? Who?*

The next morning he saw her being led through the sunlight from the annex to the Abbot's quarters. Even at this distance he could see that her cheekbones were bruised, her street clothes wrinkled and stained, and the sockets of her eyes heavily shadowed. He wondered what they had used on her—the drug that fills a person with such profound fear that *anything* is preferable, or the one that makes a person tell the truth even while believing he or she is lying, or the drum of water, or the electrodes placed carefully on the body where such things should never be placed.

She seemed to know he was looking at her and she turned to stare at him. When their eyes met, her clothes disappeared, and she was naked again in the moonlight. Before he could turn away and move down the cobblestone street to his own quarters, he felt his own robe drop away and the *shame* moved through him.

That night he dreamed of her. She was simply what she was—a woman, a woman in street clothes, with bruises—not a symbol, not a form adopted by the Prince of Lies, not an automaton for some terrorist organization. She was trying to tell him something, but he could not hear her above a recorded voice that was telling him about animals and flowers and brothers and sisters and other things.

His sheet was dry in the morning. When he saw this, a voice inside him shouted: *You have **won**, Dagnello*.

Yes, he told himself. *Yes!*

But another voice was saying: *It isn't over, Dagnello. It's never over*. And lying on the dry sheet, he knew it was true.

She escaped the next night. When he heard the news, his heart stopped beating. It wasn't fear that made it stop, he realized. It was—he realized with horror—a feeling not unlike happiness.

When he confessed this to the Abbot, the old man said calmly, "The Prince of Lies is ingenious, Dagnello. He, too, works in wondrous and mysterious ways. He has taken God's gift—our Saint's proper compassion for all creatures great or small—and through this has made you *care* for a mortal woman. In doing so, he has blinded you to the real meaning of these events. This is what he wants. As long as you understand this, he has *not* won, Dagnello, and the duel, which you fight for all of us, can continue."

Dagnello nodded. The Abbot was right, of course. He would not be Abbot were he easily deceived, as easily deceived as the Tenth Assassin who saw in this waking dream only a real woman, a real voice, a real body with blood and skin.

He dreamed that night of a woman—a woman named Olivia, a woman with a birthmark on her right hip, who laughed at him, but not unkindly, as they sat together on a marble bench in the courtyard of the abbey grounds.

Did he know her? Why was she here? She told him of her family in Florence, of the coldness of her father when she was growing up, the two water spaniels she had loved as a little girl. In turn, he told her about his own childhood in Genoa, how his older brother had entered the Navy wanting to see the world, had died in a fire on the missile frigate *Ulysses*. She told him about the first time she had bled, how scared she had been, how her mother had held her and finally said: "It is only blood—*good* blood. Men don't know this kind of blood. Stop being afraid!" How from that day on she had *not* been afraid. In turn, he told her—confessing it as he had never confessed it to anyone—how he had killed a squirrel, the first wild animal he had ever seen, in the pine forests by Lake Garda when he was ten, and how, horrified but curious, he had skinned it to see what it was like inside, how the blood had haunted him for years. How he had touched himself in a forest just like in years later, at sixteen, alone, anxious, and how the two forests, the blood and the slickness on his hand, had become one. *"Bad blood!"* she said suddenly, laughing at him but kindly. "You don't know the blood we women know!" He found himself smiling, looking at her cheekbones, at the collarbone that showed under her blouse, at the fingers of her hands, which sat in her lap, and at her eyes, which were somehow, despite his shame, accepting.

"You have very wide shoulders for a priest," she said at last, quietly, teasing, and he found himself answering: "You need wide shoulders for the work I do."

"I know," she said. "It must be a heavy thing to carry, Felice."

He began to cry, and when he awoke, he was crying. He wished he had remembered to put a towel by his bedside, because he needed to wipe his eyes. He could not remember whether he had ever killed a squirrel, had ever gotten the blood of *any* animal on him, but it did not matter, did it? They were words between human beings, and human beings were what mattered . . . for they had the power. Without human beings—their feelings for each other, their understanding of themselves—the animals were doomed. Someone had said that.

Who?

When he got up from his cot, he saw the savanna grass—a few stalks of it—on the floor by his sandals, lit by the morning light. He felt a cottony sensation in his mouth and remembered it from the other morning, too. Pulling his sleeves up quickly, he searched and finally found the needle mark. There, on the inside of his right arm, red, inflamed.

It didn't matter how she'd gotten in. What mattered was that it hadn't been a dream . . . that he hadn't been alone.

"She is in none of the computers," the Abbot told him with a sigh. "She confessed only that she belonged to a religious order, but that is surely a lie. She is a member of a brilliant terrorist cartel that has targeted our order for political annihilation. It is that simple."

He would tell the Abbot about the grass, the needle mark and what he remembered of the conversation. He would have to. But not now. He needed to think carefully, and the Abbot was talking loudly.

"Which is *not* to say, Dagnello, that the Father of Lies isn't the real weaver of this story. He works in ways as intricate as God's, but for the good of Darkness rather than Light. You know this, Dagnello. You have always—in your eternal soul—known this, Dagnello." The Abbot was staring at him, and for the first time in Dagnello's life here at the abbey, the man sounded insane.

You are wrong, Father, he wanted to tell the old man. *It is a **woman**, not the Prince of Lies. It is a flesh-and-blood woman who is trying to tell me something because she cares. Something I once knew and have somehow forgotten. Something about the animals—about **us all**. For once you are wrong, Father Abbot.*

No Abbot should sound insane, Dagnello knew, and no Tenth Assassin should feel an urge to say such things. He'd have to confess all of this, too, to the Abbot eventually. But not now.

"Your mission remains the same," the old man was saying.

"Of course."

When she appeared in the jungle that night, wearing a habit as dark as the night itself, he aimed the carbine, aimed it again, and found he could not pull the trigger. He heard her say: "The blood is the blood we *all* bleed, Father, people and animals alike. The animals—who understand our Father in Heaven better than we ever will—will always forgive us. It is we who cannot forgive ourselves.

"Have you forgiven yourself, Father," he heard her ask, "for the blood of that small animal so long ago?

"It is *people,* like you, Tenth Assassin," he heard her whispering, "we must save, for by saving you, Father, we save the animals. . . ."

At least this was what he heard. He could not be sure the voice had said it, because his heart was hammering in his ears, and he wanted to stand up, to hold her, to put his cheek

119

beside hers, find the bench again and talk, to have her listen, when all he could really do was sit in the jungle leaves and aim his weapon—the cold metal and plastic thing he held—at her.

She stood before him until at last he got up and returned to his quarters.

"She is too quick, too skilled," he explained to the Abbot. "I am simply not good enough. I am not good enough for this contest."

The Abbot looked at him, and Dagnello knew the old man knew he was lying.

The Jesuit arrived the next morning dressed in black with a Hechler and Koch 480 sniper rifle in its carrying case—the emblem that marked him as an Expedient Instrument of Rome—and retired immediately to his quarters in silence. Given the memory training Jesuits received, the man already held in his skull all intelligence accumulated to date on the events that had transpired and would need to speak to no one—not the Abbot, not the Tenth Assassin, who had, as everyone now knew, failed to excommunicate the greatest threat his order had ever known.

The man looks like death, Dagnello found himself thinking. Like someone who had never thought of squirrels or a girl's menstrual blood or a woman's hands, never placed towels on sheets at night. Like the Prince of Lies himself, walking down a cobblestone street.

Like the death I have been so afraid of, Dagnello realized.

Like my own slow dying....
Like the killing of myself....

That night he met her again in the dream that was not a dream. There was no needle. She simply appeared and sat on the edge of his bed, in his quarters, and said quietly: "I'm of the Order of Poor Clares. You know them, Father." "Yes," he answered, saying: "You broke from us in 1826. You have always been trouble." "Of course," she said, smiling, "because you and your brothers have never understood." "You're a communist," he said, raising himself on one elbow on his cot. She laughed and answered: "No." "You are mentally and spiritually ill," he insisted, and she said: "Because I have killed your animals painlessly?" "No, because you've killed them at all." "I have killed only what you have already destroyed, Father. You have remade these animals in your own image. They were not truly *alive*. Can you not see this, Father?" "I see nothing of the kind," he told her. "But you do," she said lightly. "The lions don't have teeth, do they? The snakes cannot squeeze. The monkeys cannot copulate. Even the lambs are not really lambs. You can see this, can't you, Father?"

All he could see for the moment was her face, her shoulders, her legs on the edge of his bed, as if she had been there a hundred times before, as if it were a park bench and he had known her for years.

Later he would remember her saying: "You were going to kill an old woman in Kampuchea, Father. That was why I was sent. But saving an old woman's life isn't as important as saving a soul, Father. Do you understand? Do you understand why I have stayed here with you?"

He would also, unless it was a dream, remember her whispering: *"I love the animals without you, Dagnello. I love the animals you are."*

He sat in the jungle, and when she appeared at last, he did not get up. She seemed to know he was there but did not approach him. When the Prince of Lies appeared at last—a darker darkness on the dark savanna grass, in the moonless night—he aimed the rifle he had brought with him and fired twice. As the Jesuit fell, the figure became a lion, a leopard, an animal sleeping in the grass, and everything was right again.

"*I love you,*" he said suddenly, and the loudness of his own voice embarrassed him.

"Yes, Father," she said, "you do."

He would, he knew, have to tell the Abbot everything. He would have to tell the truth, even if it meant never carrying a holy weapon again or going out on a mission, even if it meant that after he had left Assisi the weapons he had used would not appear in any museum anywhere, even if it meant that he would have never again feel the clean comforts of the monastery or the companionship of the woman who, he knew, had left his life forever.

Even if it meant having only the last words she had spoken to him—*Yes, Father, you do*—and her laughter, teasing but kind, for the briefest moment in the darkness.

The Perfect Host

by Robert Silverberg

Robert Silverberg, a transplanted New Yorker now living in
Oakland, California, has written science fiction, horror,
fantasy, historical, and erotic literature as well as non-fiction
books on science, history, and archaeology. He has won five
Nebula Awards and four Hugo Awards. His novels include
*Dying Inside, The Book of Skulls, Born With the Dead, Tom
O' Bedlam*, and *Lord Valentine's Castle*. His most recent is
The Face of the Waters (Bantam). His short fiction collec-
tions include *Unfamiliar Territory, The Best of Robert
Silverberg, Capricorn Games, Majipoor Chronicles, The
Conglomeroid Cocktail Party*, and *Beyond the Safe Zone*. He
has had thirteen stories in *Omni*, including the Hugo Award-
nominated "Our Lady of the Sauropods" (September 1980).
His most recent *Omni* story was "Hunters in the Forest"
(October 1991).

"The Perfect Host" is a departure from most of the
other stories in this book. For one thing, it could be taking
place today. Also, it's funny—at least at first. It's a good
example of Silverberg's darkly humorous wit with an edge,
which is the way I prefer my humor. It's original to this
volume.

THE PERFECT HOST

Robert Silverberg

After the third chemotherapy session a voice said, coming
from somewhere within him, apparently just back of his ribs
on the right side, "I wish you'd quit letting them give you
these treatments. It's pretty damned disagreeable for us both,
and a complete waste of time besides. You don't have
cancer."

McDermott glanced quickly around the room. No one
was there.

"Who said that?"

"I did."

"Who are you? *Where* are you?"

"I'm right in here. Inside you, not very far from your
gallbladder. I *think* this thing is your gallbladder. You've got
one hell of an incredible mess of complicated stuff inside
you, are you aware of that?"

McDermott closed his eyes and took five or six deep
breaths. They had warned him that the chemotherapy would
nauseate him and make what was left of his hair fall out, but
they hadn't said a word about hallucinations. He could
handle the nausea, most likely, and the hair was supposed to

grow back eventually if he survived at all, but he didn't like the idea of hearing voices.

"I want you to cancel these chemo sessions," the voice said firmly.

"Look, leave me alone, will you?"

"I'm serious. You're letting them pour all this deadly crap into your system, and it's very unpleasant for me. It can't be a lot of fun for you either."

"I refuse to listen to this," McDermott said. "It's bad enough to turn up with cancer at my age. To lose my mind on top of everything else is simply adding insult to injury."

"I told you. You don't have cancer."

"Then what's this lump in my abdomen?"

"Me," said the voice. "I've been living inside you for nine weeks. Establishing contact with your neural system, getting everything in shape to notify you of my presence. But you had to decide I was a malignancy, didn't you? You and that pansy doctor of yours. And now the chemotherapy. Talk about adding insult to injury, fellow. How would you like it if I called *you* a malignancy? And then started polluting your environment with vile and nasty life-threatening substances?"

"Shit," McDermott muttered. "Oh, shit, shit, shit. This is too goddamned much."

"You don't believe I'm really here?"

"Of course you're really here. You're a hideous fucking mass of inoperable carcinoma that's trying to kill me and doing a pretty good job of it, and obviously you've metastasized to my brain as well, and now I'm sliding into terminal insanity. I'm going to spend my few remaining weeks having long intimate conversations with my own cancer. That's just great. You can't imagine how happy it all makes me."

"I keep telling you and telling you, McDermott. You don't have cancer."

"What do I have, then?"

"You really want to know?"

"Sure. Why not?"

"All right. Your body is host to an intelligent alien lifeform. I'm a visitor from Cherponex VII, and I've taken up residence in your abdomen. That may sound a little unsettling to you, but I assure you, fellow, I'm the best thing that's ever happened to you. Trust me."

"Shit," McDermott said again. So he had gone out of his mind, on top of all the rest of it. "Shit, shit, shit, shit."

He began to cry. He had grown very emotional here in these days of terminal affliction.

There was no arguing with the voice's timetable, at any rate. His troubles had started exactly nine weeks before, nine weeks to the day. He had it all charted out on the calendar on his bedroom wall. Tuesday, the Fourth of July: Bill and Jan Kaiser's annual holiday cookout at the picnic grove in Taft Park, the whole gang there, beer by the keg, the usual softball game, hamburgers grilling on the charcoal fire. He played left field and didn't do such a bad job of it, considering that he hadn't been sixteen years old for the past twenty-three years, although his throwing arm wasn't what it once had been. He did proper justice to all that fine cold beer, too. And, since it was the Fourth of July, he allowed himself three nice sizzling burgers with plenty of onion, and to hell with the cholesterol count. Half an hour later he felt a stabbing pain in his gut, a little more than halfway down his right side, an icepick sensation so powerful that it knocked him to his knees. He crouched there, sweating, astonished.

"What is it, man?" Dave Brewster asked. They had gone to high school together. Brewster was an internist now. He was McDermott's doctor whenever McDermott needed a doctor, which hadn't been often.

"Pain—right—here—"

Brewster helped him up. "A little gastrointestinal discomfort, hey? That fourth hamburger sending you a message?"

"I only had three."

"But you forgot the Alka-Seltzer chaser, didn't you? You aren't a kid any more, Joey-boy."

"Thirty-nine."

"Just what I said. You aren't a kid."

Brewster always brought a first-aid kit to the Kaisers' picnic. He fixed up some fizzy-water for McDermott, and he felt better, or thought he did, though he begged off on the volleyball game that traditionally wrapped up the day's frolics. There was still a dull ache in his side when he drove home, even so, and in the morning it was worse, and he had some fever besides. He tried Maalox.

He tried more Alka-Seltzer. He lived on a bland diet for a couple of days. Things went on hurting. The pain would diminish at times, would almost disappear, and then would return worse than ever. Had there been a chunk of ground glass in that last hamburger? The following Tuesday—exactly a week after the picnic—he took a morning off—and went to see Dave Brewster.

"Still hurts?" Brewster asked, sounding surprised. "Well, let's check a few things out, now—"

He peered at McDermott's tongue. He looked down McDermott's throat. He prodded McDermott's tender abdomen. He took McDermott's temperature. He had McDermott give him blood and urine samples, just to play it safe. But he said he didn't see anything amiss.

"Could it be appendicitis?" McDermott asked, in case Brewster hadn't considered that possibility. "The appendix is on the right side, isn't it?"

"Generally. Not always. It might be appendicitis, yeah. Except that I happen to recall that you had your appendix out when you were seventeen years old, which is why I didn't explore that idea right away at the picnic. The things don't grow back, Joe. On the other hand, pain like this could be caused by a perforating ulcer of the stomach or duodenum. Or inflammation of the gallbladder. Or diverticulitis of the sigmoid colon. It could be an intestinal blockage, for that matter. Kidney stones. Shingles. Or maybe—"

"Enough," McDermott said. "Stop already. What do you think it is?"

"Let's wait for the tests, okay, Joe? The fact that the pain, while acute, doesn't seem to be getting any worse argues against most of the things I just listed. Most likely it's just some virus you picked up. Some of these viruses can be awfully stubborn."

The pain stayed. The fever came and went. There were more tests: gastric analyses, stool samples, liver-function studies. Some of the procedures were less than enjoyable. Brewster began to sound puzzled and then evasive, which McDermott didn't like at all.

"We've known each other twenty-five years," McDermott said. "Don't fuck around with me. What do you think I've got?"

"I'm not sure. I'd like to run a GI series on you with barium sulfate, just to rule a few things out."

"That means you suspect cancer, right?"

Brewster nodded. "That's one possibility, I'm afraid."

"Is there a growth in there?"

"There's a zone of irritation. I'm not sure I would call it a growth. I need a better look."

The barium sulfate was horrible, and the GI series produced no useful answers. The next step was a fiber-optic endoscopic exploration of McDermott's abdomen. Brewster reported some abnormalities in the vicinity of his liver or gallbladder.

New words entered McDermott's vocabulary as the weeks went by. The transhepatic cholangiography, which involved a long skinny needle passed through the wall of his chest, provided data about his liver ducts. The cholecystography was an unamusing X-ray study of his gallbladder. The intravenous cholangiography that followed the cholecystography sent dye into his veins to bring back information about bile production.

"I don't know, Joe," Brewster said. "I just don't know."

"That's a wonderful diagnosis, all right."

"You want to hear what I know? You've got a gallbladder inflammation that tests out malignant using one kind of methodology and as something else entirely using another kind. What the something else is, I can't tell you, because I don't know and nobody else seems to either. There's a possibility of metastasis into the liver. It may already have happened."

"If you're using words like *malignant* and *metastasis*, you're telling me that I have cancer."

"It's more like cancer than *not* like cancer, if you take my meaning."

"What are you saying, Dave?"

"That we regard this as cancer and treat it accordingly, despite the little anomalies we've seen. We may be able to knock this thing out chemotherapeutically, if we get moving now. Otherwise we're talking about surgical removal of the gallbladder, possible liver transplants, a whole raft of really problematical procedures. I'm sorry, Joe."

"That makes two of us," McDermott said.

The voice said, "It's a slow business, infiltrating an intelligent being's nervous system. First I had to get myself established, you realize, and that takes time. Negotiate some sort of truce with your white blood corpuscles, get the antibodies on my side, build my nest, settle in really snugly. That inevitably causes the host some pain, because I don't know where the neural centers are yet, so I obviously can't neutralize them. I regret that very much. It's not my intention to cause you discomfort of any sort."

"I really appreciate that," McDermott said.

"You don't have to speak out loud to me, you know. I'm plugged right into your main switchboard now."

In that case, McDermott said silently, you can hear me when I tell you that I want you to get the fuck out of my body this very minute, if you're real. And to stop bothering me anyway if you aren't.

"I assure you I'm quite real," said the voice.

"Your assuring me doesn't prove anything. If you're just a figment of my chemically disordered mind, then you can react to my thoughts just as easily as you can to what I say out loud. But none of that makes you real."

"How would you like your hair back, Joe?"

"I haven't started losing it yet. I've only had three

chemotherapy sessions."

"I mean the hair you've lost normally in the course of living your life up to this point. You want me to fill in that little bald spot in back? You want nice black hair hanging down over your forehead the way it did when you were in college? I can do that for you."

"Can you, now? Well, go right ahead."

"I can do more than that. I can metabolize those extra fifteen pounds of yours and get rid of them."

"Dying of cancer will do that too, and more."

"You aren't dying of cancer. You aren't going to die at all, as a matter of fact. Not if you don't want to. I can see to it that you live forever or as much of forever as you're interested in living into."

"You're one hell of a fine hallucination, you know?"

"What about virility? Unquenchable sexual power? Five, six, ten times a night? It would be no effort at all to arrange that. If you want me to, of course."

"You'd do that little thing for me, would you?"

"I'll make you physically perfect, Joe. It's to my advantage as well as yours, of course. I'm completely plugged into you now. I'm wired into your ganglia, your ductless glands, your autonomic nervous system, your everything. I told you, it's a slow business infiltrating a being of your complexity, but I've had nine weeks, and I've done it very thoroughly. So from now on I feel what you feel. You stub your toe, I yell "ouch." You get laid, I share the tingle. You do chemotherapy, I get nauseated. We're partners, Joe. Fifty-fifty in the well-being of your body. So naturally I'll do everything in my power to protect you from harm. And my powers are considerable. A little glandular adjustment here, a little retuning of the hormonal balance there—"

132

"Just where did you come from, anyway?"

"I told you. Cherponex VII. That's a dense and very lovely planet in the Framboin system."

"An invader from space living in my gallbladder."

"Exactly. And glad to be there, Joe. What a miserable, solitary journey I had to make! Seventeen light-years all by myself—a real pisser of an ordeal. But then at last I saw Earth ahead of me in my screen, blue and beautiful. Signs of intelligent life. Down through the atmosphere I went. Very turbulent: a terrific feat of navigation, if I have to say so myself. But I managed just fine. I landed my ship right in the middle of your hamburger no more than a tenth of a second before you put the top of the bun down on it. You swallowed me on the fourth bite, and the rest is history, Joe. The rest is history."

"I swallowed you, ship and all?"

"There was no other way. I was inside the ship; the ship was on your burger."

"So I've got a little alien spaceship attached to my gallbladder?"

"A very small vessel by your standards, let me assure you. Very *very* small. And I, naturally, am even smaller."

"Naturally."

"But quite capable, believe me. My species is not large, as Earth-species go, but we are an extremely advanced race. As I will demonstrate over the weeks ahead, if you give me permission to begin rebuilding your body according to your ideal mode."

"You want my *permission*," McDermott said bleakly.

"It seems only courteous."

"Did you ask my permission when you invaded my gallbladder?"

"I needed to find a secure place of lodging," said the alien. "That was necessary for my survival. But now that I'm safely established, I have no desire to act contrary to your wishes."

"Then get yourself out of me and find some other host."

"Unfortunately that won't be possible. Once union has been achieved there's no way to sever it."

"Then I'm stuck with you?"

"That's a harsh way of phrasing it, but, yes, you are."

"Listen to me talk," McDermott said wonderingly. "I'm actually falling into the trap of believing that you really are there."

"But I really am."

"I refuse to believe any of this. A microscopic alien in a microscopic spaceship, crossing seventeen light-years and landing on my hamburger at a Fourth of July picnic, taking up residence in my gallbladder—"

"You'd rather have cancer?" the alien asked.

The strange thing was that his hair really did start to grow back. First there was a little fuzz along the top of his forehead, and then the fuzz deepened and thickened, and by the end of the week there was no getting away from the fact that the slow erosion of his hairline that had been going on for the past seven or eight years had begun to reverse itself. He worked out a complicated arrangement of mirrors in the bathroom to see the back of his head and damn if the bothersome bald spot that he had noticed in last year's picnic photos wasn't closing over too.

He also lost a couple of pounds of the soft roll around his middle. That was easily enough explained: the cancer, the chemotherapy. But he hadn't ever heard of chemotherapy making someone grow hair.

If anybody at the Oncology Center noticed the odd things that were happening on his scalp, they didn't mention it. Probably they had other matters on their minds. McDermott, who was still on outpatient status, drove faithfully down to the Center every Tuesday and Friday for his regular sessions: the long hours in the chemoroom cubicle, the rigmarole with the IV, the increasingly familiar onset of the nausea, the wobbly time of waiting for the risks of vomiting to recede and his head to clear enough for him to go home.

Two weeks went by that way. There were no further announcements from the visitor from Cherponex VII. It must simply have been a little delusionary spell, McDermott decided. Some kind of weird one-shot drug reaction. His hair continued to grow in, dark and copious. He went on losing weight, too, but seemingly only in his gut and hips, where he had thickened a little too much in recent years. And his mental outlook seemed to have changed, also: he felt strangely exhilarated a lot of time, bouncy and vigorous in a way that seemed totally incongruous, considering the realities of his situation.

On the down side, there still were occasional little stabs of pain from the general region of his gallbladder, and when he put his hand to his side, McDermott imagined he could feel the presence of something hard and round and intrusive encapsulated within him. And the side effects of the continuing chemotherapy were very nasty indeed, just as he had been told they would be.

On the Tuesday of the third week, as he was getting ready to drive down to the Oncology Center, he heard the voice again.

"We can't go on this way any longer, Joe. You want me to keep making significant bodily improvements for you, you've absolutely got to knock off this chemotherapy crap right here and now. I tell you, it's murdering me."

"I don't want to hear anything out of you," McDermott said. "You're nothing but a drug reaction."

"The hell I am."

"And the chemotherapy is essential to my recovery."

"You've got that exactly upside down, fellow. The chemo really sucks. Maybe if you had cancer it could do you some good, I don't know, but cancer is not what you have, and you're putting up with all those foul side effects for no purpose whatsoever. All the chemo does is upset your digestion. *I'm* what's making you better and better in every way. Call Dr. Brewster and tell him that you're in remission and you want to check out of the program."

"I need proper medical help," said McDermott. "I have a mortal illness."

"In a pig's eye you do. What you have is me. Call Brewster."

"Leave me alone."

"You won't call?"

"No."

McDermott felt a sensation very much like a punch on the back of his skull. But it came from *inside*.

"Quit that!"

"You'll stop the chemotherapy?"

"Christ," McDermott muttered. "Go away!"

"All right for you, buddy. As of this minute, no more hair regrowth. As of this minute, you gain two pounds a day, and let your cancer doctors explain *that*. Tomorrow I start

136

blurring your vision. Beginning Thursday I fuck around with your hearing. As for any hope of ever getting it up again, forget all about that. Permanently."

"They said there'd be some side effects. But they didn't say I'd be having hallucinations. Nasty, vindictive ones at that."

"We don't need to be at war, Joe. I want to be your ally. Listen, just cancel the chemo, and nothing bad will ever happen to you again. Trust me."

"And if I don't?"

"I told you what I'd do. Plus this."

McDermott felt another punch against the inside of his skull.

"Every hour on the hour, one of those. Right on through the whole night."

"I don't dare stop the chemo. It would amount to committing suicide. You're putting me under duress and asking me to jeopardize my life."

"There's no suicide involved. Giving up the chemo is something that'll be good for you as well as me. And I have no choice about the duress. You're making my life hell in here, pal."

"Who invited you in the first place?"

"That's not the point. I'm here. No more chemo?"

"Jesus Christ," McDermott said. "No."

"What a stubborn son of a bitch you are. You're really compelling me to mess around with you, aren't you?"

McDermott felt the soles of his feet beginning to itch infuriatingly. His head seemed to be puffing up like a balloon. His left hand started to wriggle violently as though it wanted to jump away from his wrist. Then it slapped him hard across the face.

"I control your entire nervous system," the voice said. "You can't even imagine what I'm capable of doing to you if you won't cooperate. But you'll be sorry. Will you call Dr. Brewster?"

"No."

"I can do *this*."

"Hey!"

"And *this*. Or *this*. And if I really want to be mean—"

"Stop it!"

"Call Brewster?"

McDermott nodded. He reached for the phone.

Brewster wasn't happy about the cancellation.

"I won't mince words. It's your funeral, Joey."

"I tell you, I don't feel tender there any more. The thing is gone. Or at least it's in remission."

"You're not in any position to determine that."

"Nevertheless," McDermott said. "I'm quitting the chemo."

"Hey, nobody likes it. I know it's a miserable thing. But you've got to go through with it. At least come down here and let me check out this so-called remission of yours. You weren't looking good last time I saw you, Joe. The Oncology Center people are starting to think it's time for you to move on to radiation treatments."

McDermott felt a savage internal thump. A little warning, to keep him in line.

"I don't think radiation treatments will be necessary either, Dave."

"I want to look you over, at least. I can't just authorize cessation of therapy over the phone like this. It's completely improper."

138

Another thump, an even more agonizing one. McDermott grunted and doubled up.

"What was that?" Brewster asked.

"I didn't say anything."

"I want to see you at nine tomorrow, all right?"

"No," said McDermott. "Sorry. I just can't make it, Dave."

He put down the phone.

Brewster called back, of course. And went on calling over the next few days. McDermott had never realized before what a mistake it could be to let an old friend be your doctor. Or how persistent Dave Brewster could be when a question of medical ethics was involved. But there was no way McDermott could possibly explain the situation to him.

To escape Brewster's irritated phone messages, finally, he cashed in some unused vacation time and flew off to Hawaii for a week, telling no one where he was going.

He had the time of his life.

It was autumn now at home, a chilly, rainy autumn at that, but Hawaii's golden summer goes on and on and on. The sea was warm, the beach was sparkling, the hotel was full of hopeful single women, many of them quite attractive. McDermott, whose sex life had been on hold since the Fourth of July, quickly began making up for lost time.

That inexplicable sense of vigor and general well-being that had come over him soon after his first hallucinatory spell was still exerting its magic. He hadn't had such physical vitality since his late teens: never, perhaps. He did a couple of miles on the beach every morning at dawn, swam out to the reef and back before breakfast, ate double helpings of everything, dominated the volleyball court, spiking like a

madman, and wiped out the whole tennis-court crowd with
an invincible and faultless serve. He danced all evening and
frolicked all night and when the sun came up he was ready to
start all over again. It was unbelievable.

"Aren't you glad you listened to me?" the
Cherponexian asked.

"There's got to be a catch," McDermott replied. "And
I think I've figured out what it is. This is like having made a
deal with the devil. The Faust thing all over again. What's
really happening is that I'm having one final fling, one last
speedy go-round on the racetrack of life. In another few days
it'll be over and then I'll collapse all at once, home in a
wheelchair and six weeks of being a palsied burned-out husk
in the hospital, and then The End."

"Pal, you couldn't be wronger," said the voice within
him.

Indeed McDermott went from strength to strength as the
week moved along. Muscles he had almost forgotten he had
began to throb and swell. He tanned almost instantly. His
hair was growing so fast that he needed to have it trimmed
twice within five days, to the mystification of the hotel
barber. The little lines at the corners of his eyes were going
away, too. He looked years younger. It all seemed wondrous.
He felt blessed.

On the last night of the trip, dressing up in a suit for the
first time since his arrival for an evening of formal dancing
with a noteworthy young lady from Seattle, he was startled to
find his jacket tight across the shoulders and open space
showing between his cuffs and the top of his shoes. What the
hell was this: was he *growing?* A shiver ran down his back.
The pants legs had been the right length the last time he had
worn the suit. Could clothing shrink so fast in the warm,

humid climate here?

In the morning he hurried down to the hotel health club to check himself out on the medical scales there as soon as he and Ms. Seattle had finished breakfast. Since the age of sixteen he had been five feet eleven exactly, which had been a cause of great frustration for him then, though he had long since ceased giving a damn about having fallen just short of six feet. But when he set the scale's metal rod at the usual place it wouldn't balance. He moved it up, and up a little more. He stared. It was in balance now. Six feet one? Could it be?

"Either you aren't a hallucination after all," he told the Cherponexian, "or you've got the damndest fine sense of detail any hallucination could offer."

"Trust me," the silent voice within him said.

But he couldn't. It all seemed too good to be true. A diagnosis of cancer, followed by sudden rejuvenation, incredibly enhanced physical prowess, and two inches of new height at the age of thirty-nine, and all of it the work of a microscopic alien intelligence that had built a nice little home for itself in his gallbladder and is giving him these goodies by way of rent? Come off it, he thought. It's a pipe dream. You're actually on your deathbed in Veterans Memorial Hospital at this very moment, and everything you think you've experienced over the past few weeks is simply a medication-induced delusion that has passed through your failing mind in the last thirty seconds. Right?

"Wrong," said the Cherponexian. "What a peculiar kind of life-form you humans seem to be. Why can't you just accept your good luck and shut up about it?"

He flew home into a dreary, windy autumn day and

called Dave Brewster right away.

"I bugged out and went to Hawaii," he said. "I know you were annoyed with me, but it was something I had to do. Now I'm back, and I want you to check me out, okay?"

"You still think you're in remission, Joe?"

"I don't have the slightest idea what's going on with me," McDermott said. "I want you to tell me."

There was a look of astonishment on Brewster's face for a moment when McDermott entered his office: his eyes widened, his jaw sagged, he gaped in a highly unprofessional way. Then the amazement vanished, and anger took its place.

"Very funny, Joe," Brewster said sourly. "The wig, the elevator heels, the makeup, and all the rest. I've seen all kinds of denial mechanisms at work in my time, but this really takes the prize."

"You notice a difference, do you?"

"Are you kidding?"

McDermott pulled off his shoes. "But I'm not doing any kind of faking. Here, measure me. Stocking feet. I've grown two inches. I've dropped ten pounds around the middle and added it to my shoulders. And if you think this is a wig, take a close look."

He realized that he was trembling. "It's real, isn't it, Dave? Isn't it? What do you say? Do you know any kind of cancer that can do this to a man? Do you? Do you?"

"Get on the scale," Brewster said.

He was silent throughout the examination, which was as thorough as any McDermott could remember ever having had. When Brewster was done, he walked across the room to his desk and sat down behind it, looking up over his shoulder at the medical-school diplomas behind it. After a while he said, still looking away, "You've grown two inches, and your hair is thicker than it's been for ten years, and you check out like an Olympic athlete in everything on the chart." His voice sounded strained and hollow. "Your hemorrhoids are gone, and your blood pressure is like a kid's, and I can't find your appendectomy scar."

"So all the changes are real? I didn't just dream them?"

"They look pretty goddamned real to me, I have to say."

"That must be some cancer I have. What kind of cancer does all that to you, I wonder?"

"I wonder that too," said Brewster. He swiveled around to face him. "But the original diagnosis has to stand until we come up with a better one. So far as I can tell from manual probing, you've still got some sort of tumor in your abdomen."

"Malignant?"

"Malignant, benign, who the hell knows?" There was a stunned look in Brewster's eyes. "This situation is beyond my comprehension, and I don't mind admitting it. I'm totally bewildered by what I've seen here just now."

McDermott considered the idea of telling Brewster about the Cherponexian. But he couldn't bring himself to do it.

Brewster said, "The only thing I can suggest is a complete workup at the Oncology Center. Another GI series, a biopsy, maybe a spinal tap. And more: the whole works. As you can imagine, it won't be a lot of fun for you, Joe. But we've got to find out the precise nature of that growth by your gallbladder. We're talking medical history here."

"I understand."

"Can I set up an appointment for you for tomorrow?"

McDermott felt a thump within his skull that almost sent him to the floor. Invisible hands stroked his heart and squeezed ever so gently. An invisible finger tapped him warningly on the shoulder.

"Joe?" Brewster said. He sounded worried.

"Not tomorrow, all right? I'm just back from a vacation. Give me a day or two to get back into the swing of things, first."

"Day after tomorrow, then? This is too important to be allowed to slide."

Another thump. Another squeeze.

McDermott moistened his lips.

"I'll call you and set up a date," he said. "Is that okay, Dave? Is that okay?"

He went home, deep in humiliation and chagrin. What good was radiant health and a regenerated head of hair, if he was only the puppet of some creature from another planet no bigger than a flea? What good were two inches of extra height at his age, for Christ's sake, if he couldn't even make a doctor's appointment without getting a knock on the head from inside?

He resolved to fight back. Somehow. He had to free himself of this thing.

It wouldn't be easy, he knew. The Cherponexian—he had no doubt now that the Cherponexian was real and was really inside him—could read his every thought. It was listening in even now, McDermott suspected.

"That's right, Joe. I am."

"Fuck you."

"You won't admit that I'm the best thing that ever happened to you, will you?"

Chinga tu madre, McDermott said silently. If you have

one.

There was no response. McDermott's eyebrows rose. Maybe the alien wasn't able to read his mind when he thought in Spanish. Could that be? He was pretty fluent in Spanish. Two years in Puerto Rico on the Webster-Santos account had done that for him.

It was worth a try, anyway.

He grabbed the phone and punched in Brewster's number.

"It's me, Joe. We have to talk fast. You've got to get hold of someone who understands Spanish and have him call me back. A nurse, a doctor, anybody. And tell that person to take whatever I tell him at face value, no matter how crazy it seems. It's a matter of life and death."

"What? What?"

"Just do it. Please."

Brewster hung up. McDermott sat by the phone, waiting. He had it all worked out in his mind, in Spanish. Going over the phrases again and again, finding the words he needed. An alien creature from space has invaded me, he would say. *Un extranjero. De espacio.* The doctors think it's a cancer in my abdomen, but it isn't. It's an honest-to-God alien, and no, I'm not making this up. *Verdad. Absolutamente verdad.* It has control of my mind, only it doesn't know Spanish, which is why I'm able to tell you this. It's modifying my body. I can hardly recognize myself any more. The thing's got to be killed. Chemotherapy makes it sick. Send an ambulance for me. You'll probably have to put me under restraint. A straitjacket, yeah. Take me to the Center and get me on double chemo, the strongest dose I can stand. Triple, even. Whatever it takes. Just get rid of—

The phone rang. McDermott reached for it.

The Cherponexian did something inside his arm and it jerked back around his neck and grabbed his throat as if the alien were trying to make him strangle himself one-handed.

"Hey!" McDermott cried.

"*Y chinga tu madre tambien,*" the Cherponexian said, cackling in his brain. "*Verga estupida! Cabron!*"

As it turned out, it wouldn't have mattered much even if the alien had let McDermott pick up the phone, because that evening marked the start of the second phase of the invasion of Earth. McDermott's Cherponexian, who had served as the advance scout, had finished learning all that it needed to know about the world it had landed on and had sent the go-ahead signal to its comrades hovering just beyond the ionosphere. That night billions of Cherponexian invaders fell like snow everywhere human life was to be found. By the time morning came, there was scarcely anyone on the planet who had not been infiltrated one way or another—by inhaling an invader, or ingesting one along with the morning toast, or simply by drinking one down in water from the tap—and the process of spreading minute Cherponexian tendrils through billions of human brains and nervous systems was under way everywhere.

With the help of the guidance the scout had been able to provide, the second-wave invaders were able to establish complete somatic control in a much shorter time than the nine weeks McDermott's Cherponexian had needed. Within minutes they could locate essential neural centers and send messages to their new hosts. Within hours they had set up beachheads in ductless glands and medulla oblongatas. The whole conquest took about a day and a half.

When McDermott realized what was going on, he felt

worse than ever. He had been the gateway, after all, through which the first of the invaders had entered Earth. He felt personally responsible. If only he had been able to strike back, somehow. If only—if only—

"Look," the Cherponexian said, "why beat up on yourself like this? You're completely blameless, you know. Our arrival was an inevitable event. We're utterly invincible. Nothing you could have done would have stopped the invasion. *Nothing*."

"I don't get it," said McDermott. "You come seventeen light years just to occupy the gallbladders of an alien species? What's the point? What *use* can we possibly be to you?"

"Ah," said the Cherponexian. "You will be of great use indeed. And we will be of great use to you. What has happened is for everyone's mutual benefit. Trust me, my friend."

And, in fact, after the initial period of transition everything went on pretty much as before, except that most sickness and hunger and other forms of distress disappeared, along with bald spots, cellulite, unwanted weight, scars and birthmarks, and overly troublesome neuroses. Doctors, lawyers, and politicians suddenly had very little to do, since the Cherponexians saw to it that everyone's health was perfect and refused to allow any kind of dispute, whether between people or between nations. That created a certain amount of disruption until the members of the displaced professions could be retrained.

At the Kaisers' Fourth of July picnic the following year, McDermott hit four home runs and handled the ball magnificently in the field. So, however, did almost everyone else. They were all in terrific shape, big and strong and bursting with vitality. After the game, when the whole crowd gathered at the charcoal grill for the hamburger ritual, Dave Brewster came over to him and said, "You're looking good, kid."

"You too, man. We're all looking good, aren't we? But tell me: How's the doctor-biz?"

"What doctor-biz? Nobody gets sick these days, not even the sniffles. You know that. I'm studying classical ballet, matter of fact. A little late in life to start, but my Cherponexian has done a terrific job building up my tendons."

"That's just great, Dave," McDermott said. There wasn't much enthusiasm in his tone.

Brewster looked at him closely. "Hey, guy, what's the matter? Don't tell me you still feel guilty for—"

"Don't you?" McDermott snapped. His neck growing warm with sudden annoyance. "You who couldn't tell an alien space invader from cancer of the gallbladder? You're at least as responsible for what happened as I am."

"Hey, hey, hold on a second—" Brewster said, just as hotly.

But already McDermott felt his anger cooling. The Cherponexians took care of such things quickly.

"Yeah," he said in a milder voice. "What the hell, getting conquered by space invaders isn't so bad, really, is it?" He grinned. "And at least I don't have to worry about losing my hair anymore. Do I, Dave?"

"Right," Brewster said.

"Right," said the Cherponexian.

The Lost Sepulcher of Huascar Capac

by Paul Park

Paul Park's travel experiences throughout Southeast Asia
and the Indian subcontinent permeate the three novels that
comprise his *Starbridge Chronicles*: *Soldiers of Paradise*,
Sugar Rain, and *The Cult of Loving Kindness*. The alien
world he builds from this material is exotic and harsh and
vivid in its depiction.

He now lives in New York City, and this story has a
very different feel. "The Lost Sepulcher of Huascar Capac"
is his second published short story. The idea of a memory
palace is taken from classical and medieval times when it
was used by educated men as a mnemonic device. Memory
was then considered one of the greatest achievements in
learned people, and the memory "palace" is only one of
several memory systems they developed. Park found this
particular one striking because it is at once so spectacular
and seemingly impractical, since in order to construct one
you already need a prodigious memory. In Park's story, the
protagonist, who as a child was forced to construct a memory
palace, is so distracted by the construct's complexity and
beauty that he is unable to use his mind for practical things
(like thinking) or experience his own life firsthand.

THE LOST SEPULCHER OF HUASCAR CAPAC

Paul Park

When I was six, my eyes started to fail, for reasons no one could understand. Now tonight in this dark hole, now that I'm a man, I can appreciate the tragedy of this: a child's blindness. I can appreciate my father's sorrow, how it ate at him and finally killed him. At a certain moment in their lives, men and women find a skill for recognizing tragedy; when I was six I was too young. Too young not to accept my fate. Too young to resist my father's desperation, to refuse his legacy.

My father was one of the last practitioners of an ancient system of mnemonics. When I was six, he started teaching it to me. "Every idea, every event, can be condensed into an image," he told me in the autumn of 1951. "The point is to establish a location for these images, a space inside your memory, where they can easily be found. We will start here by conceiving of a room. We will place an image of myself against one wall. Look at me. Now shut your eyes. There I am. And perhaps there is a window behind me on the wall. Perhaps we're on an upper floor. Perhaps if you look out,

you will find evidence of streets and houses, which exist
entirely in your mind."

I go back often to that year. From September onward, I
can remember every day. I can remember every word of
every conversation with my father and can recite them, quite
literally, backwards and forwards. He died before my illness
went into its first remission. So my complete memory of him
dates from the period of my blindness, when the streets of
my mental city were still new. I used to wander them often,
particularly in the central district, looking for his live, elusive
figure among the stationary grotesques, trying to find answers to the questions that I never asked him. Especially I
want to know: What did he think he was doing? Surely his
own memory had been an ambiguous comfort to him, a
refuge and a curse.

In my city there is a street near the Hemicircle of
Deformities, perhaps a half a mile away. It is lined with stone
buildings, Central Records 1952, 1953, and so on. In all that
quarter of the city, it is perhaps the dullest street. The buildings are so big, so dull. Each is laid out around twelve square
courtyards, one courtyard for each month, three rows of four.
I was six in 1951, and that building is identical to the rest,
only most of the 30 rooms and antechambers (less or more)
which surround each courtyard are locked; it is only from
about September on that I can enter where I please and take
whatever texts I want out of the wooden cabinets that line
each wall. By September my eyesight was already very bad,
and my father was in a frenzy of imaginative labor, helping
me with the construction of these buildings.

Later I returned often to that September courtyard.
Alone in those dusty rooms, I would read over those first
conversations with my father. I would re-read his extracts

from Quintillian and Simonides, the first discoverers of his system. I would read over his descriptions of how a memory city could grow and grow. One small imaginary building, for example, could sprout towers and yards and annexes and sculpture gardens, until it was as big as a whole world. Or streets could move out from a central point, spreading past hotels, and shops, and temples, and government offices, quite literally forever. At least, I never found the end. Once I understood the principles, I could construct a whole complex of buildings in just a few minutes.

And yet, what was the point? I suppose he would have said, in his grand way, that a blind boy needs another kind of sight. Another kind of world, lit with the pure fire of reason, a place to wander and play among the bright mnemonic images as the world got dark.

Yes, surely. But it is a complicated thing, to move forever between two worlds. To do him justice, if I'd had the choice, I would never have gone back to what I was. To remind myself of why, I needed only to walk past Central Records 1945 through 1950. They are doorless, windowless hulks. Any objects or pieces of paper that I possess from those years are copies, filed elsewhere. The originals are forever inaccessible.

By contrast, in 1951, '52, and '53, the cabinets are filled with blueprints, and mimeographs, and sketches in my father's minute handwriting. At the time, the detail was bewildering to me. This section of the city is his gift—around the Central Records buildings are some of the strangest sights in the whole municipality. It is the part that we built first, and it consists of the contents of my father's own memory city, which he was transferring then to me.

A palace in an adjoining alley, for example, is built

around a sloping spiral almost forty stories tall. The spiral is lined with images, and during the years when I used to climb it, looking from one statue to another just to test myself or else just wandering or exploring, I would remember how they were first assembled, during three desperate evenings in the first week of March when I was seven years old. They are my father's reconstruction of the causes and processes of the First World War—you enter underneath a marble pediment, inscribed with the dates of the conflict. Immediately to the left, at the beginning of the spiral, stands my father's monument to Gavrilo Princip. The young man sits on the stone floor, his shoulder pressed against a grate. He holds a bloody napkin to his lips, and in his other hand he still grasps his revolver. Beside him, a Viennese newspaper, an untasted plate of sorbet, and 23 roses in a glass vase.

Although I couldn't see it at the time of the first installation, the young man is beautiful. In this way my father demonstrated his own anarchist sympathies—the memorial to Princip's victims, under the pediment on the right-hand side, is less impressive. The archduke and his wife are intensely fat. They are sprawled in the back seat of their car, covered with blood; the bullet has shattered the windscreen, shattered also the archduke's spectacles.

This is the major image, but it is surrounded by twelve small grotesques, each one a mnemonic clue. For example, a black dwarf in a beret, naked from the waist down, carrying a book entitled "6,281,914 Spanish Eggs"—an image meaningless to you, but for me it contains the location and the date and the time of the assault. A toad upon a velvet couch gives me the victims' names.

This palace contains thousands of such figures. Every six months or so, as I moved up the spiral corridor, I would pass von Schlieffen and von Kluck, Sasonov, the Kaiser, Lloyd George, von Moltke, and assorted Romanovs. This is the hall of personages—behind each of these statues is a chamber of events, loaded also with images. When I was a child, all this was overwhelming, and I dreaded my janitorial visits to the Ypres room or the Verdun exhibit—even a few seconds was too long to spend in there, and I would barely open my eyes.

Now that I consider it, I suppose some of the images in this section of the city, though obviously not these, antedate my father. I suppose some of them, perhaps some of the most grotesque and archaic ones from the Avenue of 1800 Gargoyles—that line of naked women disemboweling each other, for example—were his inheritance from the Jesuit who was his teacher. I remember my despair as they were first put in, during the first year of my blindness. These chaotic images, these strange, lopsided palaces—I was afraid they would go on forever. My father was building antechambers and additions off of every room. But I need not have worried: moving out from the origial city, one comes quite quickly to more ordered streets, laid out by myself without his help. Already when I was six, there were huge vacant places in his memory where whole blocks of his city, perhaps whole neighborhoods, had collapsed. It was for this reason, I soon realized, that he was so desperate to effect this transfer of material, to drag these statues down out of his crumbling buildings and reinstall them in my new ones. Perhaps in my encroaching blindness he saw a similarity to the darkness that was overtaking him.

Though we never discussed it, I imagine his city was constructed in Victorian Gothic style, full of 19th century homages to castles and chateaux. I imagine something northern, something dark; my city is dark too. In school that year when I was six, before my father took me out, my teacher was reading to us a child's adaptation of William Prescott's *The Conquest of Peru,* and my mind was full of visions of old Cuzco. Therefore, when I planned my city, I conceived of it as the lost capital of an Inca prince, and I located it underground in a vast system of caverns. This was partly due to my illness and my father's influence, but partly also because in this way I hoped to hide my city from Pizarro and his soldiers.

The city streets are lit with gas. A traveler can see, from the summit of the Ziggurat of Viracocha, the whole floor of the cavern picked out with light, blurring finally in the dark distance. Beyond this cavern there are others, one of which includes the tomb of the Inca Huascar Capac. It was during my search for this tomb, which I had known from the beginning was located somewhere in the city, that I quite suddenly regained my sight in January of 1954.

At that time I was living in a group home for Catholics near Elsinor, where my father had placed me during the previous November, just before his death. I lived there for ten years, as an orphan instead of as a blind boy. I went to school there, storing the contents of my education in my memory city, in images, as my father had taught me. There also I learned photography, which was to become my profession.

Perhaps this was inevitable, but I prefer to think that I had undergone a change during the time of my blindness, when I had lived almost exclusively underground. Blind, I had lived among the images, and I prefer to think that my gift of seeing, when it was returned to me, was changed by the experience. Later, when I noticed it was easier for me than for others to capture the significance in a pose, or a landscape, or a group of objects, I thanked my early training. Every image is a memory image at certain moments, as packed with significance as any montage in my city, and the trick is to isolate it then.

A photographer will discard a hundred exposures for each one he keeps. What goes into that decision? When I was working in the darkroom, it was like discovering how to look. The paper is white, and then you put it in the pan. I never got tired of it, because each time it was like opening my eyes that January, when I was nine years old. First just lumps of shade and color, the way a baby sees. A swirl of colors from a central point. A man. Six men. Sky, and then as the lines resolve, an idea resolves with it, because there is a brain behind the eye after all, a brain that knows things. Soldiers.

This is a photograph that I took years ago. Six white soldiers stand in the shade outside a primitive straw hut. I must have shot the scene a dozen times, and the differences are subtle, but this was the only one which made any sense. And it's not because it tells the story better. Other exposures show a jeep and telephone line, which account for the soldiers' presence and my presence also. But in my photo-graph—the one I kept—you just see a wall of mud and straw and the men standing in the shade smoking cigarettes. The ground is cracked into octagons, and the line of trees in the background is distorted, but it is something about the ciga-rettes that makes the heat oppressive.

Three black men dressed in t-shirts sit together in the foreground and a little to one side. Yet they are not essential. They are not what made the image important to me and important enough to other people for it to have appeared full

page in *Paris-Match,* opposite a story about Cubans in
Angola. It is not, although perhaps the editor would have
claimed it was, the stereotypically Latin insouciance of the
men against the wall. It is because the pose of two of the six
soldiers corresponds to an image in my city, an image
independent of the photograph itself, which of course is filed
in Central Records and cross-referenced in numerous other
places.

Or perhaps a combination of images, I thought. I have
thousands of soldiers down there in my city, for my father
was a student of military history. In this photograph, only
two have seen me. Or, at least, only two are reacting to my
presence. One has straightened up and is staring at me. For
him this is a portrait, and he has chosen the way he wants to
appear: cocky, stiff, his cigarette at an improbable angle. The
other has been looking at him, and at the instant the photograph was taken, has turned towards me. He must have
expected to see something specific from the way his friend
had straightened up—something good, perhaps, I don't know
what, but evidently not a dirty foreign journalist, for his
expression of disappointment is clear, the clearest thing in
the photograph. He is young, mustached, handsome, perhaps
nineteen years old.

Thirty months after I departed from Angola, I discovered, quite by accident, these two soldiers again. As it
happened, they were in the Verdun exhibition, and I saw
them in the corner of my eye as I was flickering through.
Two soldiers—French this time, though clearly of Spanish or
Italian origin—are standing in poses identical to the photograph. Their faces, their expressions of cockiness and disappointment, even their uniforms, unlikely as it seems, are
identical, and that is what disturbed me. For the first time I

contemplated the possibility that each time I printed a photograph there was some movement down below, some tiny change.

It is stupid to become obsessed with these things—I'm sure the images shift and distort over time. Memory is after all a process of the brain—only one of the processes. But the fact is, by the time I was in my early thirties, my journeys underground had taken the place of thinking, even of learning. When I was blind, other senses became more acute and were able to take over the functions of sight—as time went on, my memory was like that. I could rely on it.

It was just laziness, I suppose, as well as a new cynicism, a new dissatisfaction with my work. This trip I took hundreds of photographs, not one of which will ever be developed. A crowd, people throwing things, a building on fire. Broken windows. I've never bothered to learn Spanish. I never tried to read the papers. My editor gave me some articles; I didn't look at them. My writer knew it all, she said. She was the brains, and so I thought perhaps my pictures would be like something in a baby's eye. In the last one, a man is shooting someone in the side of the head. Who are they? I don't know. The district commissioner in Callao had warned me. He had given me a list of things I could photograph in safety—the railway station, the municipal post office—and I had thought he meant safety from him. Not that I cared one way or the other; it was hot, and we were staying in an 800-room Hyatt with about seven other guests, all newsmen. At night we sat around the huge neoclassical deserted bar, stinking drunk, listening to a pianist playing show tunes. Except for that first day, only once did I go into town. I staggered up through cold parsecs of lobby. I took a taxi. The streetlights were broken; we drove along a single narrow road. There were no other cars. We went fast at first, then slow, because gradually the street started to fill up with people—dozens, then hundreds: short men with bearded faces and white pants that would snatch at our headlights as we hesitated and went past.

All the windows were open, and from everywhere on the hot wind came smells so delicious they were almost mournful, as evocative as music. Slower and slower we went, for in some places the entire street was blocked by sudden masses of people and in some places by huge constructions of cardboard, which people would pull away to let us pass. And it was lighter, too, as we went on—the hotel was situated among dark acres of trees, but here every window had a light, and in the streets the men were carrying torches. Sometimes when we stopped, people bent down to peer into my window. Some would put their whole heads inside, and I would see their shiny skin, the shirts wet along their necks. At first I would shrink back onto the seat, but they would smile and reach out to touch me with their slippery hands. Soon I was laughing and smiling back, as if I understood what they were saying. My driver smoked a thin cigar. There was a festival tonight, he said. He leaned out of his window to spit at a dog pissing against the tire. We had come to a complete stop.

That night I dreamed about the tomb of the great Inca. It is located in the unknown part of the memory city, the part I did not build myself, and yet it's there forever in the brain. These places are always waiting, always difficult to reach. It is like descending to a new level in the darkness. I glimpsed the way when I was nine years old, during a terrible fever just before I recovered my sight, and I have never been able to retrace my steps. Though sometimes I have seen it in my dreams, as I did that night in the hotel: a stone courtyard lined with galleries, a playing field, perhaps. And in the middle, a sloping pyramid, which contains a single chamber. The body of Huascar Capac lies inside it, preserved in a glass case. He is dressed in a cloak of hummingbird feathers. His corpse is almost twelve feet long.

In my hotel I awoke suddenly and got up to stand in the darkness, staring out the window. Far away, down in the city, something was on fire.

That night the American consulate burned to the ground. This was news, and news to me until days later, when I heard it on the radio. By morning Rachel and I had already started out into the countryside, to Z—. In this we had accepted the district commissioner's compromise: The town was not in an area specifically claimed by the insurgents. It was in a different kind of turmoil, following the deaths of almost forty miners in a cave-in. The mine had been closed by strikers for a month, but, despite the urgent petitions of Euro-Bauxite and the Belgian mission, the government had not yet sent soldiers.

Possibly the district commissioner believed the miners to have legitimate grievances that deserved the attention of the international press. I don't know, and doubtless I do him an injustice to judge him by appearances, for, as I say, I speak no Spanish. All this was grudgingly interpreted for me by Rachel, my correspondent for *The Australian*. Probably he just wanted us out of the way; I don't believe that he was deliberately sending us into danger. Certainly he had seemed impressed by our credentials, even asking Rachel to point out Sydney on his globe and then muttering reflectively, "Kangourou."

We left while it was still dark. The road climbed away

from the coast as if through common sense; at sunrise it was cooler than the night, and the city was like the clog in the bottom of a basin, the hills around it ringed with residue. There is a world where water is as thin as air. I can imagine standing on a shore, the air curling and lapping at my feet, the valleys of the sea open below me, and above me not one thing, not one thing that could muddy sunlight—in a way that is the foundation of hope. You can go higher and higher. We reached little iron-roofed villages where the air seemed dry to the touch, the sky kingfisher blue. But the people were as confused as ever; we kept on getting lost. At night the mosquitoes kept us from sleeping. Once the front axle sank to the hubs in gleaming sand. I got out my Hasselblad and walked a long way, until I could look back toward the empty hills and see the car like a rock or a stump, something that hadn't budged one millimeter in a thousand years. Why am I focusing on this? Why am I finding new ways to delay? We came to Z— all right in the end, of course. As it turned out, we could have taken a bus. But that would have been too fast. Because I am avoiding this part, even in memory. The images are so painful, so recent, and so clear—perhaps the last that I will ever see under the harsh light of the sun. Now, looking back, my thoughts are the way my pictures would have been—focused on things perhaps only inches beside the point. None of them would have been worth keeping.

One of my cameras has an attachment so that you can appear to be shooting in a different direction from the one you actually are. It was as if the thing worked in reverse: you would line up your shot, and the picture would squirt out to one side. Even the last picture, the one of the man getting shot—when they smashed my camera, it was frustrating because I knew I hadn't seen what they thought I had. The

photograph would have shown the man's head, his face
strong and still. He knew what I was trying to see. Perhaps
he knew already he was just an image. The gun is poking at
him from the side. You can just see part of its black snout in
the middle of a grainy cloud; you can see the man's hair
billowing and the side of his head distended. I'm sure they
thought the picture was some kind of evidence, but if they
had asked me to point out which one had pulled the trigger, I
wouldn't have known.

The man was kneeling in the street outside the movie
theatre, his hands tied in front of him. Early in the morning
he had been released from prison and brought into the
square. He had been allowed to wash and feed himself.
Nevertheless, he made a show of sitting with his back to his
guards and ignoring what seemed to be friendly and solici-
tous remarks. He looked toward the mine, whose tower rose
from a hill of rubble a mile away. I had been up there the day
before, and I had as many pictures as I needed; Rachel was
up there still. At around six o'clock, a man came down with
news that panicked everyone. People came out of the adjoining buildings and made a semicircle around the prisoner.
That was when they bound his wrists together. An hour later,
a siren went off in the mine. It meant nothing to me, but at
the sound, the group around the kneeling man went into
some kind of a dance—some ran back and forth, others
gesticulated and slapped their chests. This went on for a
minute or more; I was taking photographs, and they did
nothing of substance until some other men appeared at the
far end of the square, yelling and throwing stones. But then
they pulled the kneeling man to his feet and tried to drag him
away. He stumbled and fell on his face in the dust, and by
that time some of the people from the new group were almost

upon them. No one had paid any attention to me, and I had shot almost a roll of film from a safe distance. But I needed a close-up of the man's face with dust on it. I had no time to change lenses, so I ran forward cursing and went down on my knees about fifteen feet away. The man raised his eyes to me, and I knew he was thinking about how he looked. If his hands had been free, he would have brushed back his hair. I saw his face out of focus through the viewer. Was that a frown, a sneer? I twisted the barrel savagely but the expression was gone, resolved into fixed staring. You could no longer see the thoughts. Then I saw the pistol coming into the picture from the right-hand side, and I pressed the shutter once, twice. The aperture closed, opened, closed, but in that fraction of a second, I saw his breaking head, perfect, framed. I heard the shot. The men around him scattered. For an instant I was alone with him, and then the square was full of people. I got to my feet, looking for Rachel, looking for a face I recognized, and I had a brief impression that there were no longer any patterns of movement in the square, no clumps of people, and everyone was standing still, posed, equidistant, repetitive, like figures on wallpaper. The man was shot to death right there, and I think I must have gotten up too fast because I bent over and put my hands to my head.

One man was dressed differently from the others—his clothes looked vaguely military. From this and from his beard I guessed he was not from that locality, a real revolutionary perhaps, or else someone from the Shining Path. But he was an idiot just the same, because he stood in front of me and pulled at my camera, as if he expected the leather strap to give way in his hand. I staggered forward, and we knocked our heads together; perhaps it is because dignity is important to such a man that after I had handed him the camera, he turned and hit me in the mouth. Or perhaps he really thought I was American. He said, "American," and then he hit me in the mouth, making me sit down. I tried to deny it, to speak a few words in my native Frisian, but my mouth was full of blood. Somebody kicked me from behind, several people—not hard, but no accident either. I had not been touched in anger since I was a child, when my father and I were building the memory city, and I was too stupid and too young. But these men were strangers.

I did not resist. In time they left me, and I settled with my back to a small tree. I sat and watched the square empty out. A policeman, a priest, and a doctor were gathered around the corpse, along with some women. They carried it to a waiting car, and then they came towards me. They said something, but I waved them away. Their accents sounded phony. If an actor on stage turns to ask you a question, no matter how pertinent, you feel no compulsion to answer. You are sitting in judgment, always.

Some olive shreds of film blew across my legs and blew across the street. A white dog came and sat beside me.

And gradually as I sat there the town came back to life. Shops that had been closed and shuttered all day opened their doors, and there were lights on inside, now that it was getting dark. The streetlights in front of the municipal building turned on, and some kids smoked cigarettes on the steps. Young men and women, some elegantly dressed, stood under the movie marquee—it shed a silver radiance. *Thunderball.* On a side street, men in soft hats played dominoes, perhaps, outside the place where I had eaten lunch. I could see the entrance to our hotel, our car parked along the curb. Someone standing on the porch looking out.

It got dark. I thought the town was making itself soft again, the way some brainless anemone or crab will stretch out after a small trauma. And I didn't want to make it clutch up tight again. So that when I stood up, I did it slowly. And in fact there was no shiver of movement, not from the kids on the steps, not from the woman on the porch. It was as if I didn't exist, and the whole way up to the mine, as I was walking I saw no one. There was no one at the gate—it was securely fastened with shiny padlocks, but to the right the chain-link fence had been trampled flat. Farther up, everything was in shadow, the cage, the showers, the pit: I had been on a tour the day before. And if I make it sound as if all these distances were short, and all these places easy to find, I am giving the wrong impression. But why drag it out? I knew what I was looking for, a place among the sidings where the rails ran straight into the rock, lit by an endless line of naked fluorescent bulbs. It was the supply shaft, and I walked in under the lights, between the tracks. I picked my way through a barricade of smashed machinery—a broken generator, a line of smashed electric cars. Huge pieces of the roof had fallen in, and in one place the floor had subsided four feet in a single step, bending the rails into greasy bows. The walls were rent and fissured, but still the line of light stretched unwavering—it was my comfort, and it buzzed and whispered as if conspiring against the dark.

I stood in a puddle of inky water. Just ahead, the tunnel had collapsed completely, and the line of lights lay buried like a vein of ore. Above, the fall had opened up a cavern, and a wall stood thirty feet high. Along its uneven surface someone had painted a huge red cross, smeared and clunky, and beneath it on a ledge stood an assortment of candles in blue and red glass jars: stubs of wax, mostly, but some still burned. Below, personal effects were gathered in careful heaps—gloves and shoes, orange helmets, framed photographs. A young man with a bad complexion. His tie is stupid, and he is looking away from the camera, but the older woman beside him is staring into it. This must have been the only picture she could find of them together, for it is flattering to neither. But it must have been she who left his clothes washed and folded in a little pile. The woman looks too old to be his wife, too young to be his mother. His sister, perhaps. In the photograph he is not touching her. I borrowed his coat, and the flashlight of another man, the father of five children.

When the tunnel collapsed, it had opened a horizontal gash in the rock above it. Into this I shined my light, and I must have seen some evidence of an opening, because I climbed into it and crawled forward on my hands and feet. I think I wanted to discover a dead body or something. But in fact there was no place to go. One lip of rock had drooped away from another, and I crawled along the gap, shining my light. It was cold—I could see my breath—and dark too. I had clambered over an outcrop that hid the tunnel from my sight. It was a glow behind some rocks, and looking back all I could see was the outline of the square cross on the wall, thirty feet high, with spots of candlelight beneath it. In front, the beam of my flashlight illuminated quick sections of the rock.

I crawled forward into the dark, and it was only by looking back that I discovered that the ledge I crept on had curled around me. I saw the glow behind me outlined by the shadow of a circle, and I found myself in a volcanic tube almost six feet in diameter, curving gently upward, and there was no reason to be cautious, either, because the rock around me was level and clean. The passage continued in the direction of the buried tunnel, but above it. But already I suspected that the passage I was in had no communication with the modern mine. Perhaps I had read somewhere that the sources of precious metals in these mountains had dried up at the end of the sixteenth century, and that Z— was built on the ruins of a much older town. When I put my light up, I saw that smoke had been cooked into the stone the length of the ceiling. It made no mark on my fingers.

I climbed this passageway for hours, I think, moving quickly because it was so cold. I walked with my neck and shoulders bent, because of the low roof. But the floor was level under a layer of crushed rock, and the air was good. Twice I had to go down on my hands and knees under a gallery of wooden supports. In the beginning, these were the only artifacts I saw: blackened chunks of wood, the mark of the axe still on them. And once I passed a crude stick figure carved into the wall. A man on a horse. There may have been others. For of course I was in total darkness, except for my flashlight, and this I used to keep myself from stumbling or from bumping my head. The light seemed to diffuse very quickly, in front and behind, although my flashlight was a strong one. But I explored only when I stopped to negotiate some difficult section or to rest. So that this part of my trip exists for me only as a series of images a few inches from my eye. The man on horseback with the light in a circle around it. A fat drop of water with the light glistening in the spray. I had stopped where I could stand and stretch, where a narrow shaft opened above me, and I could stand in a ring of wooden posts and stretch my back and knees. It was warmer here. Warm air came from above me.

At every step I had expected to turn back without

thinking, before my light failed, before I got lost, but in the warm air the difficulties seemed less urgent. It seemed far to return. Here, something was close by.

I came through a big chamber. The roof was lost in darkness. But high up along the walls I detected the outlines of painted figures, up where my light was too vague to touch. Even here, things were escaping me, I felt. Again, closer to hand, the wall had been chipped clean of significance. Is that too much to ask, I thought, to hold something in your hands for sure? Now, I don't understand what made me so dissatisfied. But I rushed forward like a drunk, hoping to catch up. It is that hope, you see. I am convinced of it. It is that drunkenness. Because I had passed holes in the floor before, places where the floor had collapsed. I had shone my flashlight into them cautiously. But with this one, I must have fallen several feet. I hurt myself, and the light snapped out. But I didn't even care, because I knew at once that I had fallen onto something real. A stone sphere the size of a bowling ball. A stone sphere covered with carvings and bumps my fingers couldn't interpret. No, it is a head, the head of an animal. The head of an animal, with something in its mouth. It is cold and heavy; I put my cheek against it.

The flashlight fell close to where I sit. Yet I am prevented from reaching for it by a confusion of hopes. Because, like a child, I am not helped to action by knowing certain things. And there is something relaxing about sitting here, blind, reading the cold stone in the ringing, breathing darkness.

It is a tiger's head. It is unusual because the sculptor has chosen to work from the outside in. Does that make sense? I mean the rock still holds its natural contours, though it looks as if it had been rolled in skin. The carving has no structure of its own. And yet the artist has taken care to select a rock that did not require much shaping. There are two holes for its eyes.

The head has broken from a larger piece, a stone image standing erect. I can sense it in the darkness near me. It is carved in the same superficial style. I am going to use it now in my description, because I know too little to make stone bones for this stone flesh. What is there to know? Only that I am sitting in the fifty-first chamber of the nineteenth court of the imperial treasury of Huascar Capac, and it is years since I have passed this way.

What is there to know? Only that in time I will get up. I will move forward. I will search among the images with ever-increasing eagerness; I will find the tomb of the great Inca, and I will sit down at his feet.

Tattoos

by Jack Dann

Jack Dann is the author or editor of over thirty books,
including *Junction, Starhiker*, and *The Man Who Melted*. His
short fiction has appeared in *Playboy, Penthouse, Omni* and
most of the leading sf magazines and anthologies. His latest
work includes *High Steel* (TOR), a novel co-authored with
Jack C. Haldeman II, and an upcoming historical novel about
Leonardo da Vinci, *The Path of Remembrance* (Doubleday/
Bantam). Dann has had seven stories in *Omni,* three of them
finalists for the Nebula Award. His most recent *Omni* story is
"Voices" (August 1991), which was chosen for Gardner
Dozois's *The Year's Best Science Fiction: Ninth Annual
Collection* (St. Martin's Press). Jack Dann lives in
Binghamton, New York.

The Nazi Holocaust has been a continuing theme
throughout Dann's short work, as demonstrated by his
classic collaboration with Gardner Dozois, "Down Among
the Dead Men," and his stories "Camps" and "Jumping
the Road," the latter a novelette recently published in *Isaac
Asimov's Science Fiction Magazine*, as well as a novella-in-
progress called "The Economy of Light." How does one
deal with the religious and cultural structure as a Jew after

the Holocaust? How do we come to terms with the past? How do we face the future?

"Tattoos," published in the November 1986 issue of *Omni*, is part of Dann's attempt to "testify" and to keep history alive (particularly in light of the creation of the Institute for Historical Review, which denies that the Holocaust ever happened). In it, a man deals with different kinds of guilt—his own and others—and takes it upon himself to expiate these feelings.

TATTOOS

Jack Dann

We are never like the angels till our passion dies.
—Decker

For the past few years we'd been going to a small fair, which wasn't really much more than a road show, in Trout Creek, a small village near Walton in upstate New York. The fair was always held in late September when the nights were chilly and the leaves had turned red and orange and dandelion yellow.

We were in the foothills of the Catskills. We drove past the Cannonsville Reservoir, which provides drinking water for New York City. My wife Laura remarked that this was as close to dry as she'd ever seen the reservoir; she had grown up in this part of the country and knew it intimately. My son Ben, who is fourteen, didn't seem to notice anything. He was listening to hard rock music through the headphones of his portable radio-cassette player.

Then we were on the fairgrounds, driving through a field of parked cars. Ben had the headphones off and was excited. I felt a surge of freedom and happiness. I wanted to ride the rides and lose myself in the arcades and exhibitions; I wanted crowds and the noise and smells of the midway. I wanted to forget my job and my recent heart attack.

We met Laura's family in the church tent. Then Laura and her Mom and sister went to look at saddles, for her sister showed horses, and Dad and Ben and I walked in the other direction.

As we walked past concession stands and through the arcade of shooting galleries, antique wooden horse-race games, slots, and topple-the-milk-bottle games, hawkers shouted and gesticulated at us. We waited for Ben to lose his change at the shooting gallery and the loop-toss where all the spindles floated on water; and we went into the funhouse, which was mostly blind alleys and a few tarnished distorting mirrors. Then we walked by the tents of the freakshow: the Palace of Wonders with the original Lobster Man, Velda the Half-Lady, and "The Most Unusual Case in Medical History: Babies Born Chest to Chest."

"Come on," Dad said, "let's go inside and see the freaks."

"Nah," I said. "Places like this depress me. I don't feel right about staring at those people."

"That's how they make their money," Dad said. "Keeps 'em off social services."

I wasn't going to get into *that* with him.

"Well, then Bennie and me'll go in," Dad said. "If that's all right with you."

It wasn't, but I wasn't going to argue, so I reached into my pocket to give Ben some money, but Dad just shook his head and paid the woman sitting in a chair outside the tent. She gave him two tickets. "I'll meet you back here in about ten minutes," I said, glad to get away by myself.

I walked through the crowds, enjoying the rattle and shake of the concessionaires, all trying to grab a buck; the filthy, but brightly painted oil canvas; the sweet smell of cotton candy; the peppery smell of potatoes frying; and the coarse shouting of the kids. I bought some french fries, which were all the more delicious because I wasn't allowed to have them. Two young girls smiled and giggled as they passed me. Goddamn if this wasn't like being sixteen again.

Then something caught my eye.

I saw a group that looked completely out of place. Bikers, punkers, and well-dressed, yuppie-looking types were standing around a tattoo parlor talking. The long-haired bikers flaunted their tattoos by wearing cut-off jean jackets to expose their arms and chests; the women who rode with them had taken off their jackets and had delicate tattoo wristlets and red and orange butterflies and flowers worked into their arms or between their breasts. In contrast, most of the yuppies, whom I assumed to be from the city, wore long-sleeved shirts or tailored jackets, including the women, who looked like they had just walked out of a New England clothes catalogue. There was also a stout woman who looked to be in her seventies. She had gray hair pulled back into a tight bun, and she wore a dark, pleated dress. I couldn't help but think that she should be home in some Jewish neighborhood in Brooklyn, sitting with friends in front of her apartment building, instead of standing here in the dust before a tattoo parlor.

I was transfixed. What had brought all these people here to the boonies? Who the hell knew, maybe they were all from here. But I couldn't believe that for a minute. And I wondered if they were *all* tattooed.

I walked over to them to hear snatches of conversation

and to investigate the tattoo parlor, which wasn't a tent, as were most of the other concessions, but a small, modern mobile home with the words TAROT TATTOO STUDIO—ORIGINAL DESIGNS, EXPERT COVER-UPS painted across the side in large letters with red serifs through the stems. Then the door opened, and a heavyset man with a bald head and a full black beard walked out. Everyone, including the yuppies, was admiring him. His entire head was tattooed in a Japanese design of a flaming dragon; the dragon's head was high on his forehead, and a stream of flame reached down to the bridge of his nose. The dragon was beautifully executed. *How the hell could someone disfigure his face like that?* I wondered.

Behind the dragon man was a man of about five feet six wearing a clean, but bloodied, white tee-shirt. He had brown curly hair, which was long overdue to be cut, a rather large nose, and a full mouth. He looked familiar, very familiar, yet I couldn't place him. This man was emaciated, as if he had given up nourishment for some cultish religious reason. Even his long, well-formed hands looked skeletal, the veins standing out like blue tattoos.

Then I remembered. He looked like Nathan Rivlin, an artist I had not seen in several years. A dear friend I had lost touch with. This man looked like Nathan, but he looked all wrong. I remembered Nathan as filled-out and full of life, an orthodox Jew who wouldn't answer the phone on Shabbes— from Friday night until sundown on Saturday—a man who loved to stay up all night and talk and drink beer and smoke strong cigars. His wife's name was Ruth, and she was a highly paid medical textbook illustrator. They had both lived in Israel for some time and came from Chicago. But the man standing before me was ethereal-looking, as if he were made out of ectoplasm instead of flesh and blood. God forbid he should be Nathan Rivlin.

Yet I couldn't keep myself from shouting, "Nate? Nate, is it you?"

He looked around, and when he saw me, a pained grin passed across his face. I stepped toward him through the crowd. Several other people were trying to gain Nathan's attention. A woman told me to wait my turn, and a few nasty stares and comments were directed at me. I ignored them. "What the hell *is* all this?" I asked Nathan after we embraced.

"What should it be? It's a business," he said. Just then he seemed like the old Nathan I remembered. He had an impish face, a mobile face capable of great expression.

"Not what I'd expect, though," I said. I could see that his arms and neck were scarred; tiny whitish welts crisscrossed his shaved skin. Perhaps he had some sort of a skin rash, I told myself, but that didn't seem right to me. I was certain that Nathan had deliberately made those hairline scars. But why. . . ? "Nate, what the hell happened to you?" I asked. "You just disappeared off the face of the earth. And Ruth too. How is Ruth?"

Nathan looked away from me, as if I had opened a recent wound. The stout, older woman who was standing a few feet away from us tried to get Nathan's attention. "Excuse me, but could I *please* talk to you?" she asked, a trace of foreign accent in her voice. "It's very important." She looked agitated and tired, and I noticed dark shadows under her eyes. But Nathan didn't seem to hear her. "It's a long story," he said to me, "and I don't think you'd want to hear it." He seemed suddenly cold and distant.

"Of course I would," I insisted.

"Excuse me, please," interrupted the older woman. "I've come a long way to see you," she said to Nathan, "and you've been talking to everyone else but me. And I've been waiting . . . ."

Nathan tried to ignore her, but she stepped right up to him and took his arm. He jerked away, as if he'd been shocked. I saw the faded, tattooed numbers just above her wrist. "Please . . ." she asked.

"Are you here for a cover-up?" Nathan asked her, glancing down at her arm.

"No," she said. "It wouldn't do any good."

"You shouldn't be here," Nathan said gently. "You should be home."

"I know you can help me."

Nathan nodded, as if accepting the inevitable. "I'll talk to you for a moment, but that's all," he said to her. "That's all." Then he looked up at me, smiled wanly, and led the woman into his trailer.

"You thinkin' about getting a tattoo?" Dad asked, catching me staring at the trailer. Ben was looking around at the punkers, sizing them up. He had persuaded his mother to let him have a "rat-tail" when he went for his last haircut. It was just a small clump of hair that hung down in the back, but it gave him the appearance of rebelliousness; the real thing would be here soon enough. He turned his back to the punkers with their orange hair and long bleach-white rat-tails, probably to exhibit his own.

"Nah, just waiting for you," I said, lying, trying to ignore my feelings of loss and depression. Seeing Nathan had unnerved me. I felt old, as if Nathan's wasting had become my own.

We spent the rest of the day at the fair, had dinner at Mom and Dad's, watched television, and left at about eleven o'clock. We were all exhausted. I hadn't said anything to Laura about seeing Nathan. I knew she would want to see him, and I didn't want her upset, at least that's what I told myself.

Ben fell asleep in the back seat. Laura watched out for deer while I drove, as my night vision is poor. She should be the one to drive, but it hurts her legs to sit—she has arthritis. Most of the time her legs are stretched out as far as possible in the foot well, or she'll prop her feet against the dashboard. I fought the numbing hypnosis of the road. Every mile felt like ten. I kept thinking about Nathan, how he looked, what he had become.

"David, what's the matter?" Laura asked when we were about half-way home. "You're so quiet tonight. Is anything wrong? Did we do anything to upset you?"

"No, I'm just tired," I said, lying. Seeing Nathan had shocked and depressed me. But there was a selfish edge to my feelings. It was as though I had looked in one of the distorting mirrors in the fun house; I had seen something of myself in Nathan.

Ben yelped, lurching out of a particularly bad nightmare. He leaned forward, hugging the back of the front seat, and asked us if we were home yet.

"We've got a ways to go," I said. "Sit back, you'll fall asleep."

"I'm cold back here."

I turned up the heat; the temperature had dropped at least fifteen degrees since the afternoon. "The freak show probably gave you nightmares; it always did me."

"That's not it," Ben insisted.

"I don't know what's wrong with your grandfather," Laura said. "He had no business taking you in there. He should have his head examined."

"I told you," Ben said, "it had nothing to do with that."

"You want to talk about it?" I asked.

"No," Ben said, but he didn't sit back in his seat; he kept his face just behind us.

"You should sit back," Laura said. "If we got into an accident—"

"*Okay*," Ben said. There was silence for a minute, and then he said, "You know who I dreamed about?"

"Who?" I asked.

"Uncle Nathan."

I straightened up, automatically looking into the rearview mirror to see Ben, but it was too dark. I felt a chill and turned up the heat another notch.

"We haven't seen him in about four years," Laura said. "Whatever made you dream about him?"

"I dunno," Ben said. "But I dreamed he was all different colors, all painted, like a monster."

I felt the hairs on the back of my neck prickle.

"You were dreaming about the freak show," Laura told him. "Sometimes old memories of people we know get mixed up with new memories."

"It wasn't just Uncle Nathan looking like that that scared me."

"What was it?" I asked.

He pulled himself toward us again. But he spoke to Laura. "He was doing something to Dad," Ben said, meaning me.

"What was he doing?" Laura asked.

"I dunno," Ben said, "but it was horrible, like he was pulling out Dad's heart or something."

"Jesus Christ," Laura said. "Look, honey, it was only a dream," she said to him. "Forget about it and try to go back to sleep."

I tried to visualize the lines on Nathan's arms and neck and keep the car on the road.

I knew that I had to go back and see him.

Monday morning I finished an overdue fund-raising report for the Binghamton Symphony with the help of my secretary. The three o'clock meeting with the board of directors went well; I was congratulated for a job well done, and my future seemed secure for another six months. I called Laura, told her I had another meeting and that I would be home later than usual. Laura had a deadline of her own—she was writing an article for a travel magazine—and was happy for the stretch of work time. She was only going to send out for a pizza anyway.

The drive to the fairgrounds seemed to take longer than usual, but that was probably because I was impatient and tense about seeing Nathan. Ben's crazy dream had spooked me; I also felt guilty about lying to Laura. We had a thing about not lying to each other, although there were some things we didn't talk about, radioactive spots from the past which still burned, but which we pretended were dead.

There weren't as many people on the fairgrounds as last night, but that was to be expected, and I was glad for it. I parked close to the arcades, walked through the huckster's alley and came to Nathan Rivlin's trailer. It was dusk, and there was a chill in the air—a harbinger of the hard winter that was to come. A few kids wearing army jackets were loitering, looking at the designs of tattoos on paper, called flash, which were displayed under plexiglas on a table secured to the trailer. The designs were nicely executed but ordinary stuff to attract the passersby: anchors, hearts, butterflies, stylized women in profile, eagles, dragons, stars, various military insignia, cartoon characters, death's-heads, flags, black panthers and lions, snakes, spiders—nothing to indicate the kind of fine work that had been sported by the people hanging around the trailer yesterday.

I knocked on the door. Nathan didn't seem surprised to see me; he welcomed me inside. It was warm inside the trailer, close, and Nathan was wearing a sixties hippie-style white gauze shirt; the sleeves were long and the cuffs buttoned, hiding the scars I had seen on his arms yesterday. Once again I felt a shock at seeing him so gaunt, at seeing the webbed scars on his neck. Was I returning to my friend's out of just a morbid fascination to see what he had become? I felt guilty and ashamed. Why hadn't I sought out Nathan before this? If I had been a better friend, I probably would have.

Walking into his studio was like stepping into his paintings, which covered most of the available wall space. Nathan was known for working on large canvases, and some of his best work was in here—paintings I had seen in process years ago. On the wall opposite the door was a painting of a nude man weaving a cat's cradle. The light was directed from behind, highlighting shoulders and arms and the large, peasant hands. The features of the face were blurred, but unmistakably Nathan's. Beside it was a huge painting of three circus people, two jugglers standing beside a woman. Behind them, in large red letters was the word CIRCUS. The faces were ordinary, and disturbing, perhaps because of that.

There was another painting on the wall where Nathan had set up his tattoo studio. A self-portrait. Nathan wearing a blue worker's hat, red shirt, and apron and standing beside a laboratory skeleton. And there were many paintings I had never seen, a whole series of tattoo paintings, which at first glance looked to be nonrepresentational, until the designs of figures on flesh came into focus. There were several paintings of Gypsies. One, in particular, seemed to be staring directly at me over tarot cards, which were laid out on a table strewn with glasses. There was another painting of an old man being carried from his death bed by a sad faced demon. Nathan had a luminous technique, an execution like that of the old masters. Between the paintings, and covering every available space, was flash; not the flash that I had seen outside, but detailed colored designs and drawings of men and animals and mythical beasts, as grotesque as anything by Goya. I was staring into my own nightmares.

The bluish light that comes just before dark suffused the trailer, and the shadows seemed to become more concrete than the walls or paintings.

The older woman I had seen on Sunday was back. She was sitting in Nathan's studio, in what looked like a variation of a dentist chair. Beside the chair was a cabinet and a sink with a high, elongated faucet, the kind usually seen in examination rooms. Pigments, dyes, paper towels, napkins, bandages, charcoal for stencils, needle tubes, and bottles of soap and alcohol were neatly displayed beside an autoclave. I was surprised to see this woman in the chair, even though I knew she had been desperate to see Nathan. But she just didn't seem the sort to be getting a tattoo, although that probably didn't mean a thing: anyone could have hidden tattoos—old ladies, senators, presidents. Didn't Barry

Goldwater brag that he had two dots tattooed on his hand to represent the bite of a snake? Who the hell knew why.

"I'll be done in a few minutes," Nathan said to me. "Sit down. Would you like a drink? I've got some beer, I think. If you're hungry, I've got soup on the stove." Nathan was a vegetarian; he always used to make the same miso soup, which he'd start when he got up in the morning, every morning.

"If you don't mind, I'll just sit," I said, and I sat down on an old green art deco couch. The living room was made up of the couch, two slat-back chairs, and a television set on a battered oak desk. The kitchenette behind Nathan's work area had a stove, a small refrigerator, and a table attached to the wall. And, indeed, I could smell the familiar aroma of Nathan's soup.

"David, this is Mrs. Stramm," Nathan said, and he seemed to be drawn toward me, away from Mrs. Stramm, who looked nervous. I wanted to talk with him . . . connect with him . . . find the man I used to know.

"Mister Tarot," the woman said, "I'm ready now; you can go ahead."

Nathan sat down in the chair beside her and switched on a gooseneck adjustable lamp, which produced a strong, intense white light. The flash and paintings in the room lost their fire and brilliance, as the darkness in the trailer seemed to gain substance.

"Do you think you can help me?" she asked. "Do you think it will work?"

"If you wish to believe in it," Nathan said. He picked up his electrical tattoo machine, examined it, and then examined her wrist, where the concentration-camp tattoo had faded into seven smudgy blue marks.

"You know, when I got these numbers at the camp, it was a doctor who put them on. He was a prisoner, like I was. He didn't have a machine like yours. He worked for Dr. Mengele." She looked away from Nathan while she spoke, just as many people look away from a nurse about to stick a needle in their vein. But she seemed to have a need to talk. Perhaps it was just nerves.

Nathan turned on his instrument, which made a staticky, electric noise, and began tattooing her wrist. I watched him work; he didn't seem to have heard a word she said. He looked tense and bit his lip, as if it were his own wrist that was being tattooed. "I knew Mengele," the woman continued. "Do you know who he was?" she asked Nathan. Nathan didn't answer. "Of course you do," she said. "He was such a nice-looking man. Kept his hair very neat, clipped his mustache, and he had blue eyes. Like the sky. Everything else in the camp was gray, and the sky would get black from the furnaces, like the world was turned upside down." She continued to talk while Nathan worked. She grimaced from the pain of the tattoo needle.

I tried to imagine what she might have looked like when she was young, when she was in the camp. It would have been Auschwitz, I surmised, if Mengele was there.

But why was a Jew getting a tattoo?

Perhaps she wasn't Jewish.

And then I noticed that Nathan's wrist was bleeding. Tiny beads of blood soaked through his shirt, which was like a blotter.

"Nathan—" I said, as I reflexively stood up.

But Nathan looked at me sharply and shook his head, indicating that I should stay where I was. "It's all right, David. We'll talk about it later."

I sat back down and watched them, mesmerized.

Mrs. Stramm stopped talking; she seemed calmer now. There was only the sound of the machine and the background noise of the fair. The air seemed heavier in the darkness, almost smothering. "Yesterday you told me that you came here to see me to find out about your husband," Nathan said to her. "You lied to me, didn't you."

"I had to know if he was alive," she said. "He was a strong man, he could have survived. I left messages through the agencies for him when I was in Italy. I couldn't stand to go back to Germany. I thought to go to South America, I had friends in São Paulo."

"You came to America to cut yourself off from the past," Nathan said in a low voice. "You knew your husband had died. I can feel that you buried him . . . in your heart. But you couldn't bury everything. The tattoo is changing. Do you want me to stop? I have covered the numbers."

I couldn't see what design he had made. Her wrist was bleeding, though . . . as was his.

Then she began to cry and suddenly seemed angry. But she was directing her pain and anger at herself. Nathan stopped working but made no move to comfort her. When Mrs. Stramm's crying subsided and she regained control of her breathing, she said, "I murdered my infant. I had help from another, who thought she was saving my life." She seemed surprised at her own words.

"Do you want me to stop," Nathan asked again, but his voice was gentle.

"You do what you think, you're the tattooist."

Nathan began again. The noise of his machine was teeth-jarring. Mrs. Stramm continued talking to him, even though she still looked away from the machine. But she

talked in a low voice now. I had to lean forward and strain to
hear her. My eyes were fixed on Nathan's wrist; the dots of
blood had connected into a large bright stain on his shirt
cuff.

"I was only seventeen," Mrs. Stramm continued. "Just
married and pregnant. I had my baby in the camp, and Dr.
Mengele delivered it himself. It wasn't so bad in the hospital.
I was taken care of as if I were in a hospital in Berlin. Everything was nice, clean. I even pretended that what was going
on outside the hospital in the camp, in the ovens, wasn't true.
When I had the baby—his name was Stefan—everything was
perfect. Dr. Mengele was very careful when he cut the cord;
and another doctor assisted him, a Jewish doctor from the
camp. Ach!" she said, flinching; she looked down at her
wrist, where Nathan was working, but she didn't say a word
about the blood soaking through his shirtsleeve. She seemed
to accept it as part of the process. Nathan must have told her
what to expect. He stopped and refilled his instrument with
another ink pigment.

"But then I was sent to a barracks, which was filthy but
not terribly crowded," she continued. "There were other
children in there, mutilated. One set of twins had been sewn
together, back to back, arm to arm, and they smelled terrible.
They were an experiment, of course. I knew that my baby
and I were going to be an experiment. There was a woman in
the barracks looking after us. She couldn't do much but
watch the children die. She felt sorry for me. She told me
that nothing could be done for my baby. And after they had
finished their experiment and killed my son, then I would be
killed also; it was the way it was done. Dr. Mengele killed all
surviving parents and healthy siblings for comparison. My
only hope, she said, was to kill my baby myself. If my baby

died 'naturally' before Mengele began his experiment, then he might let me live. I remember thinking to myself that it was the only way I could save my baby the agony of a terrible death at the hands of Mengele.

"So I suffocated my baby. I pinched his nose and held his mouth shut while my friend held us both and cried for us. I remember that very well. Dr. Mengele learned of my baby's death and came to the barracks himself. He said he was very sorry, and, you know, I believed him. I took comfort from the man who had made me kill my child. I should have begged him to kill *me*. But I said nothing."

"What could you have done?" Nathan asked, as he was working. "Your child would have died no matter what. You saved yourself; that's all you could do under the circumstances."

"Is that how *you* would have felt, if you were me?"

"No," Nathan said, and a sad smile appeared for an instant, an inappropriate response, yet somehow telling.

Mrs. Stramm stopped talking and closed her eyes. It was as if she and Nathan were praying together. I could feel that, and I sensed that something else was happening between them. Something seemed to be passing out of her, a dark, palpable spirit. I could feel its presence in the room. And Nathan looked somehow different, more defined. It was the light from the lamp, no doubt, but some kind of exchange seemed to be taking place. Stolid, solid Mrs. Stramm looked softer, as if lighter, while Nathan looked as ravaged as an internee. It was as if he were becoming defined by this woman's past.

When Nathan was finished, he put his instrument down on the cabinet and taped some gauze over his own bleeding wrist. Then he just stared at his work on Mrs. Stramm. I couldn't see the tattoo from where I was sitting, so I stood up and walked over. "Is it all right if I take a look?" I asked, but neither one answered me . . . neither one seemed to notice me.

The tattoo was beautiful, lifelike in a way I had not thought possible for a marking on the flesh. It was the cherubic face of an angel with thin, curly hair. One of the numbers had now become the shading for the angel's fine, straight nose. Surrounding the face were dark feathered wings that crossed each other; an impossible figure, but a hauntingly sad and beautiful one. The eyes seemed to be looking upward and out, as if contemplating a high station of paradise. The numbers were lost in the blue-blackness of lifting wings. This figure looked familiar, which was not surprising, as Nathan had studied the work of the masters. I remembered a Madonna, which was attributed to the Renaissance artist Lorenzo di Credi, that had two angels with wings such as those on the tattoo. But the tattooed wings were so dark they reminded me of death; and they were bleeding, an incongruous testament to life.

I thought about Nathan's bleeding wrist, and wondered . . . .

"It's beautiful," Mrs. Stramm said, staring at her tattoo. "It's the right face; it's the way his face would have looked . . . had he lived." Then she stood up abruptly. Nathan sat where he was; he looked exhausted, which was how I suddenly felt.

"I must put a gauze wrap over it," Nathan said.

"No, I wish to look at him."

"Can you see the old numbers?" Nathan asked.

"No," she said at first, then, "Yes, I can see them."

"Good," Nathan said.

She stood before Nathan, and I could now see that she had once been beautiful: big-boned, proud, full-bodied, with a strong chin and regal face. Her fine gray hair had probably been blond, since her eyebrows were light. And she looked relieved, released. I couldn't help but think that she seemed now like a woman who had just given birth. The strain was gone. She no longer seemed gravid with the burden of sorrow. But the heaviness had not disappeared from the room, for I could feel the psychic closeness of grief like stale, humid air. Nathan looked wasted in the sharp, cleansing, focused light.

"Would you mind if I looked at *your* tattoo?" Mrs. Stramm asked.

"I'm sorry," Nathan said.

Mrs. Stramm nodded, then picked up her handbag and took out her checkbook. She moved toward the light and began to scribble out a check. "Will you accept three hundred dollars?"

"No, I cannot. Consider it paid."

She started to argue, but Nathan turned away from her. "Thank you," she said, and walked to the door.

Nathan didn't answer.

Nathan turned on the overhead light; the sudden change from darkness to light unnerved me.

"Tell me what the hell's going on," I said. "Why did your wrist start bleeding when you were tattooing that woman?"

"It's part of the process," Nathan said vaguely. "Do you want coffee?" he asked, changing the subject—Nathan had a way of talking around any subject, peeling away layers as if conversation was an onion; he eschewed directness.

Perhaps it was his rabbinical heritage. At any rate, he wasn't going to tell me anything until he was ready. I nodded, and he took a bag of ground coffee out of his freezer and dripped a pot in the Melitta. Someone knocked at the door and demanded a tattoo, and Nathan told him that he would have to wait until tomorrow.

We sat at the table and sipped coffee. I felt an overwhelming lassitude come over me. My shoulder began to ache . . . to throb. I worried that this might be the onset of another heart attack (I try not to pay attention to my hypochondria, but those thoughts still flash through my mind, no matter how rational I try to be). Surely it was muscular, I told myself: I had been wrestling with my son last night. I needed to start swimming again at the Y. I was out of shape, and right now I felt more like sixty-two that forty-two. After a while, the coffee cleared my head a bit—it was a very, very strong blend, Pico, I think—but the atmosphere inside the trailer was still oppressive, even with the overhead light turned on. It was as if I could *feel* the shadows.

"I saw Mrs. Stramm here yesterday afternoon," I said, trying to lead Nathan. "She seems Jewish, strange that she should be getting a tattoo. Although maybe not so strange, since she came to a Jewish tattooist." I forced a laugh and tried not to stare at the thin webbing of scars on his neck.

"She's not Jewish," Nathan said. "Catholic. She was interred in the camp for political reasons. Her family was caught hiding Jews."

"It seems odd that she'd come to you for a tattoo to cover up her numbers," I said. "She could have had surgery. You would hardly be able to tell they'd ever been there."

"That's not why she came."

"Nathan . . . ."

"Most of the people just want tattoos," Nathan said. He seemed slightly defensive, and then he sighed and said, "But sometimes I get people like Mrs. Stramm. Word gets around, word-of-mouth. Sometimes I can sense things, see things about people when I'm tattooing. It's something like automatic writing, maybe. Then the tattoo takes on a life of its own, and sometimes it changes the person I tattoo."

"This whole thing . . . it seems completely crazy," I said, remembering his paintings, the large canvases of circus people, carny people. He had made his reputation with those melancholy, poignant oil paintings. He had traveled, followed the carnies. Ruth didn't seem to mind. She was independent, and used to travel quite a bit by herself also; she was fond of taking grueling, long day-trips. Like Nathan, she was full of energy. I remember that Nathan had been drawn to tattooing through circus people. He visited tattoo studios and used them for his settings. The paintings he produced then were haunted, and he became interested in the idea of living art, the relationship of art to society, the numinous, symbolic quality of primitive art. It was only natural that he'd want to try tattooing, which he did. He had even tattooed himself: a tiny raven that seemed to be forever nestled in his palm. But that had been a phase, and once he had had his big New York show, he went on to paint ordinary people in parks and shopping malls and in movies houses, and his paintings were selling at over five thousand dollars apiece. I remembered ribbing him for tattooing himself. I had told him he couldn't be buried in a Jewish cemetery. He had said that he had already bought his plot. Money talks.

"How's Ruth?" I asked, afraid of what he would tell

me. He would never be here, he would never look like this, if everything was all right between them.

"She's dead," he whispered, and he took a sip of his coffee.

"What?" I asked, shocked. "How?"

"Cancer, as she was always afraid of."

The pain in my shoulder became worse, and I started to sweat. It seemed to be getting warmer; he must have turned the heat up.

"How could all this happen without Laura or me knowing about it?" I asked. "I just can't believe it."

"Ruth went back to Connecticut to stay with her parents."

"Why?"

"David," Nathan said, "I knew she had cancer, even when she went in for tests and they all turned out negative. I kept dreaming about it, and I could *see* it burning inside her. I thought I was going crazy . . . I probably was. I couldn't stand it. I couldn't be near her. I couldn't help her. I couldn't do anything. So I started traveling, got back into the tattoo culture. The paintings were selling, especially the tattoo stuff—I did a lot of close-up work, you wouldn't even know it was tattoos I was painting; I got into some beautiful oriental stuff—so I stayed away."

"And she died without you?" I asked, incredulous.

"In Stamford. The dreams got worse. It got so I couldn't even talk to her over the phone. I could see what was happening inside her, and I was helpless. And I was a coward. I'm paying for it now."

"What do you mean?" I asked. Goddammit, it was hot. He didn't answer.

"Tell me about the scars on your neck and your arms."

"And my chest, everywhere," Nathan confessed. "They're tattoos. It started when I ran away, when I left Ruth. I started tattooing myself. I used the tattoo gun, but no ink."

"Why?" I asked.

"At first, I guess I did it as practice, but then it became a sort of punishment. It was painful. I was painting without pigments. I was inflicting my own punishment. Sometimes I can see the tattoos, as if they were paintings. I'm a map of what I've done to my wife, to my family; and then around that time I discovered I could see into other people and sort of draw their lives differently. Most people I'd just give a tattoo, good work, sometimes even great work, maybe, but every once in a while I'd see something when I was working. I could see if someone was sick, I could see what was wrong with him. I was going the carny route and living with some Gypsy people. A woman, a friend of mine, saw my 'talent'"—he laughed when he said that—"and helped me develop it. That's when I started bleeding when I worked. As my friend used to tell me, 'Everything has a price.'"

I looked at Nathan. His life was draining away. He was turning into a ghost or a shadow. Not even his tattoos had color.

My whole arm was aching. I couldn't ignore it any longer. And it was so close in the trailer that I couldn't *breathe*. "I've got to get some air," I said as I forced myself to get up. I felt as if I hadn't slept in days. Then I felt a burning in my neck and a stabbing pain in my chest. I tried to shout to Nathan, who was standing up, who looked shocked, who was coming toward me.

But I couldn't move; I was as leaden as a statue. I could only see Nathan, and it was as if he were lit by a tensor lamp.

194

The pigments of living tattoos glowed under his shirt and resolved themselves like paintings under a stage scrim. He was a living, radiant landscape of scenes and figures, terrestrial and heavenly and demonic. I could see a grotesque caricature of Mrs. Stramm's tattoo on Nathan's wrist. It was a howling, tortured, winged child. Most of the other tattoos expressed the ugly, minor sins of people Nathan had tattooed, but there were also figures of Nathan and Ruth. All of Ruth's faces were Madonna-like, but Nathan was rendered perfectly, and terribly; he was a monster portrayed in entirely human terms, a visage of greed and cowardice and hardness. But there was a central tattoo on Nathan's chest that looked like a Dürer engraving—such was the sureness and delicacy of the work. Ruth lay upon the ground, amid grasses and plants and flowers, which seemed surreal in their juxtaposition. She had opened her arms, as if begging for Nathan, who was depicted also, to return. Her chest and stomach and neck were bleeding, and one could look into the cavities of the open wounds. And marching away, descending under the nipple of Nathan's chest, was the figure of Nathan. He was followed by cherubs riding fabulous beasts, some of which were the skeletons of horses and dogs and goats with feathery wings ... wings such as Nathan had tattooed on Mrs. Stramm. But the figure of Nathan was running away. His face, which had always seemed askew—a large nose, deep-set engaging eyes, tousled hair, the combination of features that made him look like a seedy Puck, the very embodiment of generous friendliness—was rendered formally. His nose was straight and long, rather than crooked, as it was in real life, and his eyes were narrow and tilted, rather than wide and roundish; and his mouth, which in real life, even now, was full, was drawn as a mere line. In his hands, Nathan was carrying Ruth's heart and other organs, while a child riding a skeleton Pegasus was waving a thighbone.

The colors were like an explosion, and the tattoos filled my entire field of vision; and then the pain took me, wrapped like a snake around my chest. My heart was pounding. It seemed to be echoing in a huge hall. It was all I could hear. The burning in my chest increased, and I felt myself screaming, even if it might be soundless. I felt my entire being straining in fright, and then the colors dimmed. Fainting, falling, I caught one last glimpse of the walls and ceiling, all pulsing, glowing, all coalescing into one grand tattoo, which was all around me, and I followed those inky, pigment paths into grayness and then darkness. I thought of Laura and Ben, and I felt an overwhelming sense of sorrow for Nathan.

For once, I didn't seem to matter, and my sense of rushing sadness became a universe in which I was suspended.

I thought I was dying, but it seemed that it would take an eternity, an eternity to think, to worry back over my life, to relive it once more, but from a higher perspective, from an aerial view. But then I felt a pressure, as if I were under water and a faraway explosion had fomented a strong current. I was being pulled away, jostled, and I felt the tearing of pain and saw bright light and heard an electrical sparking, a sawing. And I saw Nathan's face, as large as a continent gazing down upon me.

I woke up on his couch. My head was pounding, but I was breathing naturally, evenly. My arm and shoulder and chest no longer ached, although I felt a needle-like burning over my heart. Reflexively, I touched the spot where I had felt the tearing pain, and found it had been bandaged. "What the hell's this?" I asked Nathan, who was sitting beside me. Although I could make out the scars on his neck, I could no longer find the outlines of the tattoos I had seen, nor could I make out the brilliant pigments that I had imagined or hallucinated. "Why do I have a bandage on?" I felt panic.

"Do you remember what happened?" he asked. Nathan looked ill. Even more wasted. His face was shiny with sweat. But it wasn't warm in here now; it was comfortable. Yet when Mrs. Stramm was sitting for her tattoo, it was stifling. I had felt the closeness of dead air like claustrophobia.

"Christ, I thought I was having a heart attack. I blacked out. I fell."

"I caught you. You did have a heart attack."

"Then why the hell am I here instead of in a hospital?" I asked, remembering how it felt to be completely helpless in the emergency room, machines whirring and making ticking and just-audible beeping noises as they monitored vital signs.

"It could have been very bad," Nathan said, ignoring my question.

"Then what am I doing here?" I asked again. I sat up. This was all wrong. Goddammit, it was wrong. I felt a rush in my head, and the headache became sharp and then withdrew back into dull pain.

"I took care of it," he said.

"How?"

"How do you feel?"

"I have a headache, that's all," I said, "and I want to know what you did on my chest."

"Don't worry, I didn't use pigment. They'll let you into a Jewish cemetery." Nathan smiled.

"I want to know what you did." I started to pull off the gauze, but he stopped me.

"Let it heal for a few days. Change the bandage. That's all."

"And what the hell am I supposed to tell Laura?" I asked.

"That you're alive."

I felt weak, yet it was as if I had sloughed something off, something heavy and deadening.

And I just walked out the door.

After I was outside, shivering, for the weather had turned unseasonably cold, I realized that I had not said goodbye. I had left, as if in a daze. Yet I could not turn around and go back. This whole night was crazy, I told myself. I'd come back tomorrow and apologize . . . and try to find out what had really happened.

I drove home, and it began to snow, a freakish wet, heavy snow that turned everything bluish-white, luminescent.

My chest began to itch under the bandage.

I didn't get home until after twelve. Understandably, Laura was worried and anxious. We both sat down to talk in the upholstered chairs in front of the fireplace in the living room, facing each other; that was where we always sat when we were arguing or working out problems. Normally, we'd sit on the sofa and chat and watch the fire. Laura had a fire crackling in the fireplace; and, as there were only a few small lamps on downstairs, the ruddy light from the fire flickered in our large white carpeted living room. Laura wore a robe with large cuffs on the sleeves and her thick black hair was long and shiny, still damp from a shower. Her small face was tight, as she was upset, and she wore her glasses, another give-away that she was going to get to the bottom of this.

She almost never wore her glasses, and the lenses were scratched from being tossed here and there and being banged about in various drawers; she only used them when she had to "focus her thoughts."

I looked a sight: My once starched white shirt was wrinkled and grimy, and I smelled rancid, the particular odor of nervous sweat. My trousers were dirty, especially at the knees, where I had fallen to the floor, and I had somehow torn out the hem of my right pantleg.

I told Laura the whole story, what had happened from the time I had seen Nathan Sunday until tonight. At first she seemed relieved that I had been with Nathan—she had never been entirely sure of me, and I'm certain she thought I'd had a rendezvous with some twenty-two year old receptionist or perhaps the woman who played the French horn in the orchestra —I had once made a remark about her to Laura. But she was more upset than I had expected when I told her that Ruth had died. We were friends, certainly, although I was much closer to Nathan than she was to Ruth.

We moved over to the couch, and I held her until she stopped crying. I got up, fixed us both a drink, and finished the story.

"How could you let him tattoo your skin?" Laura asked; and then, exposing what she was really thinking about, she said in a whisper, "I can't believe Ruth's gone. We were good friends; you didn't know that, did you?"

"I guess I didn't." After a pause, I said, "I didn't *let* Nathan tattoo me. I told you, I was unconscious. I'd had an attack or something." I don't know if Laura really believed that. She had been a nurse for fifteen years.

"Well, let me take a look at what's under the gauze."

I let her unbutton my shirt; with one quick motion, she

tore the gauze away. Looking down, I just saw the crisscrossings and curlicues and random lines that were thin raised welts over my heart.

"What the hell did he *do* to you? This whole area could get infected. Who knows if his needle was even clean. You could get hepatitis, or AIDS, considering the kinds of people who go in for tattoos."

"No, he kept everything clean," I said.

"Did he have an autoclave?" she asked.

"Yes, I think he did."

Laura went to the downstairs bathroom and came back with Betadine and a clean bandage. Her fuzzy blue bathrobe was slightly open, and I felt myself becoming excited. She was a tiny woman, small-boned and delicate-featured, yet big-busted, which I liked. When we first lived together, before we married, she was extremely shy in bed, even though she'd already been married before; yet she soon became aggressive, open, and frank, and to my astonishment I found that *I* had grown more conservative.

I touched her breasts as she cleaned the tattoo, or more precisely, the welts, for he used no pigment. The Betadine and the touch of her hands felt cool on my chest.

"Can you make anything out of this?" she asked, meaning the marks Nathan had made.

I looked down but couldn't make anything more out of them than she could. I wanted to look at the marks closely in the mirror, but Laura had become excited, as I was, and we started making love on the couch. She was on top of me, we still had our clothes on, and we were kissing each other so hard that we ground our teeth. I pressed myself inside her. Our lovemaking was urgent and cleansing. It was as if we had recovered something, and I felt my heart beating, clear and strong. After we came and lay locked together, still intimate, she whispered, "Poor Nathan."

I dreamed about him that night. I dreamed of the tattoo I had seen on his chest, the parade of demons and fabulous creatures. I was inside his tattoo, watching him walking off with Ruth's heart. I could hear the demon angels shouting and snarling and waving pieces of bone as they rode atop unicorns and skeleton dragons flapping canvas-skinned pterodactyl wings. Then Nathan saw me, and he stopped. He looked as skeletal as the creatures around him, as if his life and musculature and fat had been worn away, leaving nothing but bones to be buried.

He smiled at me and gave me Ruth's heart.

It was warm and still beating. I could feel the blood clotting in my hand.

I woke up with a jolt. I was shaking and sweating. Although I had turned up the thermostat before going to bed, it was cold in the bedroom. Laura was turned away from me, moving restlessly, her legs raised toward her chest in a semi-foetal position. All the lights were off, and as it was a moonlit night, the snow reflected a wan light; everything in the room looked shadowy blue. And I felt my heart pumping fast.

I got up and went into the bathroom. Two large dormer windows over the tub to my left let in the dim light of a streetlamp near the southern corner of the house. I looked in the mirror at my chest and could see my tattoo. The lines were etched in blue, as if my body were snow reflecting moonlight. I could see a heart; it was luminescent. I saw an angel wrapped in deathly wings, an angel such as the one Nathan had put on Mrs. Stramm's wrist to heal her; but this angel, who seemed to have some of Nathan's features—his crooked nose and full mouth, had spread his wings, and his perfect infant hands held out Ruth's heart to me.

Staring, I leaned on the white porcelain sink. I felt a surging of life, as if I was being given a gift, and then the living image of the tattoo died. I shivered naked in the cold bathroom. I could feel the chill passing through the ill-fitting storms of the dormer windows. It was as if the chill were passing right through me, as if I had been opened up wide.

And I knew that Nathan was in trouble. The thought came to me like a shock of cold water. But I could *feel* Nathan's presence, and I suddenly felt pain shoot through my chest, concentrated in the tattoo, and then I felt a great sadness, an oceanic grief.

I dressed quickly and drove back to Trout Creek. The fairgrounds were well-lit, but deserted. It had stopped snowing. The lights were on in Nathan's trailer. I knocked on the door, but there was no answer. The door was unlocked, as I had left it, and I walked in.

Nathan was dead on the floor. His shirt was open, and his chest was bleeding—he had the same tattoo I did. But his face was calm, his demons finally exorcised. I picked him up, carried him to the couch, and kissed him goodbye.

As I left, I could feel his strength and sadness and love pumping inside me. The wind blew against my face, drying my tears . . . it was the cold fluttering of angel's wings.

The Heart's Own Country

by J.R. Dunn

J.R. Dunn's second story, "The Gates of Babel," published in May 1989, in *Omni*, is a remarkable piece of work that seems all the more so having been produced by a relatively unseasoned writer. It was chosen by editor David S. Garnett for *The Orbit Science Fiction Yearbook #3*. Since then Dunn has had stories in *Isaac Asimov's Science Fiction Magazine* and *Amazing Stories*. He has recently finished a novel called *This Side of Judgment*.

Dunn's most recent piece in *Omni* is the short story "Overtures" (September 1992).

"The Heart's Own Country" is the second story of the series Dunn began with "The Other Shore" (*Omni*, December 1991), about a future in which a small group of men set out to play god, unleashing a selective plague in an attempt to solve the overpopulation problem. Here, one can see some of the less obvious consequences of that immoral decision.

THE HEART'S OWN COUNTRY

J.R. Dunn

1)
The cover of the report bore only the BuTech symbol and a
black SECRET stamp. Crozier opened it again to study the
photo on the second page. A normal-enough face, nothing
demented or vicious about it. Hard to believe that somebody
who looked like the kid down the street had been fooling
with the dark sciences.

Turning the page, he ran his eyes down the single-
spaced lines. Anthony Ricelli, age twenty-three. Detected
while doing research at a university lab—the name of the
school was blacked out. He'd been accessing the restricted
sections of the lab DB. Crozier smiled to himself. So the
Bureau of Technological Investigation was tapping private
databases—interesting. They also appeared to be using
banned biological data as bait. Damn close to entrapment, as
far as Crozier could see, but there was no such thing as
legality where biotech was concerned.

The BuTech agent, Howard Alton, was talking to Noah
Singletary. "Grad student," he was saying. "That's the age
where they pop up, when they know it all, think they can

take on the world. I'll tell you, we don't teach 'em enough about the Greening these days. If it was up to me . . . ."

Crozier cleared his throat. "This Ricelli," he said, tapping the photo. "He's definitely in Phoenix?"

"The area. If I knew exactly where I wouldn't be sitting here." Alton paused, perhaps remembering who he was talking to. "We'd have picked him up already, commissioner."

Crozier let it pass. "The connection with Reclamation," he said. "How'd you figure that out?"

"We knew what the scumbag was working on and kept an eye open for any materials he'd need. Small market for that stuff. One order cropped up paid for by your Reclamation Department and sent to a P.O. box here."

Crozier flicked a few pages on. "A hypercentrifuge."

"Right. Obsolete model, used. He probably thought we'd miss it." Alton smiled, cold and harsh, not touching anything past his lips.

"But you couldn't trace the check."

"Issued from accounts, like a hundred-fifty others that same day," Alton said. "Since we were poaching on your territory, we decided we'd better bring you in."

Crozier looked up. His territory—had there been a shift in tone with those words, a touch more emphasis than necessary? He met Alton's eyes. The agent stared back coolly.

"I appreciate that," Crozier said. "Now what's the program?"

He said little while Alton outlined the strategy. Noah made a few comments, each one cutting to the heart of some problem Alton hadn't seen or was trying to skip over. Crozier eyed the agent with amusement. He hadn't even introduced Noah as head of security. By now Alton must have figured it out for himself.

"How do we contact you?" Crozier said as he finished, reaching for the switch on the phone memory.

Alton hesitated. "Uh . . . we don't like anything on file during an investigation. Too easy to tap it . . . ."

"Our system is swept five times a day. I don't see a problem."

Shrugging, Alton rattled off a motel name. "Save that," Crozier said. The call button flashed green. "Tomorrow, then," he told Alton. The agent nodded sharply and left.

Brusque, Crozier thought—hadn't even bothered to shake hands. He turned to Singletary. "A bit intense, isn't he?"

The skin around Noah's eyes crinkled slightly. Once again it occurred to Crozier how little he knew the man. Noah Singletary had been with him twelve years, before he'd been appointed Commissioner Southwest, and he was nearly as much a stranger as the day they'd met. Crozier hadn't ever been to his home, had seen his wife twice, maybe three times . . . and his children—there were two, he believed—never. But there were reasons for that.

He got up and went to the window. A fine day; he could see all the way across the Salt Valley. From up here Phoenix looked pristine: a model city, clean, prosperous, and old-fashioned. Below him stood the boxy, glassed-in buildings of the late 20th, the inhuman monuments of a bitter era. Many were empty, and there hadn't been any new construction since the Greening. No need to build—the population was now a third of what it had been during the city's prime, an all-time high for this century.

It wasn't only the result of the Greening. Lack of water

was the major reason—the exhaustion of the Rocky Mountain aquifer, millions of years worth of stored water poured away in just three generations. That was the problem Reclamation was trying to lick.

A thought teased him: One of the fantasies of the biotechs had been creating plant life to thrive on next to no moisture. He dismissed the notion. That wasn't what Ricelli had been working on.

Behind him Noah spoke. "Odd that Alton is running this solo."

"Agreed. But who knows what standard procedure is with the biocops?" He turned to see Noah gazing at him quizzically, an expression he'd grown used to over the years. "What else?"

"Reclamation," Noah said quietly.

Looking away, Crozier returned to the desk. He knew what Noah was getting at: Start poking around, go through the department DB, put somebody in. "Let it go for now," he muttered. "I'll see to it."

"Sir," Noah said. "I'll get the wheels turning."

"Do that." He looked up to see the security chief reach the door just as it slid open.

He sank back in the chair, feeling an obscure sense of guilt. What could Singletary think? The specter of the Greening suddenly rises on a sunny afternoon, and he shows no sign. The Zero years, the Oughts, the first decade of the century. All the names: the Greening, the Salvaging, the Plague, and not one able to match the simple reality of a man-made holocaust carried out in favor of an insane ideal of ecological balance. Four-fifths of humanity dead, the brown people, what had once been called the Third World. The plague had been tailored to kill only non-whites.

Could it just be another job to Noah, part of a day's
work? Impossible. And yet Crozier couldn't ask him. It was
one of those things you didn't talk about.

What does a black man think? For the thousandth time
he wondered where the term had come from. The ones he'd
met—not many, there weren't many around—had been
various shades of brown. Noah, now, could be called dark
tan . . . .

And as for Reclamation . . . . He looked across the desk
at the picture in the opposite corner. A holo displaying the
face of a woman, smiling broadly, hair scarcely graying.
Aggie, dead these three years. At his wave the holo changed,
revealing another face, one heartbreakingly similar to the
first.

He knew the director of Reclamation. Knew her well. In
fact, he'd paid for her degree in dry-land ecology. She gazed
at him gravely: his daughter, Melissa Crozier.

The comp screen showed calls accumulating. Twelve,
no, thirteen now. Plenty of work waiting. Well, it could wait.

He picked up the phone and spoke a number. A voice
answered, and his eyes darted to the holo. "Hello, Mel," he
said quietly.

2)

Taking a sip of rye, Crozier scowled at the photo on the
wall. A flat shot of a snowy day out east, Mel in the arms of
a tall, dark-haired young man, both bundled in long coats,
both laughing.

He realized that Mel had spoken. "What?"

"I said," she called from the kitchen. "It's been a
month since you've been over."

"Well . . . I've been busy."

"Good answer, Pop."

He flushed: It was a great answer, wasn't it? He wondered if she'd been lonely, shooting another sour glance at the photo. No thanks to you, Walsh. A typical Easterner, Larry Walsh, all sensitive, poetic romanticism, no spine whatsoever. Things get rough and off he runs, as if this were still the 20th and vows meant nothing. Where was it he was hiding? Some artists colony in SoCal, the place where they used to make films . . . .

Mel appeared in the kitchen door, holding a bowl and pouting at him.

"Now, Mel," he said as he walked toward her. "You've had a lot to do too . . . ."

She smiled: honey hair, cowgirl's face, the image of Aggie. "I know. Just teasing."

"So we're both to blame," he said as he followed her into the kitchen.

She grimaced at him. "Daboatovus."

He threw his head back and laughed. Mel had spent four years at Columbia. You had to know the dialect to get around Old New York, and she'd picked it up rather well.

"Funny," she said as she set the bowl down. "At the department they probably think we get together every night to plot how to conquer another chunk of the bureaucracy. The Crozier dynasty."

"You're still hearing that?" There had been a lot of grumbling five years ago when she'd taken the job. Crozier hadn't actually arranged it for her, but he'd made his wishes known when the slot opened up. With her troubles—darling Larry running out, and the child—he'd wanted her near him.

"No," she said. "They know better."

She went on to tell him what had been happening in the department the past few weeks. He listened with interest. His own position as commissioner was limited to overall policy and public order, and he seldom heard about administrative matters in detail.

She was talking about her last trip to Washington. The Southwest Reclamation District covered a lot of ground—everything from West Texas to the Coast—and Arizona-New Mexico was at the bottom of the list. Mel had to fight for everything she got.

"... so they're cutting the desalination budget again—a stretch-out, they call it, but it's a cut—and guess who takes the slack? And when I bring it up, the secretary says, 'Who wants to live in the desert anyway?' So I told him it's all desert. The L.A. basin is as much a desert as here. And you know what he said? 'It can't be. It's next to the ocean.' "

She opened a cabinet. "I mean . . . goddamn."

"Yes," Crozier shook the ice in his drink. "Goddamn."

"No," Mel said. "Not that." She took off her paper apron and crumpled it. "I need jalapeños."

As she walked out muttering about how she was sure she'd had them, he put the glass down and said, "I'll get them. You stay here and . . . ."

Mel turned to him, biting her lip in the are-you-serious expression she'd used since she'd been about three. He waited, smiling in spite of himself.

"Poppy, do you know what a jalapeño is?"

He waved his hands vaguely. "It's a kind of pepper."

"And that's what you'll come back with. Pepper." She swept on. "I remember what poor Mom used to go through. You sit down and get another drink."

The door closed before he was able to protest, and he went to do as he was told. From the photo Larry beamed at him. "How could you give her up, fool?" he asked it. Even considering the boy . . . .

He meandered around the room. A nice house, built a long time ago, much better constructed than most housing of the immediate pre-Greening era. Low, everything on one level, what was called a "ranch" though there was little resemblance to the actual thing that he could see. There was a pool out back, half-filled with gravel to prevent it from popping out of the ground. A standard item last century; most had been filled in completely, but Mel had kept this one as it was, as a challenge.

His gaze moved to the hallway leading to the bedrooms. An old feeling arose, a leaden ache too simple for words. They hadn't mentioned it tonight, either of them, but it was always there.

"It," he repeated to himself, with more than a touch of self-contempt. That's how I think of him now. And Mel? No; he knew what she thought.

He found himself at the door of the nearest bedroom, studying the readout screen pinned there. It told him nothing. There, at the bottom, a series of lines jumping across a graph—could those be brainwaves? Perhaps the boy was dreaming.

But what did he have to dream about, Crozier asked himself as he pushed the door open. What had he ever known to be translated into dreams?

The boy made a small sound as Crozier approached the bed. He paused, staring at the equipment shedding the only light in the room. He did not want to disturb him; Larry would be afraid if he awoke with his mother not there.

He lay on his side, curled into a fetal position. He was eight but looked four years younger. Mentally he was no age at all.

This was what his father had run from. Cystic fibrosis, complicated—Crozier admired that term—by an allergic antibiotic reaction when he'd been two.

Leaning over the bed, Crozier rested a hand on the covers. Ricelli had been investigating congenital diseases.

He felt a sudden dampness and looked down. The hand holding the glass was shaking. A chunk of ice leapt out and fell to the rug. He turned from the bed. If that son of a bitch was using his little girl . . . .

He started as he saw Mel in the doorway. She gazed back, her hands clasped, then stepped inside. At the bed she did what Crozier had not dared, fixing the covers and stroking her son's head.

Crozier walked into the hall. They never spoke of it much. Every few weeks he'd ask her how the boy was, and she always gave the same answer: that he was all right. As if it were a ritual.

She'd broken down only once, just after Aggie died. For a short time as he'd held her then he'd thought it was her mother she was crying for, but it had been everything. Aggie, that coward fleeing, but above all the boy. "I only want him to be like everybody else," she'd said, as though it were in his power to grant that gift.

The phrase echoed, as if he'd just now heard it: like everybody else.

He felt her hand on his arm. "You shouldn't get so upset, Poppy."

Gazing at her, he thought of what he'd planned to do: question her, manipulate her, trick her into admitting what it

213

was she'd gotten involved in. He dropped his eyes. "My grandson, Mel."

"I hate seeing you like this."

He threw his arm around her and smiled. "Then you won't. Now come on. Your old man is starving."

As she went into the kitchen, he got himself another drink. The shame of what he'd planned lingered, but that was unnecessary now. Her expression as she'd bent over the bed told him all he needed to know. Tenderness, and love, but for the first time in years something else: hope.

He eyed the old photo again. Hollywood: That was the place where Walsh had bunkered down. He added another shot to the glass. Good place for him, he thought as he turned to go to the kitchen.

3)

"He hasn't told us everything, Steve."

Crozier narrowed his eyes. "How's that?"

"Alton is holding something back," Berg said. "We're not sure what it is." He glanced at Noah, sitting next to Luke Tyner, one of the Tac Squad officers. Crozier had called them in to congratulate Tyner on the quick job he'd made of the bandits who'd crossed into Arizona last week. There weren't many Mexicans left, even these days, but those there were congregated on the border. Easy pickings, the settlements isolated and lonely, lots of rough country to hide in. Tyner had disarmed this latest gang and sent them home without a casualty on either side, a fine piece of work.

"He may be trailing an accomplice," Noah said. "Vanished yesterday, no explanation. We got a report from the city traffic system today. He was tagged in front of the

Reclamation offices."

Keeping his face steady, Crozier nodded. "No surprise there," Tyner said. "Biocops got a bad rep for cooperation."

Crozier turned to him. Good man, Tyner. Young, bright, ambitious. He got the impression that Noah was grooming him for bigger things. He regarded Tyner's smiling face and thought of the popular myth about blacks being cold and emotionless. About as true as all the other stories: their superhuman strength, quick intelligence, ability to prevail over any circumstances. Ridiculous, but understandable: The average man could go through his whole life without ever meeting a black. That was why they made such outstanding security officers: It was a brave rioter who stood up against a black Tac Squad, a gutsy suspect who held out under interrogation.

They were waiting for him to speak. "All right," he said. "What do we do about it?"

"No use bugging his car," Berg said. "He'll detect it."

"Surveillance? He's been trained." He turned to Noah. "Our people good enough to beat him?"

"We can try."

"Fine. But don't pressure him. If they're seen, pull 'em off."

"Understood."

"Beyond that, any other ideas on what he's up to?"

Pursing his lips, Berg shifted in his seat. "It occurred to me that he might have contacted the target."

"Noah?"

"Considered it. Doesn't make much sense."

"Is there any record of BuTech agents cutting deals with suspects?"

"That's just it," Berg said. "There's no record on

biocops at all."

"Always one rotten apple," Noah said.

"Right. We'll go worst case." Crozier tapped the desktop. "Noah, contact his home office. It's in Virginia, I believe?"

"Langley. The old intelligence HQ. Electronically isolated, I'm afraid . . . ."

"So we'll have to go through channels?"

"Take a day or so."

"We'll live with it. Felix, Luke . . . ." The two of them got up. As they reached the door Crozier called out, "Again, Luke, outstanding work on that incursion." Tyner smiled as he went through the door.

"Up and coming," Crozier said. "You think a promotion's due?"

Noah nodded silently.

"What about Berg?"

"Felix is fine at ops. He knows it. He's not looking higher."

It relieved Crozier to hear that. Berg was an Easterner, white and Jewish, unusual for a security man, to say the least. He got along well with the rest of the staff. They called him "brother," a damned high honorific. It would be a pity if he thought he were being overlooked.

Noah sat quietly, aware that more was coming. Crozier waited a moment, the words like ashes on his tongue. "My daughter's involved."

There was no reply, for which he was grateful. "We'll need sensors on her car. Full spectrum."

The chair squeaked as Noah got up. "I'll see to it. Speak to Luke."

Understanding, Crozier nodded. Noah would keep it

quiet. Nobody else would know until the whole world did.

"Keep me informed," he called out as Noah went to the door.

"Sir."

He turned to the window. Another clear day. The valley would have been filled with smog a century ago, cutting visibility to nothing. That had been one of the excuses for the Greening, one of the many, many excuses. There wasn't anything like smog anymore.

The scene darkened. Crozier glanced at the sun. Something had eclipsed it, one of the big orbital platforms, most likely. He smiled. As if it could be anything else.

The sun reappeared, dazzling him. He turned back to the office, blinking away afterimages. His vision cleared to show Melissa smiling from the holo. He dropped his eyes and changed the image to Aggie's.

4)

He planned to turn in early that night after wrapping up some overdue paperwork in the hope it would settle his mind. An hour passed before he admitted it wasn't working. He kept glancing at the phone key, even reaching once to touch it. Finally he cleared the screen and sat back.

Alton was following his daughter. No direct evidence, but gut feeling told him it had to be so. She might be working with someone else or running it through channels as if it were legitimate business, but that was metaphysics. Mel was the one behind it, and if Alton didn't know that yet he soon would.

But what to do? Warn her, confront her, get her away from here? He didn't have that right. He was a security commissioner, pledged to enforce the martial law in place since the Greening. It was his career, his life work, his vocation.

A parade of images flashed through his mind: piles of dark-skinned bodies burning, burning; hordes of doomed refugees trying to flee the death they carried within them; dead cities, dead countries, dead continents.

You had to grow up under that shadow to know what it meant. Crozier had, and he understood. Mel didn't. How could she, if she was doing this thing, aiding an arrogant fool in developing the same black science used to commit the worst crime in history?

The penalty for unauthorized biotech research was death. Immediate execution, all cases. No appeal, no consideration, no mercy.

. . . *but she is my daughter.*

He dropped his head. At least she was safe tonight. At home, away from the office, with no one to . . . .

He looked up at the monitor then bent over the keyboard. Tapping into the office DB he entered his code and waited to be cleared. The screen blinked, he put his palm against it and then he was in.

Two minutes later he had what he needed. Telling the comp to exit, he got up and went for his coat.

A low knoll stood opposite Mel's place with a road running across it. Switching off his headlights, he nosed past a clump of brush far enough to see downhill.

Her lights were on and at least a half-dozen cars were parked on the block, a lot more than usual. He called the car system up and told it to set the windows to IR. A second later the night flared into ghastly daylight, greenish and sickly. He leaned forward to survey the street.

There it was, half a block down. A late-model Morovich, dark blue. "Give me a plate readout on the third car down, right side," he said. "Don't query its system."

The heads-up display flashed the number. His jaw tightened. It was Alton, all right.

He thumped back in the seat. He'd like to go down there and . . . . But that was senseless, and besides, there was a better way.

Picking up the mike, he called for a secure channel and then the city cops. "911" a woman's voice said.

He rattled off his code, followed by a description of the car. "I want a lifter to roust him, pronto."

There was a pause. "Who is this?"

"This is Commissioner Crozier."

"Bullshit."

"Patrolman," he said patiently. "Enter that code I gave you, please."

"I'm sorry, sir," the voice whispered a second later. "I'll get a bod over right away."

"Thank you," Crozier said.

The lifting body appeared sooner than he expected. He nearly missed its approach: a black shape gliding stealthily over the hills, lighting up and letting loose a whoop as it drew above the street. A spotlight speared the car, and Crozier smiled to himself. He'd dearly love to see the expression on Alton's face right now.

The lifter settled onto the pavement, blocking his line of sight. He leaned forward anxiously. Alton might ID himself and send them packing. Not likely, but it could happen.

The drapes in Mel's front window were pulled back, and someone looked out. He glanced over, feeling a sense of warmth, but then realized that it wasn't Melissa. He squinted in puzzlement as two more figures appeared, then a movement from the lifter drew his attention.

It was the car, pulling away. He watched it with satisfaction, paying no attention as the bod took off. He was about to tell his car to start when it occurred to him that Alton just might come back.

He sighed and looked over at the house. The drapes were back in place, no one in sight. It seemed that he'd be making a night of it, just like old times before he'd wound up behind a desk. Too bad he didn't smoke anymore.

A half hour passed and Mel's door opened. A procession of young women emerged, waving and calling goodbyes. Crozier smiled to himself. A bit of a party—he sometimes forgot that she had a life of her own.

A short time later the lights went out and Crozier settled back to wait. It was early hours before he left for home.

5)
"Thought you'd want to see this right away, Steve, " Noah said. They were in the vid room, two floors down from Crozier's office. The door was locked, and they were alone.

At the front of the room the screen was lit up—there hadn't been time to process the footage for holo projection. The bug had been placed on the rear bumper of the car, giving a clear view of the street.

Crozier jerked forward as a figure walked up to the car. Short jacket, khaki pants, sunglasses. There had been no attempt at disguise: It was Ricelli, all right.

He passed the sensor, and a second later the car door whined open. Crozier heard Mel's voice. "What is it? I thought you didn't want to . . . ."

". . . need more money."

There was a pause before Mel spoke again. When she did her voice was high-pitched and throaty. "But you said . . . ."

"What I said was that the prelim work was nearly complete." Ricelli's voice was blasé, almost sarcastic. "You want application, it's another story . . . ." He went on, using terms that Crozier was not familiar with: plasmids, nucleotides, replicons.

"Oh, God, I don't know."

"Hey," Ricelli said, "I don't want to sound blunt, but it's a little rougher for me . . . ."

Crozier looked away. Blackmail: That was the only word for it. The bastard had hooked her and was now bleeding her. He fought back an urge to leap to his feet and demand to know where Ricelli was this minute...

Noah cut the sound off. "The important thing is this." He adjusted the projector controls. The picture shifted a few feet to show the opposite side of the street. There, thirty yards back, was a Morovich, nearly black in the morning sunlight. "That's . . . ."

"Alton," Crozier said.

"Right." The picture froze, then faded. Crozier swung to face Noah. "And you haven't heard from him."

"Not a damn thing," Noah said, his face set as if carved from wood.

"Have we been able to trail him?"

Noah grimaced. "Shook us twice. Smooth. Don't know if it was deliberate or not." He pulled out the film cartridge and put it in his pocket. "I've authorized a lifter to track him from the air. Tyner will be piloting."

"Good." Crozier got up and walked to the door. "Keep me posted. And Noah . . . ."

There was no answer from behind him.

"If things go to hell . . . do what you have to."

"Sir." Noah's voice was barely audible.

Back upstairs Crozier queried his schedule and then cleared it. Lot of work piling up but only one handshaker scheduled for today, a delegation from a town called Truth or Consequences come around on a courtesy visit. He told the system to make his regrets.

A blank, miserable time later he looked at the clock. After three. Mel would be leaving her office in less than an hour.

Without thinking about it he found himself walking to the elevator.

It was a good thing he'd left when he had; Mel was heading home early. He watched her cross the lot, the cool breeze of early March ruffling her hair. As he got out of the car he noticed that the building he was facing—an old bar or restaurant—had deteriorated badly. It seemed ready to collapse at a touch. Lot of shoddy construction at the end of the 20th—he'd make a note to have it looked into.

He reached Mel as she was telling the car door to unlock. "Poppy!" she cried as she caught sight of him. "What's wrong?"

"Let's . . . ." He faltered, then found the words again. "Let's go somewhere and talk. Coffee, something . . . ."

Her face went cold. "What is it?"

Forcing himself to meet her eyes, he said, "Mel . . . Melissa. They know."

A flash of pain struck him as her eyes moved around

the lot. Did she actually think he'd lead them here? Could she really believe that?

She was staring into the open door, mouth a bitter line. "Who's 'they'?" she said. "That aide of yours, the one who never talks?"

Crozier said nothing. She threw her head back, defiant. "Dad, you've got to hold him off for me."

Closing his eyes, Crozier shook his head.

"A few days, that's all. I've got it worked out. Once Larry gets the treatment, I'll take him south, across the wild country. The roads are still good. Straight through to Greater Brazil, where there's people . . . ."

"No, Mel . . . ."

"Poppy, please! I don't want much."

"Mel, if there was any chance at all, I would, believe me. But there isn't. There is no treatment. Ricelli lied to you."

She stared at him, teeth clenched. "Your grandson," she spat. "You care about your grandson."

She slid into the front seat, and the door began to close. The whine of the motor went up in pitch as Crozier grabbed the frame.

Mel was crying now. "They were working on it," she said. "He showed me research papers. They were near a breakthrough . . . ."

"They were working on nothing!" Crozier slapped the roof. "The Greening, that's what they were working on. Olbers and his pack of fiends. They made a killer plague and that's all!"

She raised her head and the look in her eyes silenced him. "The Greening." Her voice was bitter. "I don't want to hear about that. It was a long time ago, and I didn't have

223

anything to do with it. And Larry didn't have anything to do with it."

"Do you know what you're saying, Mel? Four billion . . . ."

"I didn't kill those people, Daddy."

He straightened up, trying to think of something else. The door motor whined on. "You're going to burn it out," Mel said.

He hesitated before stepping away. The door shut, the noise dying with a note that sounded like relief. Mel didn't turn her head as the car hummed to life, but when it pulled out, she glanced back at him, a second's look, packed full of meaning.

Aggie used to do that, he told himself. A parting shot: You will do what I want. He lifted his arm as if to wave. And I would, honey, I would.

Head down, he turned back to his car. He sensed something off, without quite being aware of it, and when he looked up, it was directly at the blue-black car parked at the end of the street.

Clenching his fists, he walked toward it. As it pulled away, he broke into a run, but when he reached the corner, it was gone.

Back at the office he accessed the classified files and got the name and code of the government's top authority on biotech. A Dr. Vincent, in Minneapolis. Setting the comp to vid mode, he keyed in the code and waited. The screen lit up with a message symbol, but he ordered it to bull on through.

A moment passed before anyone appeared. Crozier inspected the room: a library, with a lot of esoteric-looking books and discpaks on the shelves. A man came into sight, middle-aged, gray-haired, an untied ascot and a jacket across his arm. "Yes?" he said, sounding annoyed.

Crozier identified himself, adding that he had a question. "Well, I'm due for dinner . . . ." Vincent said, but peered intently at the screen and shrugged. "But go ahead."

As he poured out the story, Vincent interrupted him with questions about the shape that Larry was in, the progress of the disease, the nature of the treatment Ricelli had promised. Crozier answered as best he could.

". . . so what I'm asking is this: is it possible? Can it be done?" He realized he was nearly shouting and forced calm on himself.

Vincent sighed. "Eight years old," he muttered. "Commissioner, I'll put this in layman's terms as well as I can. What you're talking about is gene therapy, from the DNA level up. There were experiments done with that technique at the turn of the century, some successful, some not. But at best they cured only the disease itself. Long-term damage, in particular from the antibiotic reaction . . . ." He shook his head. "There are a lot of tales about what biotechnology was capable of . . . ."

"I've heard them."

". . . but they're only tales. That type of treatment was in its infancy before the Plague. If research had continued unbroken over the past five decades, maybe. A good chance. But as it stands, no. Utterly out of the question."

"Could this research have been done underground?"

A slight smile appeared on Vincent's face. "What is sometimes called the Invisible College doesn't actually exist. A few cranks, a researcher trying an experiment or two, the occasional self- styled Prometheus, as in this case. The problem has been grossly exaggerated for bureaucratic reasons, which I'm sure you understand better than I. It could easily be answered by opening up limited research under strict controls . . . . But that's heresy, of course."

"I see. Thank you."

Vincent nodded. "Good luck."

After he signed off, Crozier tried Mel's home comp. The call had been recorded; he'd play it for her and then . . . .

But he couldn't get through. The screen displayed a do-not-disturb signal and that was all. It was no use trying to break in—the software she had was as good as his own.

He got his coat; the day was growing cold. Driving over he switched on the car's law signal so that the lights turned green as he neared them. He reached the house in ten minutes.

It was dark, and Mel's car was gone. Of course, he told himself. You didn't expect her to wait, did you? For the guy who doesn't talk much to kick the door in, with Poppy right behind.

When he got home he poured a drink and tossed it down. The next he sipped, deciding to limit himself to two. He needed a clear head, and he couldn't put it away like he used to.

He sat down at his desk, trying to see a way out. His eyes fell on a picture of Aggie, an early one, taken right after they were married. God, she looked so young. I could use that steady head of yours now, darling. But thank Christ you didn't live to see this.

He lifted the glass but found it empty. Pushing the chair back he stared at the lower desk drawer. He asked it to unlock and pulled it open. Inside there was a pistol, a box of ammo, and a stubby metal tube resembling an old-style electric razor.

He picked it up. A stungun, of a type called a tickler. A nasty weapon, throwing an electric charge along an ionized beam. Kill a grizzly from ten feet away with no sign of what had done it. But you had to be within ten feet.

He squeezed the cold alloy. He could get ten feet from Alton.

The phone rang as he was getting up. When he lifted the receiver the voice was crisp and cool: "Sir."

6)

"When did you find him?"

"Half past four," Noah said. "Old Chicano neighborhood north of town. Abandoned house, just like we thought."

Crozier was about to ask why he hadn't been told immediately but held back. Whatever reasons Noah had were bound to be good ones. He looked out the car window. Noah seemed to be driving awful slowly but that was probably only his own anxiety working on him.

"Heard from BuTech," Noah was saying. "Real interested. Seems that Alton has a rep as a bully. They're sending some people . . . ."

"Fine. But what about Ricelli?"

"Alton left a half-hour ago. To eat, evidently. Tyner broke in, found the suspect in the back room handcuffed to a radiator. Badly beaten." Noah paused. "Near dead, in fact. Alton was asking him questions."

"About me."

Noah's expression remained unchanged, but his eyes flicked to Crozier. "Right. Ties in with what BuTech told me. Alton was supposed to bring Ricelli in, but he likes toying

227

with suspects. It blew back on him this time. Ricelli got spooked and skipped."

Crozier nodded. It all fit: Alton had botched the hunt back east and headed out here as soon as the prey had been tracked down, probably suppressing the info, planning to bring the trophy in on his own. Once here and aware of the situation he'd decided to increase his bag. What better way to make amends for a fumbled investigation, to save a threatened career? A sector commissioner involved in a biotech conspiracy and his daughter, too. Welcome home, Alton. All is forgiven.

In his coat pocket the weight of the tickler seemed to increase. He reached down and squeezed it through the fabric.

They were driving through a lost neighborhood now. Old homes, long abandoned and falling to the years. Some of them burnt out, some with roofs collapsed and walls slumped into the street. Those who had lived here were long buried, victims of a foul and never-ending crime. In the fading light it looked like nothing less than the city of Dis itself.

Noah pulled into a driveway. A ranch house, much like Mel's. They drove past the building into the yard beyond. As they came to a stop, a man appeared from behind the ruined garage. Tyner, Crozier saw as he got out of the car.

A lifter was parked in the next yard, crushing a stand of dead, sand-choked bushes. One of Tyner's men stood next to it, a figure of menace in the bleak twilight. Crozier ignored him and went on to what lay sprawled in the dry grass.

Ricelli. Badly beaten, but that wasn't what had killed him, Crozier was certain of that. He said nothing as he stepped away from the body. The penalty for biotech was always death.

There was a shout from the street, the sound of a scuffle. Crozier turned in that direction.

"What the hell," a voice cried out, more fearful than angry. It was followed by low mutters and then footsteps. Alton came into sight, half-dragged by two more men.

"What is this, Crozier?" Alton yelled, trying for fury but failing miserably. "What do you . . . ." He caught sight of the body and his eyes went wide.

One of the men holding him handed something to Noah. A gun: an old-style piece called an automatic. Noah looked it over, hefting it in his hand.

"I called you, Crozier," Alton said rapidly. "Just now. They told me you weren't around . . . ."

He fell silent as Noah snapped a cartridge into the chamber, took a step and fired into Ricelli's body. The corpse jumped slightly, as if just now giving up the ghost.

Swinging toward Alton, Noah dropped the gun on the dead grass then reached into his jacket and pulled out another.

Staring at him open-mouthed, Alton let out a moan. The men at his side dropped their visors and moved away. "Oh, my God . . . ." Alton said, looking around at the dark men who ringed him in, the remnants, the figures who carried the image of a race's guilt.

"Crozier . . . ." His voice was barely audible.

Stepping up to Noah, Crozier raised his hand. Noah gave him the gun. He found the safety and clicked it off.

Alton collapsed, his fingers digging into the drifted sand. "*Crozier!*" he shrieked, his voice distorted beyond measure.

Crozier met the man's eyes. Alton gazed back, shaking

his head at what he found there. As Crozier moved, he covered his face and wailed.

After a moment Crozier turned and handed the pistol to Noah. The men moved away, one of them lifting his visor. It was Tyner, and Crozier saw that he was grinning. He held out his palm, and another trooper slapped it, a ritual Crozier had never quite understood.

Alton's hands dropped, and he looked up at them, his face wet. He tried to speak, but all that emerged was a croak. Swallowing harshly, he forced the words out. "What do I tell them?"

"Straight cooperation, first to last," Noah said. "Track, apprehension, attempted escape. You can have the kill."

Alton nodded and got shakily to his feet.

"Report's already entered. You'd better read it well before they debrief you, sonny."

Turning to the lifter, Noah gestured at the body. "Let's get this cleaned up." Crozier watched as they brought out a stretcher, feeling the chill air for the first time. A cold night, as only the desert could make it.

Alton was wiping his face with his sleeve. He stooped for his gun, then raised his head fearfully before picking it up and slipping it in his waistband.

There was a screech of brakes from the street and a moment later voices. Crozier recognized one of them as Berg's and turned to see him leading two people around the garage, a short redheaded woman and a man who appeared to be Latin. As Berg studied the scene in puzzlement, the woman went over to Alton. She pointed at the stretcher. "Ricelli?"

Alton nodded. He'd nearly pulled himself together, but a trace of his terror remained.

"Well, it's a damn good thing you got him." She glanced at Crozier. "Or did you?"

"It's his," Crozier said.

"Come on then," the woman said. "You've got a lot of explaining to do."

"My office," Crozier said loudly. She made a face and shrugged.

Noah appeared beside him, quiet as night, and they walked out of the yard. As they reached the car Crozier said, "Is my daughter . . . ."

"Old house in the high country, sir. She'll be okay."

Crozier sighed and got in. As the motor started he turned his head. "My thanks, Noah."

The car was too dark to see his expression. "Sir."

It was morning before he talked to Mel. He got as far as telling her that everything was all right before she hung up.

(7)

Two weeks passed before he saw her again. It was early afternoon, and he was preparing for a meeting with the governor-elect of New Mexico, the first since the Greening. A get-acquainted session, more or less—there would be quite a few more before she was ready to take office. The woman was a professor of sociotechnics from a second-rate engineering college and had some strange ideas about what a governorship involved. It wouldn't be easy.

The door opened as he was going over some resource data. When he looked up, Mel had already reached the desk. She's growing old, was his first thought: Her hair was getting thin, her skin starting to fade . . . .

He got up and was smiling before he caught her expression. "Mel?"

"He's dead, Poppy." She stepped around the desk and gazed up at him, eyes narrowed to slits, mouth twisted. "Larry's dead."

Her husband, he thought, but behind that he knew. "How?"

"That night out in the mountains . . . ." Her voice broke. "It was so cold. He got sick and then it was pneumonia . . . ."

You didn't call me, Crozier thought. My grandson dying, dead, and you alone, and you didn't let me know.

She was staring at a point below his face, hand covering her mouth as if to hold back the sounds of grief. He said the first thing he could think of. "Now he's like everyone else."

Her face changed as she turned away. He reached after her. "Melissa . . . ."

When she swung around all he saw was rage. She struck him full-handed across the face. He took it unmoving and the one that followed as well.

"Mel," he called as she ran to the door. "Wait . . . ." But his hand was raised to nothing, and after a time he sat back down.

Aggie's gaze was fixed on him, with no more reproach in it than there ever had been. He moved his head, and as her smile broadened he recalled how she had looked those last days, as the cancer had taken her. They'd been working on cancer before the Greening. A cure had been right around the corner.

He touched the still-aching skin of his face. A line occurred to him, or half of one, an old quotation from somewhere. The heart has reasons . . . .

He didn't know that he'd said it aloud until a voice

232

completed it "... that reason knows not."

Noah was standing in the doorway, hands behind his back. He nodded at Crozier. "Our governor is waiting, sir."

"So she is." Crozier rose from the chair, then paused to lift his hand to the holo. He didn't look as it changed to the face that would be waiting when he returned but walked across the office and followed Noah out into the hall.

Listening to Brahms

by Suzy McKee Charnas

Charnas is best known for her classic vampire novel, *The Vampire Tapestry*. Her other novels include *Motherlines*, *Walk to the End of the World*, and *Dorothea Dreams*. Although only an occasional writer of short fiction, most of the stories she does write receive critical acclaim. "Boobs," a teenage-girl-as-werewolf story, won the Hugo Award, and "Advocates," a novelette co-authored with Chelsea Quinn Yarbro and featuring both authors' most famous vampires, was nominated for the Bram Stoker Award.

"Listening to Brahms" (*Omni*, September 1986), one of her finest achievements in fiction, was nominated for the Nebula Award. The novelette is reminiscent in scope of Olaf Stapledon's classic novel *Last and First Men*. Despite its satirical aspect, "Listening to Brahms" is ultimately tragic (at least for humanity) and is a lovely melancholy ode to Earth.

LISTENING TO BRAHMS

Suzy McKee Charnas

Entry 1: They had already woken up Chandler and Ross. They did me third. I was supposed to be up first so I could check the data on the rest of our crew during their cold sleep, but how would a bunch of aliens know that?

Our ship is full of creatures with peculiar eyes and wrinkled skin covered with tiny scales, a lot like lizards walking around on their hind legs. Their skins are grayish or greenish or even bluish sometimes. They have naked-looking faces—no hair—with features that seem polished smooth. The first ones I met had wigs on, and they wore evening clothes and watered-silk sashes with medals. I was too numb-brained to laugh, and now I don't feel like it. They all switched to jumpsuits once the formalities were over. I keep waiting for them to unzip their jumpsuits and then their lizard suits and climb out, regular human beings. I keep waiting for the joke to be over.

They speak English, some with accents, some not. They have breathy voices and talk very softly to us. That may be because of what they have to say. They say Earth burned itself up, which is why we never got our wake-up signal and

were still in the freezer when they found us. Chandler be-
lieves them. Ross doesn't. I won't know what the others
think until they're unfrozen.

I sit looking through the view plate at Earth, such as it
is. I know what the lizards say is true, but I don't think I
really believe it. I think mostly that I'm dead or having a
terrible dream.

Entry 2: Steinbrunner killed himself (despite their best
efforts to prevent anything like that, the lizards say). Sue
Anne Beamish, fifth to be thawed, won't talk to anybody.
She grits her teeth all the time. I can hear them grinding
whenever she's around. It's very annoying.

The lead lizard's name is Captain Midnight. He says he
knows it's not the most appropriate name for a spaceflight
commander, but he likes the sound of it.

It seems that on their home planet the lizards have been
fielding our various Earth transmissions, both radio and TV,
and they borrow freely from what they've found there. They
are given native names, but if they feel like it later they take
Earth-type names instead. Those on Captain Midnight's ship
all have Earth-type names. Luckily the names are pretty
memorable, because I can't tell one alien from another
except by the name badges they wear on their jumpsuits. I
look at them sometimes and I wonder if I'm crazy. Can't
afford to be, not if I've got to deal on a daily basis with
things that look as if they walked out of a Walt Disney
cartoon feature.

They revive us one by one and try to make sure nobody
else cuts their wrists like Steinbrunner. He cut the only way
that can't be fixed.

I look out the viewplate at what's left of the earth and
let the talk slide over me. We can't raise anything from down

there. I can't raise anything inside me either. I can only look and look and let the talk slide over me. Could I be dead after all? I feel dead.

Entry 3: Captain Midnight says now that we're all up he would be honored beyond expression of we would consent to come back to Kondra with him and his crew in their ship. *Kondra* is their name for their world. Chu says she's worked out where and what it is in our terms, and she keeps trying to show me on the star charts. I don't look; I don't care. I came up here to do studies on cryogenic nutrition in space, not to look at star charts.

It doesn't matter what I came up here to do. Earth is a moon with a moon now. *Nutrition* doesn't mean anything, not in connection with anything human. There's nothing to nourish. There's just this airless rock, like all the other airless rocks rolling around in space.

I took the data the machines recorded about us while we slept, and I junked it. Chu says I did a lot of damage to some of our equipment in the process. I didn't set out to do that, but it felt good, or something like good, to go on from wiping out information to smashing metal. I've assured everybody that I won't freak out like that again. It doesn't accomplish anything, and I felt foolish afterward. I'm not sure they believe me. I'm not sure I believe my own promise.

Morris and Myers say they won't go with the Kondrai. They say they want to stay here in our vessel just in case something happens down there or in case some other space mission survived and shows up looking for whatever's left, which is probably only us.

Captain Midnight says they can rig a beacon system on our craft to attract anybody who does come around and let them know where we've gone. I can tell the lizards are not going to let Morris and Myers stay here and die.

They say, the Kondrai do, that they didn't actually come here for us. After several generations of receiving and enjoying Earth's transmissions, Kondran authorities decided to borrow a ship from a neighboring world and send Earth an embassy from Kondra, a mission of goodwill.

First contact at last, and there's nobody here but the seven of us. Tough on the Kondrai. They expected to find a whole worldful of us, glued to our screens and speakers. Tough shit all around.

I have dreams so terrible there are no words.

Entry 4: There's nothing for us to do on the Kondran ship, which is soft and leathery inside its alloy shell. I have long talks with Walter Drake, who is head of mission. Walter Drake is female, I think. Walter Duck.

If I can make a joke, does that mean I'm crazy?

It took me a while to figure out what was wrong with the name. Then I said, "Look, it's Sir Walter *Raleigh* or Sir *Francis* Drake."

She said, "But we don't always just copy. I have chosen to commemorate two great voyagers."

I said, "And they were both males."

She said, "That's why I dropped the *Sir*."

Afterward I can't believe these conversations. I resent the end of the world—my world, going on as a bad joke with Edgar Rice Burroughs aliens.

Myers and Morris play chess with each other all day and won't talk to anybody. Most of us don't like to talk to each other right now. We can't look in each others eyes, for some reason. There's an excuse in the case of not looking the lizards in the eyes. They have this nictitating membrane. It's unsettling to look at that.

All the lizards speak English and at least one other Earth language. Walter Drake says there are several native languages on Kondra, but they aren't spoken in the population centers anymore. Kondran culture, in its several major branches, is very old. It was once greater and more complex than our own, she says, but then it got simple again, and the population began to drop. The whole species was, in effect, beginning to close down. When our signals were first picked up, something else began to happen: a growing trend toward population increase and a young generation fascinated by Earth culture. The older Kondrai, who had gone back to living like their ancestors in the desert, didn't object. They said fine, let the youngsters do as they choose as long as they let the oldsters do likewise.

I had to walk away when Walter Drake told me about this. It started me thinking about my own people I left back on Earth, all dead now. I won't put their names down. I was crying. Now I've stopped, and I don't want to start again. It makes my eyes hurt.

Walter Drake brought me some tapes of music that they've recorded from our broadcasts. They collect our signals, everything they can, through something they call the Retrieval Project. They reconstruct the broadcasts and record them and store the recordings in a huge library for study. Our classical music has a great following there.

I've been listening to some Bach partitas. My mother played the piano. She sometimes played Bach.

Entry 5: Sibelius, Symphony No. 2 in D, Op. 43; Tchaikovsky, Variations on a Rococo Theme, Op.33; Rachmaninoff, Symphonic Dances, Op.45; Mozart, Clarinet Quintet in A major, K581; Sibelius, Symphony No.2 in D, Op. 43; Sibelius, Symphony No. 2 in D, Op. 43

Entry 6: Chandler is alive, Ross is alive, Beamish is alive, Chu is alive, Morris is alive, Myers is alive, and I am alive. But that doesn't count. I mean I can't count it. Up. To mean anything. *Why* are we alive?

Entry 7: Myers swallowed a chess piece. The lizards operated on him somehow and saved his life.

Entry 8: Woke up from a dream wondering if maybe we did die in our ship and my "waking life" in the Kondran ship is really just some kind of after-death hallucination. Suppose I died, suppose we all actually died at the same moment Earth died? It wouldn't make any difference. Earth's people are all dead and someplace else or nowhere, but we are *here*. We are separate.

They're in contact with their home planet all the time. Chu is fascinated by their communications technology, which is wild, she says. Skips over time or folds up space—I don't know, I'm just a nutrition expert. Apparently on Kondra now they are making up their own human-style names instead of lifting them ready-made. (Walter Drake was a pioneer in this, I might point out.) Captain Midnight has changed his name. He is henceforth to be known as Vernon Zeno Ellerman.

Bruckner and Mahler symphonies, over and over, fill a lot of time. Walter Drake says she is going to get me some fresh music, though I haven't asked for any.

Entry 9: Beamish came and had a talk with me. She looked fierce.

"Listen, Flynn," she said, "we're not going to give up."

"Give up what?" I said.

"Don't be so obtuse," she said between her teeth. "The human race isn't ended as long as even a handful of us are still alive and kicking."

I am alive, though I don't know why (I now honestly do not recall the exact nature of the experiments I was onboard our craft to conduct). I'm not sure I'm kicking, and I told her so.

She grinned and patted my knee. "Don't worry about it, Flynn. I don't mean you should take up where you left off with Lily Chu." That happened back in training. I didn't even remember it until Beamish said this. "Nobody's capable right now, which is just as well. Besides, the women in this group are not going to be anybody's goddamn brood mares, science-fiction traditions to the contrary."

"Oh," I said. I think.

She went on to say that the Kondrai have or can borrow the technology to develop children for us in vitro. All we have to do is furnish the raw materials.

I said fine. I had developed another terrible headache. I've been having headaches lately.

After she left I tried some music. Walter Drake got me *Boris Godunov*, but I can't listen to it. I can't listen to anything with people's voices. I don't know how to tell this to Walter Drake. Don't want to tell her. It's none of her business anyhow.

Entry 10: Chu and Morris are sleeping together. So much for Beamish's theory that nobody is capable. With Myers not up to playing chess yet, I guess Morris had to find something to do.

Chu said to me, "I'm sorry, Michael."

I felt this little, far-off sputtering like anger somewhere deep down, and then it went out. "That's okay," I said. And it is.

Chandler has been spending all his time in the communications cell of the ship with another lizard, one with a French name that I can't remember. Chandler tells us he's learning a lot about Kondran life. I tune him out when he talks like this. I never go to the communications cell. The whole thing gives me a headache. Everything gives me a headache except music.

Entry 11: I was sure it would be like landing in some kind of imitation world, a hodgepodge of phony bits and pieces copied from Earth. That's why I wouldn't go out for two K-days after we landed.

Everybody was very understanding. Walter Drake stayed onboard with me.

"We have fixed up a nice hotel where you can all be together," she told me, "like the honored guests that you are."

I finally got off and went with the others when she gave me the music recordings to take with me. She got me a playback machine. I left the Mozart clarinet quintet behind, and she found it and brought it after me. But I won't listen to it. The clarinet sound was made by somebody's living breath, somebody who's dead now, like all of them. I can't stand to hear that sound.

The hotel was in a suburb of a city, which looked a little like L.A., though not as much as I had expected. Later sometime I should try to describe the city. There's a hilly part, something like San Francisco, by the sea. We asked to go over there instead. They found us a sort of rooming house of painted wood with a basement. Morris and Chu have taken the top floor, though I don't think they sleep together anymore.

Ross has the apartment next door to me. She's got her own problems. She threw up when she first set foot on

Kondra. She throws up almost every day, says she can't help it.

There are invitations for us to go meet the locals and participate in this and that, but the lizards do not push. They are so damned considerate and respectful. I don't go anywhere. I stay in my room and listen to music. Handel helps me sleep.

Entry 12: Four and a half K-years have passed. I stopped doing this log because Chandler showed me his. He was keeping a detailed record of what was happening to us, what had happened, what he thought was going to happen. Then Beamish circulated her version, and Dr. Birgit Nilson, the lizard in charge of our mental health, started encouraging us all to contribute what we could to a "living history" project.

I was embarrassed to show anybody my comments. I am not a writer or an artist like Myers has turned out to be. (His pictures are in huge demand here, and he has a whole flock of Kondran students.) If Chandler and Beamish were writing everything down, why should I waste my time doing the same thing?

Living history of what, for whom?

Also I didn't like what Chandler wrote about me and Walter Drake. Yes, I slept with her. One of us would have tried it, sooner or later, with one lizard or another. I just happened to be the one who did. I had better reasons than any of the others. Walter Drake had been very kind to me.

I was capable all right (still am). But the thought of going to bed with Lily or Sue Anne made my skin creep, though I couldn't have said why. On the Kondran ship I used to jerk off and look at the stuff in my hand and wonder what the hell it was doing there: Didn't my body know that my world is gone, my race, my species?

Sex with Walter Drake is different from sex with a woman. That's part of what I like about it. And another thing. Walter Drake doesn't cry in her sleep.

Walter and I did all right. For a couple of years I went traveling alone, at the government's expense—like everything we do here—all over Kondra. Walter was waiting when I got back. So we went to live together away from the rooming house. The time passed like a story or a dream. Not much sticks in my head now from that period. We listened to a lot of music together. Nothing with flutes or clarinet, though. String music, percussion, piano music, horns only if they're blended with other sounds—that's what I like. Lots of light stuff, Dukas and Vivaldi and Milhaud.

Anyway, that period is over. After all this time Chu and Morris have committed suicide together. They used a huge old pistol one of them must have smuggled all this way. Morris, probably. He always had a macho hang-up.

Beamish goes around saying, "Why? Why?" At first I thought this was the stupidest question I'd ever heard. I was seriously worried that maybe these years on Kondran food and water had addled her mind through some weird allergic reaction.

Then she said, "We're so close, Flynn. Why couldn't they have waited? I wouldn't have let them down."

I keep forgetting about her in vitro project. It's going well, she says. She works very hard with a whole team of Kondrai under Dr. Boleslav Singh, preparing a cultural surround for the babies she's developing. She comes in exhausted from long discussions with Dr. Boleslav Singh and Dr. Birgit Nilson and others about the balance of Earth information and Kondran information to be given to the human babies. Beamish wants to make little visitors out of the babies. She says it's providential that we were found by the Kondrai—a race that has neatly caught and preserved everything transmitted by us about our own culture and our past. So now all that stuff is just waiting to be used, she says, to bridge the gap in our race's history. "The gap," that's what she calls it. She has a long-range plan of getting a ship for the in vitros to use when they grow up and want to go find a planet they can turn into another Earth. This seems crazy to me. But she is entitled. We all are.

I've moved back into the rooming house. I feel it's my duty, now that we're so few. Walter has come with me.

Entry 13: Mozart's piano concertos, especially Alfred Brendel's renditions, all afternoon. I have carried out my mission after all—to answer the question: What does a frozen Earthman eat for breakfast? The answer is music. For lunch? Music. Dinner? Music. This frozen Earthman stays alive on music.

Entry 14: A year and a half together in the rooming house, and Walter Drake and I have split up. Maybe it has nothing to do with being in the rooming house with the other humans. Divorce is becoming very common among young Kondrai. So is something like hair. They used to wear wigs. Now they have developed a means of growing featherlike down on their heads and in their armpits, etc.

When Walter came in with a fine dusting of pale fuzz on her pate, I told her to pack up and get out. She says she understands, she's not bitter. She doesn't understand one gaddamned thing.

Entry 15: Beamish's babies, which I never went to see, have died of an infection that whipped through the whole lot of them in three days. The Kondran medical team taking care of them caught it, too, though none of them died. A few are blind from it, perhaps permanently.

Myers took pictures of the little corpses. He is making paints from his photos. Did I put it in here that swallowing a chess piece did not kill Myers? Maybe it should have, but it seems nothing can kill Myers. He is a tough as rawhide. But he doesn't play chess, not since Morris killed himself. There are Kondrai who play very well, but Myers refuses their invitations. You can say that for him at least.

He just takes photographs and paints.

I'm not really too sorry about the babies. I don't know which would be worse, seeing them grow up as a little clutch of homeless aliens among the lizards or seeing them adapt and become pseudo-Kondrai. I don't like to think about explaining to them how the world they really belong to blew itself to hell. (Lily Chu is the one who went over the signals the Kondrai salvaged about that and sorted out the sequence of events. That was right before she killed herself.) We slept through the end of our world. Bad enough to do it, worse to have to talk about it. I never talk about it now, not even with the Kondrai. With Dr. Birgit Nilson I discuss food, of course, and health. I find these boring and absurd subjects, though I cooperate out of politeness. I also don't want to get stuck on health problems, like Chandler, who has gone through one hypochondriacal frenzy after another in the past few years.

Beamish says she will try again. Nothing will stop her. She confided to Ross that she thinks the Kondrai deliberately let the babies die, maybe even infected them on purpose. "They don't want us to revive our race," she said to Ross. "They're trying to take our place. Why should they encourage the return of the real thing?"

Ross told me Beamish wants her to help arrange some kind of escape from Kondra, God knows to where. Ross is worried about Beamish. "What," she says, "if she goes off the deep end and knifes some innocent lizard medico? They might lock us all up permanently."

Ross does not want to be locked up. She plays the cello all the time, which used to be a hobby of hers. The lizards were only too pleased to furnish her an instrument. A damn good one, too, she says. What's more, she now has three Kondrai studying with her.

I don't care what she does. I walk around watching the Kondrai behave like us.

I have terrible dreams, still.

Symphonic music doesn't do it for me anymore, not even Sibelius. I can't hear enough of the music itself; there are too many voices. I listen to chamber pieces. There you can hear each sound, everything that happens between each sound and each other sound near it.

They gave me a free pass to the Library of the Retrieval Project. I spend a lot of time there, listening.

Entry 16: Fourteen K-years later. Beamish eventually did get three viable Earth-style children out of her last lot. Two of them drowned in a freak accident at the beach a week ago. The third one, a girl named Melissa, ran away. They haven't been able to find her.

Our tissue contributions no longer respond, though Beamish keeps trying. She calls the Kondrai "Snakefaces" behind their backs.

Her hair is gray. So is mine.

Kondran news is all about the growing tensions between Kondra and the neighbor world it does most of its trading with. I don't know how that used to work in eco-

249

nomic terms, but apparently it's begun to break down. I never saw any of the inhabitants of that world, called Chadondal, except in pictures and Kondran TV news reports. Now I guess I never will. I don't care.

Something funny happened with the flu that killed all of Beamish's first babies. It seems to have mutated into something that afflicts the Kondrai the way cancer used to afflict human beings. This disease doesn't respond to the cure human researchers developed once they figured out that our cancer was actually a set of symptoms of an underlying disease. Kondran cancer is something all their own.

They are welcome to it.

Entry 17: I went up into the sandhills to have a look at a few of the Old Kondrai, the ones who never did buy into imitation Earth ways. Most of them don't talk English (they don't even talk much Kondran to each other), but they don't seem to mind if you hang around and watch them awhile.

They live alone or else in very small settlements on a very primitive level, pared down to basics. Your individual Old Kondran will have a small, roundish stone house or even a burrow or cave and will go fetch water every day and cook on a little cell-powered stove or a wood fire. They usually don't even have TV. They walk around looking at things or sit and meditate or dig in their flower gardens or carve things out of the local wood. Once in a while they'll get together for a dance or a sort of mass bask in the sun or to put on plays and skits and so on. These performances can go on for days. They have a sort of swap economy, which is honored elsewhere when they travel. You sometimes see these pilgrims in the city streets, just wandering around. They never stay long.

Some of the younger Kondrai have begun harking back to this sort of life, trying to create the same conditions in the cities, which is ridiculous. These youngsters act as if it's something absolutely basic they have to try to hang on to in the face of an invasion of alien ways. Earth ways.

This is obviously a backlash against the effects of the Retrieval Project. I keep an eye on developments. It's all fascinating and actually creepy. To me the backlash is uncannily reminiscent of those fundamentalist-nationalist movements—Christian American or Middle-Eastern Muslim or whatever—that made life such hell for so many people toward the end of our planet's life. But if you point this resemblance out, the anti-Retrieval Kondrai get furious because, after all, anything Earth-like is what they're reacting against.

I sometimes bring this up in conversation just to get a rise out of them.

If I'm talking to Kondrai who are part of the backlash, they invariably get furious. "No," they say, "we're just trying to turn back to our old, native ways!" They don't recognize this passion itself as something that humans, not Kondrai, were prone to. From what I can gather and observe, fervor, either reactionary or progressive, is something alien to native Kondran culture as it was before they started retrieving our signals. Their life was very quiet and individu-alized and pretty dull, as a matter of fact.

Sometimes I wish we'd found it like that instead of the way it had already become by the time we got here. Of course the Old Kondrai never would have sent us an em-bassy in the first place.

I talk to Dr. Birgit Nilson about all this a lot. We aren't exactly friends, but we communicate pretty well for a man and a lizard.

She says they have simply used human culture to

revitalize themselves.

I think about the Old Kondrai I saw poking around, growing the kind of flowers that attract the flying grazers they eat, or just sitting. I like that better. If they were a dying culture, they should have just gone ahead and died.

Entry 18: Ross has roped Chandler into her music making. Turns out he played the violin as a kid. They practice a lot in the rooming house. Sometimes Ross plays the piano, too. She's better on the cello. I sit on my porch, looking at the bay, and I sit.

Ross says the Kondrai as a group are fascinated by performance. Certainly they perform being human better and better all the time. They think of Earth's twentieth century as the Golden Age of Human Performance. How would they know? It's all secondhand here, everything.

I've been asked to join a nutritional-study team heading for Kondra-South, where some trouble spots are developing. I have declined. I don't care if they starve or why they starve. I had enough of looking at images of starvation on Earth, where we did it on a terrific scale. What a performance that was!

Also I don't want to leave here because then I wouldn't get to hear Ross and Chandler play. They do sonatas and duets and they experiment, not always very successfully, with adapting music written for other instruments. It's very interesting. Now that Ross is working on playing the piano as well as the cello, their repertoire has been greatly expanded.

They aren't nearly as good as the great musical performers of the Golden Age, of course. But I listen to them anyway whenever I can. There's something about live music. You get a hunger for it.

Entry 19: Myers has gone on a world tour. He is so

famous as an artist that he has rivals, and there are rival schools led by artists he himself has trained. He spends all his time with the snakes now, the ones masquerading as artists and critics and aesthetes. He hardly ever stops at the rooming house or comes by here to visit.

Sue Anne Beamish and I have set up house together across the bay from the rooming house. She's needed somebody around her ever since they found the dessicated corpse of little Melissa in the rubbish dump and worked out what had been done to her.

The Kondran authorities say they think some of the Kondrachalikipon (as the anti-Retrieval-backlash members call themselves now, meaning "return to Kondran essence") were responsible. The idea is that these Kondracha meant what they did as a symbolic rejection of everything the Retrieval Project has retrieved and a warning that Kondra will not be tuned into an imitation Earth without a fight.

When Dr. Birgit Nilson and I talked about this, I pointed out that the Kondracha, if it was them, didn't get it right. They should have dumped the kid's body on the Center House steps and then called a press conference. Next time they'll do it better, though, being such devoted students of our ways.

"I know that," she said. "What is becoming of us?"

Us meant "us Kondrai," of course, not her and me. She likes to think that we Earth guests have a special wisdom that comes from our loss and from a mystical blood connection with the culture that the Kondrai are absorbing. As if I spend my time thinking about that kind of thing. Dr. Birgit Nilson is a romantic.

I don't talk to Sue Anne about Melissa's death. I don't feel it enough, and she would know that. So many died before, what's one more kid's death now? A kid who could never have been human anyway because a human being is born on Earth and raised in a human society, like Sue Anne and me.

"We should have blown their ship up and us with it," she says, "on the way here."

She won't come with me to the rooming house to listen to Ross and Chandler play. They give informal concert evenings now. I go, even though the audience is ninety-eight percent lizard, because by now I know every recording of chamber music in the Retrieval Library down to the last scrape of somebody's chair during a live recital. The recordings are too faithful. I can just about tolerate the breath intake you hear sometimes when the first violinist cues a phrase. It's different with Ross and Chandler. Their live music makes the live sounds all right. Concerts are given by Kondran "artists" all the time, but I won't go to those.

For one thing, I know perfectly well that we don't hear sounds, we human beings, not sounds from outside. Our inner ear vibrates to the sound from outside, and we hear the sound that our own ear creates inside the head in response to that vibration. Now, how can the Kondran ear be exactly the same as ours? No matter how closely they've learned to mimic the sounds that our musicians produced, Kondran ears can't be hearing what human ears do when human music is played. A Kondran concert of human music is a farce.

Poor Myers. He missed the chance to take pictures of Melissa's dead body so he could make paintings of it later.

Entry 20: They are saying that the reason there's so much crime and violence now on Kondra isn't because of the population explosion at all. Some snake who calls himself Swami Nanda has worked out how the demographic growth is only a sign of the underlying situation.

According to him Kondra made an "astral agreement" to take in not only us living human survivors but the souls of all the dead of Earth. Earth souls on the astral plane, seeing that there were soon going to be no more human bodies on Earth to get born into, sent out a call for new bodies and a new world to inhabit. The Kondran souls on the astral plane, having pretty much finished their work on the material world of Kondra, agreed to let human souls take over the physical plant here, as it were. Now the younger generation is all Earth souls reborn as Kondrai on this planet, and they're re-creating conditions familiar to them from Earth.

I have sent this "Swami" four furious letters. He answered the last one very politely and at great length, explaining it all very clearly with the words he has stolen for his stolen metaphysical concepts.

Oh, yes: Another dozen K-years have passed. I might as well just say *years*. Kondran years are only a few days off our own, and Chandler has stopped keeping his Earth-time calendar since he's gotten so deep into music.

Chandler is now doing some composing, Ross tells me.

Ross rebukes me when I call the Kondrai snakes, talking to me as gently and reasonably as the Kondrai themselves always talk to us. That makes me sick, which is pretty funny when I recall how she used to vomit every day when we first came here. So she can stop telling me how to talk and warning me that it's no good to be a recluse. No good for what? And what would be better?

Nobody ever taught me to play any instrument. My parents said I had no talent, and they were right. I'm a listener, so I listen. I'm doing my job. I wouldn't go to the rooming house and talk to Ross at all except for the music.

255

They are getting really good. It's amazing. Once in a while I
spend a week at the Retrieval Library listening to the really
great performances that are recorded there, to make sure my
taste hasn't become degraded.

It hasn't. My two crew mates are converting themselves, by some miracle of dedication, into fine performers.

Last night I had to walk out in the middle of a
Beethoven sonata to be alone.

Entry 21: Sue Anne had a stroke last week. She is
paralyzed down her left side. I am staying with her almost
constantly because I know she can't stand having the snakes
around her anymore.

She blames me, I know, for having cooperated with
them. We all spent hours and hours with their researchers,
filling out their information about our dead planet. How
could we have refused? In the face of their courtesy and
considering how worried we all were about forgetting Earth
ourselves, how could we? Besides, we really had nothing
else to do.

She blames me anyhow, but I don't mind.

A wave of self-immolation is going on among young
Kondrai. They find themselves an audience and set themselves afire, and the watching Kondrai generally stand there
as if hypnotized by the flames and do nothing.

Dr. Birgit Nilson told me, "Your entire population died
out; many of them burnt up in an instant. This created much
karma, and those who are responsible must be allowed to
pay."

"You're a Nandist, then," I said. "Swami Nanda and
his reincarnation crap."

"I see no other explanation," she said.

"It all makes sense to you?" I said.

"Yes." She stroked her cheek with her orange-polished talons. "It's a loan: We have lent our beautiful material world and our species' bodies in exchange for your energetic souls and your rich, passionate culture."

They are the crazy ones, not us.

Entry 22: Some wild-eyed young snake with this top feathers dyed blue took a shot at the swami this morning with an old-fashioned thorn gun.

They caught him. We watched on the news. The would-be assassin sneers at the camera like a real Earth punk. Sue Anne glares back and snorts derisively.

Entry 23: Dreamed of my mother at her piano, but her hands were Kondran hands. The fingers were too long, and the nails were set like claws, and her skin was covered in minute, grayish scales.

I think she was playing Chopin.

Entry 24: Sometimes I wish I were a writer, to do all this justice. I might have some function as a survivor.

Look at Sue Anne: Except for some terrible luck, she would have created out of us a new posterity.

Myers is doing prints these days, but not on Earth themes anymore, though the Kondrai beg him to concentrate on what's "native" to him. He says his memory of Earth is no longer trustworthy, and besides, images of Kondra are native to the eyes of reborn Earth souls now. He accepts Nandism openly and goes around doing Kondran landscapes and portraits and so on. Well, nobody will have to miss any of that in my account, then. They can always look at Myers's pictures.

Walter Drake died last winter of Kondran cancer. I went to the funeral. For the first time I wore makeup.

Myers, the arrogant son of a bitch, condescended to

share a secret with me. He used this face paint, plus a close haircut or a feathered cap, to go out incognito among the snakes so he can observe them undisturbed. Age has smoothed his features and made him thin, like most Kondrai, and he's been getting away with it for years. Well, good for him. Look at what *they're* trying to get away with along those lines!

Being disguised has its advantages. I hadn't realized the pressure of being stared at all the time in public until I moved around without it.

They said, "Ashes to ashes and dust to dust," and I got dizzy and had to sit down on a bench

Entry 25: Four more years. My heart still checks out, Dr. Birgit Nilson tells me. I put on makeup and hang out in the bars, watching TV with the Kondrai, but not too often. Sometimes they make me so damn nervous, even after so long here. I forget what they are and what I am. I forget myself. I get scared that I'm turning senile.

When I get home Sue Anne gives me this cynical look, and my perspective is restored. I play copy-tapes of Dvorák for her. Also Schubert. She likes the French, though. I find them superficial.

To hear Brahms and Beethoven and Mozart, I go to the rooming house. I go whenever Ross and Chandler play. While the music sounds the constant crying inside me gets so big and so painful and beautiful that I can't contain it. So it moves outside me for a while, and I feel rested and changed. This is only an illusion, but wonderful.

Entry 26: Poor Myers got caught in a religious riot on the other side of the world. He was beaten to death by a Kondracha mob. I guess his makeup job was careless. Dr. Birgit Nilson, much aged and using a cane, came to make a personal apology, which I accepted for old times' sake.

"We caught two of them," she said. "the ringleaders of the Kondracha group that killed your poor Mr. Myers."

"Kondrachalations," I said. Couldn't help myself.

Dr. Birgit looked at me. "Forgive me," she said. "I shouldn't have come."

When I told Sue Anne about this, she slapped my face. She hasn't much strength even in her good arm these days. But I resented being hit and asked her why she did it.

"Because you were smiling, Michael."

"You can't cry all the time," I said.

"No," she said. "I wish we could."

Dr. Birgit Nilson says that Kondrai are now composing music in classical, popular, and "primitive" styles, all modeled on Earth music. I have not heard any of this new music. I do not want to.

Entry 27: At least Sue Anne didn't live to see this: They are now grafting lobes onto their ugly ear holes.

No, that's not the real news. The real news is about Kondra-South, where a splinter group of Kondracha extremists set up a sort of purist, Ur-Kondran state some years ago. They use only their version of Old Kondran farming methods, which is apparently not an accurate version. Their topsoil has been rapidly washing away in the summer floods.

Now they are killing newborns down there to have fewer mouths to feed. The pretext is that these newborns look like humans and are part of the great taint that everything Earthish represents to the pure. The official Kondrachalikipon line is that they are feeding themselves just fine, thank you. The truth seems to be mass starvation and infanticide.

After Sue Anne died, I moved back into the rooming

house. I have a whole floor to myself and scarcely ever go out. I watch Kondran TV a lot, which is how I keep track of their politics and so on. I stop looking for false notes that would reveal to any intelligent observer the hollowness of their performance of humanity. There isn't much except for my gut reaction. The Kondran claim to have preserved human culture by making it their own would be very convincing to anyone who didn't know better. Even their game shows look familiar. Young Kondrai go mad for music videos and deafening concerts by their own groups like the Bear Minimum and Dead Boring. I stare and stare at the screen, looking for slip ups. I am not sure that I would recognize one now if I saw one.

I hate the lizards. I miss her. I hate them.

Entry 28: Ross and Chandler have done the unthinkable. At last night's musicale they sprang one hell of a surprise.

They have trained two young Kondrai to a degree that satisfies them (particularly Gillokan Chukchonturanfis, who plays both violin and viola).

Now the four of them are planning to go out and perform in public together as the Retrieval String Quartet.

The Lost Earth String Quartet I could stomach, maybe. Or the Ghost String Quartet, or the Remnant String Quartet. But then, of course, how could Kondran musicians be in it?

I walked out in protest.

Ross says I am being unreasonable and cutting off my nose to spite my face, since as a quartet they have so much more music they can play. To hell with Ross. The traitress. Chandler, too.

Entry 29: I cut my hair and put on my makeup and managed to get myself one ticket, not as Michael Flynn the

Earthman but as a nameless Kondran. The debut concert of
the Retrieval String Quartet is the event of the year in the
city: a symbol of the passing of the torch of human culture,
they say. An outrage, the Kondracha scream. I keep my
thoughts to myself and lay my plans.

Lizards are pouring into the city for the event. Two
bombings have already occurred, credit for them claimed by
the Kondrachalikipon, of course.

As long as the scaly bastards don't blow me up before I
do my job.

The gun is in my pocket, Morris's gun that I took after
he and Chu killed themselves. I was a good shot once. My
seat is close to the stage and on the aisle, leaving my right
hand free. I have had too much bitterness in my life. I will
not be mocked and betrayed in the one place where I find
some comfort.

Entry 30: Now I know who I wrote all this for. Dear Dr.
Herbert Akonditichilka: You do not know me. Until a little
while ago I didn't know you either. I am the man who sat
next to you in Carnegie Hall last night. Your Kondran
version of Carnegie Hall, that is: constructed from TV
pictures; all sparkling in crystal and cream and red velvet—
handsomer than the real place was, but in my judgment
slightly inferior acoustically.

You didn't notice me, Doctor, because of my makeup. I
noticed you. All evening I noticed everything, starting with
the police and the Kondracha demonstration outside the hall.
But you I noticed in particular. You managed to wreck my
concentration during the last piece of fine music I expected
to hear in my life.

It was the Haydn String Quartet Number One in G,
Opus 77. I sat trying to hear the effect of having two Kondrai

among the players, but your damned fidgeting distracted me. *Just my luck*, I thought. *A Kondran who came for a historic event, though he has no feeling for classical Earth music at all.* All through the Haydn you sat locked tight except for these tiny, spasmodic movements of your head, arms, and hands. It was a great relief to me when the music ended and you joined the crashing applause. I was so busy glaring at you that I missed seeing the musicians leave the stage.

I watched you all through the interval. I needed something to fix my attention on while I waited. The second piece was to be one of my favorites, the Brahms String Quartet Number Two in A minor, Opus 51. I had chosen the opening of that quartet as my signal. I meant to see to it that the Brahms would never be played by the traitors Ross and Chandler and the two snakes they had trained. In fact, no one was ever going to hear Ross and Chandler play anything again.

What would happen to me afterward I didn't know or care (though it crossed my mind in a farcical moment that I might be rescued as a hero by the Kondracha).

I wondered if you would be a problem—an effective interference, once the first note of the Brahms piece sounded and I began to make my move. I thought not.

You were small and thin, Dr. Akonditichilka, neatly dressed in you fake blazer with the fake gold buttons; a thick thatch of white top feathers; a round face, for a lizard; and glasses that made your eyes enormous. I wondered if you had ruined your eyesight studying facsimile texts taken from Earth transmissions. I could see by the grayed-off skin color that you were elderly, like so many in this audience, though probably not as old as I am.

You fell into conversation with the Kondran on your

left. I realized from what I could overhear that the two of you had met for the first time earlier that same day. She was now exploring the contact. "Oh," she said, "you're a doctor?"

"Retired," you said.

"You must meet Mischa Two Hawks," she said, "my escort tonight. He's a retired doctor, too."

The seat to her left was empty. Retired doctor Mischa Two Hawks may have withdrawn to the men's room or gone out in the lobby for a smoke.

You must understand; my mind made automatic translations as fast as the thought finished: Imitation retired, imitation doctor Mischa S. (for Stolen names) Two Hawks was in the imitation men's room or smoking an imitation cigarette.

His companion, an imitation woman in a green, imitation wool dress, wore a white wig with a blue-rinse tint. God, how Beamish used to rage over the tendency of Kondran females to choose the most traditional women's styles as models! Beamish would have been proud of my work tonight, I thought.

Green Wool Dress, whose name I had not caught, said to you, "The lady with you this afternoon at the gallery—is she your wife? And where is she tonight?"

You shook your head, and your glasses flashed. It pleases me that the nictitating membrane prevents you snakes from wearing contact lenses.

"We used to go to every concert in the city together," you said. "We both love good music, and there is no replacement for hearing it live. But she's been losing her hearing. She doesn't go anymore; it's too painful for her."

"What a pity," Green Wool Dress said. "To miss such a great event! Wasn't the first violinist wonderful just now? And, so young, too. It was amazing to hear him."

Damned right it was. Chandler had literally played second fiddle to his own student, Chukchonturanfis. For that alone I could have killed my old crew mate.

I shut my eyes and thought about the gun in my pocket. It was a heavy goddamned thing. I thought about the danger of getting it caught in the cloth as I pulled it out, of missing my aim, of my elderly self being jumped by you two elderly aliens before I could complete my job. I thought of Chandler and Ross, no spring chickens themselves anymore, soon to die and leave me alone among you. The whole thing was a sort of doddering comedy.

Another Kondran, heavyset for a lizard and bald, worked his way along the row of seats. He hovered next to Green Wool Dress, clearly wanting to sit down. She wouldn't let him until she had made introductions. This was, of course, retired doctor Mischa Two Hawks.

"Akonditichilka," you said with a little bow. "Herbert." And the two of you shook hands across Green Wool Dress. All three of you settled back to chat.

Suddenly I heard your voices as music. You, Doctor, were the first violin, with your clear, light tenor. Dr. Two Hawks's lower register made a reasonable cello. Green Wool Dress, who scarcely spoke, was second violin, of course, noodling busily along among her own thoughts. And I was the viola, hidden and dark.

If this didn't stop I knew I would use the gun right now, on you and then on myself. I listened to the words you were saying instead of your voices. I grabbed onto the words to keep control.

"A beautiful piece, the Haydn," you were saying. "I have played it. Oh, not like these musicians, of course. But I used to belong to an amateur chamber group." (How like you thieving snakes, to mimic our own medical doctors' affinity for music-making as a hobby!) You went on to explain how it was that you no longer played. Some slow, crippling Kondran bone disease. Of course—your lizard claws were never meant to handle a bow and strings. What was your instrument? I missed that. You said you had not played for six or seven years now. No wonder you had twitched all through the Haydn, remembering.

Some snake in a velvet suit pushed past, managing to step on both my feet. We traded insincere apologies, and he went on to trample past you and your companions. They were all hurrying back in now. My moment was coming. The row was fully occupied, so I sat down and pretended to skim the program notes for the next piece.

On you went, in the clear, distantly regretful tone. I couldn't stop hearing. "It's been a terrible season for me," you said. "My only grandchild died last month. He was fifteen."

Your voice was not music. It was just a voice, taking a tone I remembered from when I and my crew mates first began to be able to say to each other, "Well, it's all gone, blown up—mankind and womankind and whalekind and everykind smashed to smithereens while we were sleeping." It's how you sound instead of screaming. You have no more acute screaming left in your throat, but you can't stop talking about what is making you scream, because the screaming of your spirit is going on and on.

My eyes locked on the page in front of me. Had you really spoken this way, to two strangers, at a concert? The other two were making sounds of shock and sympathy.

"Cancer," you said, though of course you meant not our kind of cancer but Kondran cancer, and of course even if you were screaming inside it wasn't the same as the spirit of a human being screaming that way.

You leaned forward in your seat to talk across Green Wool Dress to Dr. Two Hawks. "It was terrible," you said. "It started in his right leg. None of the therapy even slowed it down. They did three operations."

I sneaked a look at you to see what kind of expression you wore on your imitation human face while you recited your afflictions. But you were leaning outward to address your fellow doctor, and the back of your narrow lizard shoulders was turned toward me.

Between you two, Green Wool Dress sat with a blank social smile, completely withdrawn into herself. I tried to follow what you were saying, but you got into technical terms, one doctor to another.

The musicians were tuning up their instruments backstage. The gun felt like a battleship in my pocket. Under the dimming lights I could make out the face of Dr. Two Hawks, sympathetic and earnest. Amazing, I thought, how they've learned to produce the effect of expressions like our own with their alien musculature and their alien skin.

"But it's better now than it was at first," Dr. Two Hawks protested (I thought of Beamish's babies and the death of Walter Drake). "I can remember when there was nothing to do but cut and cut, and even then—there was a young patient I remember, we removed the entire hip—oh, we were desperate. Dreadful things were done. It's better now."

All around, oblivious, members of the audience settled expectantly into their seats, whispering to each other, rustling program pages. Apparently I was your only involuntary eavesdropper, and soon that ordeal would be over.

The audience quieted, and here they came: Ross first, then Chandler (the Kondran players didn't matter). Ross first: You wouldn't see the blood on her red dress. No one would understand exactly what was happening, and that would give me time to get Chandler, too. I needed my concentration. My moment was here.

On you went, inexorably, in your quiet, melancholy tone: "As a last resort they castrated him. He lost most of his skin at the end, and he was too weak to sip fluids through a tube. I think now it was all a mistake. We should never have fought so hard. We should have let him die at the start."

"But we can't just give up!" cried Dr. Two Hawks over the applause for the returning musicians. "We must do *something!*"

And you sighed, Dr. Akonditichilka. "Aaah," you said softly, a long curve of sounded breath in the silence before the players began. You leaned there an instant longer, looking across at him.

Then you said gently (and how clearly your voice still sounds in my mind)—each word a steep, sweet fall in pitch from the one before—"Let's listen to Brahms."

And you sat back slowly in your seat as the first notes rippled into the hall. After a little I managed to uncramp my fingers from around the gun and take my empty hand out of my pocket. We sat there together in the dimness, our eyes stinging with tears past shedding, and we listened.